He had an itchy feeling, something he had seen that his memory had recorded but that he wasn't paying attention to...

Lagarde filled Black in on his interview with Emma over a cup of coffee in the office. The best way he knew to figure out what was bothering him was to talk it through with his partner.

"Are we missing something obvious?" he asked Black as they took the back road from Kearneysville to Wodehouse's Charles Town office. They had filed the initial paperwork for the Wodehouse murder and dropped off the compass Lagarde found in the hayloft and Wodehouse's cell phone for processing. "I have this weird feeling that there was something right in our faces and we missed it this morning, something big, important, that we should have seen."

Black glanced over at his partner. It was his turn to drive while Lagarde went through his notes. The first part of the trip would be through hilly farmland with large open pastures and fields. There would be fewer S turns, but this was still a two-lane road with rises high enough to conceal a vehicle charging toward him in the oncoming lane. He kept his eyes on the road while he speculated out loud. "Let's see, a guy goes out to his barn in the early morning to let out his horses. His wife gets up to make them breakfast. She can see the barn from her kitchen window, which means she can see who approaches the barn at the stable level. But, she can't see if someone drives or walks up to the barn from the other side, the entrance to the upper level hayloft. So, while she's making coffee and frying up eggs, or boiling them or whatever she does with them—and, wait a minute, where were the eggs she said she called down to the barn to tell him were getting cold? Why didn't you see them on the table? Did she dump them in the trash before she went down to the barn to find him, or before we got there? Or were they metaphorical?"

Lagarde looked at him. Black never ceased to surprise him. "Right! Problem number one with what I observed at the house and what we were told: metaphorical eggs. So, was Emma lying about the course of events this morning, or the timing of those events, or omitting something? Or all of the above?"

When Grant Wodehouse went to the barn that fine morning, he had no idea what good, bad, or ugly would happen—saddle a couple of horses, a little S&M with his neighbor, get a pitchfork rammed through his chest, pinning him to the wall...He never expected the latter.

Who would *not* want him dead? Having bedded every female he'd ever laid eyes on, swindled anyone he had ever had business dealings with, and ignored and ostracized his children, one person said it was time for Grant to meet his maker...but who?

ated his children and ex-wives, so Lagarde has to add them to the mix as well. And what about the neighbor woman with whom he was having an affair? When she ends up murdered as well, her husband jumps to the top of the list. But he has an alibi. Can they break it? *No Good Deed Left Undone* explores the life, and death, of a not-very-nice man. It's the story of a man addicted to sex, who swindled people in his business dealings, cheated on his wife, and ostracized his children, but was surprised when someone finally had enough. It will make you laugh, cry, and struggle to guess "who done it." It's one you will want to keep on your shelf and read again and again to catch what you missed the first time. ~ *Regan Murphy, Reviewer*

ACKNOWLEDGEMENTS

Many thanks to my fellow writers, K.P. Robbins, Tara Bell, Katherine Cobb, and Catherine Baldau for their continual encouragement, support, and critical listening. Deep gratitude to my sons Hal and Peter whose willing imaginations helped me find my way through the plot. Thanks to artists Joe Bourgeois and Patricia Perry for teaching me what's important to a reader. Always, I am indebted to Carolyn Bross, whose sharp eye misses nothing, to Carmen Procida who reads everything and, therefore, knows much and Dr. Eileen Fenrich who showed me how a woman of courage grieves. I owe a bow to my agent Jeanie Loiacono, whose enthusiasm is a tonic, and to the astonishing staff at Black Opal Books who wave their collective magic wands and a book appears.

NO GOOD DEED LEFT UNDONE

Ginny Fite

A Black Opal Books Publication

GENRE: MYSTERY-DETECTIVE/THRILLER

NO GOOD DEED LEFT UNDONE
Copyright © 2016 by Ginny Fite
Cover Design by Jackson Cover Designs
All cover art copyright © 2016
All Rights Reserved
Print ISBN: 978-1-626945-21-0

First Publication: SEPTEMBER 2016

Published by Black Opal Books **http://www.blackopalbooks.com**

DEDICATION

To my husband, David,
who taught me what was important.

All suffering comes from the wish for ourselves to be happy, and all happiness comes from the wish for others to be happy ~ *Eighth-Century Buddhist Monk Shantideva*

CHAPTER 1

October 12, 8:15 a.m.:

By the time Detective Sam Lagarde got to the body, the horses were long out of the barn. Grant Wodehouse, the dead guy, was pinned to his barn wall by a pitchfork. The cement floor all around him was awash in blood. Lagarde's first assessment was that this murder was a crime of passion with an available weapon. The victim had been skewered in a single powerful lunge and driven back to the wooden wall behind him with such force that his boots dragged on the cement barn floor, leaving little piles of straw behind his heels.

There were no tentative holes in the man's clothing. The murderer didn't hesitate, didn't test out his weapon, didn't taunt his victim, just went straight for the kill. And yet, the murder had the look of the unexpected, as if it might have surprised even the killer. There'd been no attempt to hide the body, to conceal the crime, or delay detection. Lagarde thought the murder might be a one-off killing by someone who'd never killed before and had no plans to continue. On the other hand, the killer could be so depraved that he left bodies as gifts for the police to find, the way cats left dead mice for their owners.

Lagarde knew from long experience that there was no telling what he might uncover about the killer.

Four neighbors, including two teenagers, one toddler and her mother, three sheriff's deputies, the new widow, and perhaps a few horses had trampled through the crime scene, obliterating any small clues that might have led to the immediate identification of the murderer. Not that Lagarde expected such a miracle, but he could always hope.

He took off his hat, a tan felt Stetson Outback that he wore in all seasons, pushed back hair now more gray than blond from his receding hairline, put his hat back on, squeezed the top of his nose, as if that gesture would improve his eyesight, and looked around at the scene in front of him.

There were too many people for him to expect a pristine crime scene. Everyone had their excuses for being there. The wife came out to the barn to see what was taking her husband so long with his morning chores. The boys said they were there to feed the horses and let them out into the pasture. The toddler's mother said she came outside after her child and ran down toward the barn when she heard Mrs. Wodehouse screaming. The deputies were first on the scene in response to the nine-one-one call, and, of course, they had to walk through the barn to see what was going on. The stories rolled over each other, small whirlwinds of fallen leaves in an autumn storm, more reasons for being there than there were witnesses.

The deputy pointed out the boy who had called emergency dispatch on his cell phone.

Lagarde told Deputy Sheriff Dennis Harbaugh to move everyone away from the area, corralling them twenty feet from the barn, where they huddled fearfully together waiting to be questioned. Their horror hung in the air above them, their own personal weather system. The next-door neighbor had her arm around the newly made widow, who stared stone-faced at the barn, her arms wrapped around her body. She shivered in her sweater, although this October morning had begun at sixty degrees and was headed higher. Around the property, the dense woods were acquiring the yellows, reds and orange colors of autumn.

If this weren't a murder scene, it would be very pretty here, Lagarde mused.

"The wife stopped screaming, thank God," Deputy Harbaugh said, interrupting Lagarde's surveillance of the site. "She was loud. Now she's calm as death."

Lagarde looked the man over carefully. Short, out of shape, unable to run farther than forty feet, probably balding under that black baseball cap with the sheriff's department insignia emblazoned on the crown, with heavy bags under his eyes, the deputy didn't immediately fill Lagarde with confidence. His callous comment made him wonder about the accuracy of anything else the deputy might say.

The widow was clearly in shock. At least she had company almost immediately after finding her husband impaled like an insect on exhibit. More people contaminated the whole area, but it was better for Mrs. Wodehouse. At least he assumed it was, even when he knew he shouldn't assume anything. She might be the kind of woman who'd rather be left alone. For that matter, she might be the kind of woman who kills her husband.

Lagarde walked up and down the barn's center aisle between the stalls trying to get his bearings, to sort out what had been added with all those footfalls and what had been subtracted—a dropped glove or a dirty tissue that had fallen out of a pocket in the struggle and from which they could have DNA extracted. There might even have been clues on the horses themselves or the gates to their stalls. The whole damn barn would have to be dusted for the hundreds of fingerprints, the floor in every stall swept for physical evidence. They would have to comb through every stalk of bedding straw and feed hay. *Talk about trying to find a needle.*

The cadaver was located near the sliding barn door. It was easier for Lagarde if he didn't call the deceased by name. Blood ran down the body and was splashed across the wall in a way remarkably similar to paint spatters on a Jackson Pollock painting. The minute Lagarde made that connection in his mind, he realized he would always look at Pollock's paintings that way, as blood spray. The victim was stabbed from the front. Wodehouse had seen his killer, perhaps confronted him. The body was not yet in rigor. His head drooped, and his eyes and mouth were open, as if to express his deep astonishment at having been killed in this manner. Someone had flipped on the barn lights, maybe the deputies, but maybe Mr. Wodehouse in the normal course of morning chores. The murder scene was also illuminated by sheaves of morning light coming through the roof skylight. Barn swallows, completely impervious to the human turmoil below, performed their acrobatic flights above Lagarde's head.

It was a good stable, Lagarde observed, neatly organized with halters, bridles, bits and reins on hooks, with saddle pads and blankets on racks for each animal set out against the front wall between each of the stalls. The old bank barn—part stone, part timber frame, about the same age as the nineteenth-century stone house up the hill— had been handsomely refurbished with electricity, running water and roomy stalls with wrought iron gates. There were stalls for eight horses, four on each side of the alley, a grooming area, a tack room off the lower entrance and ladder stairs to the hayloft, which could also be accessed from the outside via the drive-up door a level above. A graveled lane, about one hundred yards from the primary driveway that led from Ridge Road to the house, ran behind the house and up to the hayloft entrance. It wouldn't be hard to enter the barn through the outside hay door on the upper level, come down the stairs and surprise someone who was occupied with leading a horse out of its stall. Lagarde couldn't help comparing the elegance and organization of this barn with his own more slap-dash way of stabling his horses.

Well, whatever works. He immediately forgave himself all kinds of sins.

The detective walked into the tack room, checking the area to see if it would yield any clues. The room had six tall cubbies with shelves and hooks that held helmets, boots, crops, barn jackets, riding and work gloves and other sundry equipment a rider might store there if they rode frequently. Only three of the cubbies had rider's equipment in them. Saddle racks holding English saddles of varying quality, some for every day work and some for showing, racing, or hunting, occupied the center of the room. Lagarde counted five saddles. A portable tack box for the horseman to take with him to events was against the wall under the window, its lid open. It had the appearance of having been rifled through. Someone in a hurry was looking for something, and they were pretty serious about it.

Could the murder have been in pursuance of a theft? What on earth could be so valuable in a barn that someone would kill for it?

Wodehouse's silks for steeplechase racing were thrown on top of other supplies in the box. *Did Wodehouse ride in the races himself or did he have a rider who took the risk of galloping at full speed over bushes, stone walls, and water trenches?* Wodehouse obviously thought a lot of himself. He had invented a crest for the rider's shirt that included a griffin and a peacock. His colors were purple and blue. Maybe that told Lagarde all he needed to know about the man. An old leather couch, a low stool where riders could put on boots, two boot jacks for removing tight boots—one modern wood, the other an antique brass—and an antique chest of drawers, which had been pulled out and not closed completely, and had a jumble of grooming equipment piled on the top of it, completed his quick inventory of the space.

This was not a huge operation, but it was expensive nonetheless.

There were only four horses in the paddock next to the barn. A large, fenced, four-acre pasture with two run-in sheds stretched out behind the barn. Perhaps there were more horses there. Or, maybe Wodehouse leased out space in the barn from time to time. He would have been able to make a couple hundred bucks extra each month boarding horses. People would pay at least four hundred dollars a month to have their horse boarded in this grand style, particularly some of the former city-dwellers who now made rural Jefferson County, West Virginia their home and commuted on the train every day to Washington, D.C. It was clear that Wodehouse made his money some other way than raising, training and selling horses. You had horses for the love of it, Lagarde knew from personal experience, not because it made you any money.

The barn had that deeply satisfying smell of sweet hay, animals and manure. Wodehouse must have just finished his morning routine when he was attacked. The stalls had not yet been mucked out. *That would be what those youngsters were for,* Lagarde figured. Low-lying fog, typical in early fall, would have been clinging to the fields, the dew sparkling in the early morning light when Wodehouse walked the two hundred yards from his house to the barn. *I bet Wodehouse enjoyed that time of the morning, just like I do.*

With much left to learn, if he wanted to find the killer, he needed to know why this particular man had been the target. According to Lagarde, the only way of accomplishing this task was to ask questions, follow the clues and keep his eyes open. He preferred hunches to science. It helped that his partner, Sergeant Lawrence Black, knew how to use all the twenty-first-century technology available.

At twenty-seven, Black had told him he was now thinking about applying to the FBI, but Lagarde didn't hold Black's ambitions against him. The man was smart, quiet when he was supposed to be, and could put two-and-two together and get four when it was required. Those were the essential characteristics of a good detective, as far as Lagarde was concerned.

They had been working together for two years and had developed a certain rhythm that helped them to solve crimes too complicated, or too messy, for local sheriff's departments. They had a system that worked.

Thanks to Black, even before they arrived on the scene, they had learned some interesting facts. While Lagarde drove their unmarked state trooper vehicle, Sergeant Black typed "Grant Wodehouse Jefferson County WV" into the Google app on his smart phone and read out loud the information he found on the Internet. "Wodehouse belonged to every hunt club in the three-state area. He must have been busy every weekend of the year. If he wasn't riding to hounds," Black put on his best posh British accent, "he had horses entered in events like point-to-point and cross country racing." He paused and scrolled through the information with his thumb. "It says here that Grant Wodehouse raised and rode only hunters." He looked over at Lagarde. "That means the horses, right? A quarter horse, a thoroughbred? It's not talking about people."

Lagarde nodded. "Yes, horses." He had always admired the twelve-hundred-pound, seventeen-hand horses bred for looks, speed, and strength that could jump a six-foot stone wall without breaking a sweat, but they were too much horse for him. He'd stick to his easy going American Quarter Horse and his Paint. His horses weren't chic enough for the hunt club crowd, but they were reliable and didn't give him a lot of attitude. When all else failed him, when he couldn't get the grisly images out of his mind, Lagarde got on his horse and rode out. After a few miles, all there was in the world was the easy movement of his body synchronized with the horse's canter across the open fields. Even in the winter with snow crunching under his horse's hooves, riding at night to the top of a hill from which he could see lights, jewels on black velvet, from the far town laid out in the valley, Lagarde found solace in quiet companionship with his horse. Horses, he had found after several failed marriages, were better companions than women. They didn't talk back.

"Wodehouse should have been dead three times over before this. He fell from his horse on two hunts then on one cross-country race when he nearly got trampled, but only broke his hip or got a concussion. The man was living on borrowed time." Black scrolled through more information on the phone screen. "Oh, here's something you'll be interested in. The couple was known for their after-hunt parties during which everyone got drunk and slept with everyone else's wife."

Lagarde, navigating the many complicated turns up and down the hilly country on the back roads to the Wodehouse property, quickly looked over at Black. "Wait. What? It actually said that on Google?"

"Facebook, man, the view into people's very souls, the personal diaries of a billion people, with pictures."

Lagarde looked blank. He had never been on Facebook. He couldn't imagine why anyone would put their personal diary where everyone in the world could see it. *Wasn't the point of a diary that it was secret? When had the world decided that hanging their dirty laundry out in public was better?* Lagarde shook his head. *'Going to hell in a hand basket,' Mom would have said.*

Black explained that he was looking at Wodehouse's Facebook profile and extrapolating from the photographs about the man's party behavior. "These people look pretty blotto to me—all those low-cut dresses, people with their arms around each other, men leering at cleavage, lots of booze to loosen social conventions. Draw your own conclusions."

Women who rode to the hounds were not known to be shy, Lagarde knew. He had met a few of them at horse auctions—and briefly bedded a few. The phenomenon of bold horsewomen had something to do with being the master of a giant animal.

Being in command gave women a sense of power, which they extrapolated to other areas of their lives. They knew how to use a crop, when to dig in their heels and how to dismount in a hurry. All of them were predators as far as Sam Lagarde was concerned. Of course, he was a tad gun shy since his fourth divorce. He was off women for a while and that was a good thing, Lagarde told himself.

As far as members of hunt clubs were concerned, he considered them to be spoiled brats who complained bitterly that they weren't allowed to ride over their neighbors' land at a gallop, horses' hooves flipping up clods of soil as they pounded across the fields after a tiny red animal fleeing for its life. The era of lords of the manor was over, as Lagarde saw it, and one of the last of them had been killed in a decidedly eighteenth-century way.

Shaking off his prejudices, he realized there really were only four questions: who committed this heinous crime, why, how and when. If he could answer those questions, find evidence that proved the answers and locate the perpetrator, he could make an arrest and pass the case to the county prosecutor.

That was his whole job. People had been killing each other even before someone wrote down the story of Cain and Abel.

It was a grim thought that, even in the twenty-first century, so-called civilized nations expected people to kill each other. The whole point of police departments was the expectation of crime, and that the people who were guilty should be found and punished. Sometimes it seemed as if he was engaged in a hopeless exercise, sticking his thumb in the dike against an increasing wave of violence that was threatening to flood the world. Nevertheless, this was the career he had chosen and he was determined to see it through to the end, which every day he hoped would come sooner than the day before.

In the Wodehouse murder case, the "how" of the killing looked pretty obvious, although it was possible they'd hear from the medical examiner that Grant Wodehouse had been poisoned first, or drugged to slow him down, or hit on the head with a shovel and then run through with a handy, sharp object. On the other hand, Lagarde had learned long ago, nothing was what it seemed.

Lagarde walked out of the barn and over to the gaggle of witnesses. He took Black aside. "The first thing we're going to need is a clear timeline. After that, we'll need a few good clues and a lot of luck."

Black nodded. "The killer in this case has to be a man, and not a small man, to ram an old iron pitchfork through

Wodehouse's body with such force that the tines entered the barn wall."

"Right. He'd have to be taller than Wodehouse, to have the weapon enter the body at the angle it did, *and* take Wodehouse by surprise. Otherwise, why hadn't Wodehouse turned around and run back to the house, or picked up the shovel leaning against the opposite wall to defend himself, or try to jump out of the way?"

Did Wodehouse yell for help? The murder method suggested a crime of passion and random opportunity. Wodehouse couldn't have been holding a horse's halter to lead him out to the paddock. A horse would have spooked, whinnied, warned Wodehouse in some way about an intruder running at him. The horse could easily have gotten in the way, or given Wodehouse an opportunity to mount and ride out of the barn. If he'd been leading a horse out of the barn, Wodehouse would have been facing the barn door, not have his back to the wall. Unless the killer was known to Wodehouse, was helping him with the horses, and then something went hideously awry. Lagarde's mind raced through scenarios.

The medical examiner was looking at the body now. They would do a thorough autopsy later to identify the cause and time of death. The forensics team had pulled out the pitchfork and bagged it for evidence. Maybe the perp hadn't been wearing gloves and there would be good prints on the shaft. But everyone who normally touched the implement would have to be finger printed to establish a baseline. Wodehouse had on rubber boots and his hands were bare. He wore jeans, a work shirt and a quilted vest. He must have walked down to the barn with the boots on, or entered the barn and had time to put them on before he started his chores.

It wasn't clear if Wodehouse was the one who led the horses out to the paddock or someone else did. Lagarde left the medical examiner to do her job and walked out of the barn. Some of his colleagues saw Lagarde as morose, a little bit of a curmudgeon. He wasn't really a pessimist, he would constantly have to remind them. He just didn't like people and he didn't have a lot of hope that life would turn out well.

One of the parts of his job Lagarde hated most was talking to witnesses to try to gather useful information, but he had to do it. Maybe he could divide the job of interviewing them.

Black's six feet gave him an advantage in a crowd. Maybe Black was a bit too smart for a detective, but Lagarde enjoyed his company and his ability to speculate about what had happened with almost no evidence.

"Hey, Larry, make sure all those folks get fingerprinted. You question the kids and neighbor lady. I'm going to take Mrs. Wodehouse back into her kitchen and talk to her there without all the confusion. Okay?"

"No problem, but try not to get involved with her." Black smirked at Lagarde.

Lagarde gave him a scowl but he wasn't offended. Black was right. He had, in fact, gotten too attached to Beverly Wilson, the grandmother of a murder victim in a complicated case a year before.

Black hardly let a day go by when he didn't rag Lagarde about his infatuation. Truth be told, Lagarde still thought about the lovely Beverly, but he did nothing about it. The lady had made it clear she was off limits. He hadn't talked to her since they closed the case.

He shook off the image of Beverly and focused on the task at hand. He had to interview the victim's wife, Mrs. Emma Wodehouse, not so much because he suspected she was her husband's killer but because, at least theoretically, she knew her husband better than anyone else did.

Lagarde needed to know who Grant Wodehouse was in order to catch his killer.

CHAPTER 2

6:30 a.m.:

In spite of trouble with his son, Kyle, and a few glitches with his law practice, right up until a few minutes before he was killed, Grant Wodehouse thought of himself as a lucky guy. He cherished his quiet time, the early morning, dealing with his horses, the physical labor of it, their huffing and the sound of their hooves on the barn floor impatient for him to release them into paddock or pasture. He had walked down to the barn, slid the door open and let the smell of animals in close proximity envelope him.

Grant always got what he wanted. Mostly what he wanted was women. He already had money. Even women other men dismissed without a second glance had something lovely about them as far as he was concerned. It wasn't the obvious things he loved.

Other men were obsessed with breasts and butts, with pretty faces and long silky hair, but for Grant it could be the shape of her neck that lured him, the way she turned her head to look at him, the bones in her slender feet, or the way her eyelashes lay against her cheeks when she lowered her lids. He was sure a woman crossing her legs at a meeting was inviting him to know her intimately.

Short, a little stocky now, and lately near-sighted, he was a nearly handsome man, close enough to Hollywood's ideal for a woman to catch her breath when she spotted him across a room full of ordinary mortals. But it was his attention to women that was as compelling to them as another conquest was to him. He had discovered early in his life that women wanted to be listened to, to be looked at when they spoke to him, to have their feelings and observations mirrored back to them. They wanted, in short, to feel understood. He had developed into an excellent mirror by the time he was twenty. At sixty, he considered himself to be at the height of his seductive powers.

Grant cut open a new bale of hay and peeled off a flake. He carried it out to the hay feeder in the paddock, looked out toward the pasture and decided there was still enough grass for the horses that he didn't need to add hay. He'd often marveled at the fact that he looked forward to these menial tasks. He could see himself retiring, settling down to work only with his horses. The idea alone gave him a sense of contentment.

He knew that his preoccupation with women was mildly debilitating. It took his mind off work. He often daydreamed about a woman he had seen in line waiting for a table at the café or walking up an aisle in the market. A woman standing in the queue next to him at the bank, just a few feet away, could make him vibrate with longing. It was possible that eighty percent of the time he was thinking about having sex with some woman, well, maybe *more* than eighty percent. The difference between Grant and other men was that Grant would act on his fantasies. He took pride in this fact. As a result, he had many vivid memories of sex in odd places: janitor's closets, under the stairs in the courthouse, over the back of a bench in a national park. When he didn't have a woman handy, he would call on these memories for his own satisfaction.

He walked back into the barn, peeled off two more leaves of hay and then carried them out to the paddock. He picked up the hose attached to the side of the barn, turned on the tap and walked to the trough to fill it with water for the horses.

Emma had said, "You know, Grant, you might have an overabundance of testosterone or some other hormonal imbalance. You should get tested." But he told himself she didn't seem to mind his dalliances. When they had sex, she would always stop and say, "Put on a condom." She even made sure that he showered and gargled with a strong mouthwash before they went to bed. He told her about his escapades in great detail. He enjoyed telling his stories to Emma while he undressed her and stroked her body. It was a threesome without the hassle of having to deal with a third person's feelings. He felt he was Scheherazade, in an interesting role reversal, and had to regale his monarch with a story every night in order to keep his head. For her part, Emma seemed to treat the stories as just that, fantasies he made up for her delectation. She never asked him if they were real, never asked the woman's name, never asked if he had seen the woman more than once. She seemed immune to jealousy.

Grant had to hide his joy rides from his two previous wives. His problem, as he saw it, was that he wasn't good at hiding anything. Hiding his affairs meant he was late to dinner with no excuse or a transparently bad one. His previous wives were annoyed when he ran off to the store after receiving a phone call or suddenly had to go back to the office to do some work for a client in the middle of a Sunday afternoon. His first wife was particularly furious with him when he was unable to visit her in the hospital while she was dying of cancer because he needed to satisfy his cravings, sometimes with nurses who came in to take her vitals or adjust her intravenous medications.

Although Grant loved his children, fruit of his loins and all that, he was careless about his relationships with them. He expected them to know that he loved them and thought that would be enough. If they asked, he would give them anything. But he didn't have a lot of time to spend with them, or chat on the phone, email or text, and he didn't think he needed to be the one to make the first move. All they had to do was call him. He was quick with a hug and a pat on the back. He went to all their events when they were young. He had his law practice and his extracurricular activities, all of which took up a fair amount of time. His children should understand, yet one of the more sorrowful results of his behavior was that he didn't see his daughter, Rebecca, very often after she turned eighteen.

"You're scum, Daddy," she'd said to him minutes after she descended the stage after receiving her diploma. Furious at Grant for abandoning her mother while she was dying of cancer, Rebecca went away to college and never came home.

Grant was not one to fault himself, however. He thought of his daughter as a prude and was completely unaware that she thought of him as a faithless monster. Grant carried on as best he could, in his own estimation, always making sure that Rebecca always got cards and expensive gifts on the appropriate holidays.

He consoled himself with the fact that Emma understood him and, therefore, his behavior was understandable. Emma was the complete opposite of his other wives. Rhonda would have screaming fits. "How can you do this to me?" He'd found her going through his briefcase and check book, pawing through all his papers. "Who's *this*?"

she screamed, "And *this* one? How many women are you seeing?" Tears spurted from her eyes like juice from a cut lemon. He backed away and walked out of the room. It was exhausting living with them.

With Emma, he could text her and say, "I'll be late" or "Nature calls." Somehow, her acceptance of his extracurricular passions made him love her more. Perhaps Emma didn't care about his affairs because she didn't really love him, but he dismissed that thought as absurd. He couldn't help himself. He knew his friends thought he had some kind of mental illness but he had been having too much fun to consider that he needed help overcoming an addiction. Emma made sure that he regularly checked in with a physician to ensure that he hadn't contracted any social diseases, as she called them. She would get a strange look on her face when she said that, as if he were something disgusting she had found in the garbage that needed to be discarded quickly before it smelled up the house. Yet, he dutifully went for the checkups. It was a small price to pay for so much freedom.

Grant shook off his reverie. Getting old was making him think too much. He walked into the first stall to check out Emma's horse. He ran a hand over her back and down her legs. Annie's Way was favoring one hoof. He examined her fetlock and ankle. He'd have to call the vet. She couldn't be ridden.

"It's okay, old girl," he said to the horse. "No exercise for you today. Let's take you out into the sunshine and you can munch on grass and watch the birds."

The horse nodded. Grant stroked her long neck, attached a lead to her halter, then walked her out of the stall and over to the paddock. He opened the gate, led the horse inside, unclipped the lead and she walked off toward the new hay in the feeder.

Grant watched her walk for a bit and then went back

into the barn to let the other horses out one at a time.

The last few years, Emma had invited Rebecca and her family, his son Kyle, and her own son William to come with them on various vacations, skiing in Beaver Creek or the beach in the Hamptons, even first class European jaunts. His joy was to see them smile at him, joking and laughing among themselves. He had come around the corner in a restaurant, having excused himself to take a phone call, and saw them all at a large table, leaning toward each other, having a great time, listening to some joke Kyle was telling. The sight made his heart smile. Emma had somehow pulled it off, made all the disparate parts into one family. He enjoyed snowboarding with Kyle and talking religion with William. They were the typical American family when they were all together...at least from the outside.

Enjoying glimpses of his family together never distracted Grant from his primary preoccupation. Each woman he seduced felt that she was the only woman in the world who could delight him, even if the actual coupling had resembled the activity of stray dogs in heat. That glaze of delight lasted until they saw him on the street with his arm around another woman, leaning down toward her, looking into her eyes.

"Forget *you*, schmuck," the smart ones said, dropping him immediately.

The needy ones held on for dear life. Either way worked for Grant. He was not above pity sex now and then. His weakness reinforced theirs.

That was one of the reasons Rhonda Morewood, wife number two and Kyle's mother, still called him. "Oh, Grant," she would say as she opened her door in a skimpy negligee, "you have no idea how much I need you." He simply took her where she stood. Then he wrote a large check for whatever it was she said Kyle needed at that moment, plus a little something for her, and left. Grant saw himself as munificent after these encounters, having done a good deed for which he'd been amply rewarded by his own satisfaction.

He wasn't the kind of man who examined his own actions. If he did something, then that was the right thing for him to do. His ethical universe consisted only of himself and occasionally his wife, who he sometimes consulted but not always. His training as a lawyer had not given him strong convictions about right and wrong. On the contrary, it had taught him that the position of a single word in a sentence, when moved from one phrase to another, could completely change the meaning of the document and the outcome for his client. He was an expert at defining the word "is" advantageously.

Only two people could intrude on Grant's closed circle of self-regard: his wife, Emma, and his son. His son's intrusions completely frustrated him. Recent reports from Kyle's school had not been good. They embarrassed him. This was the boy's third private school. He had been thrown out of the previous two. Last spring, Dean Bergen had said Kyle wasn't concentrating and his teachers thought he had attention deficit disorder. For this kind of insight, Grant was paying $50,000 a year in tuition, plus room and board for his son. The solution presented by the dean was simple, however, and Grant approved a prescription for a drug that was supposed to help Kyle do better in school. A month ago, the school doctor said Kyle was prone to panic attacks and anxiety. Grant approved another prescription to deal with that. It never occurred to Grant to drive out to the school and talk to his son directly. It never occurred to him that the school was the wrong place for Kyle. Taking care of this problem was what Grant was paying the school to do, after all.

"The meds aren't helping your son," the dean reported

last week. "Kyle's in trouble almost every week. He fights with other students, threatens teachers, and periodically tears apart his dorm room."

It was too much for Grant. He put a local Pennsylvania lawyer on retainer to deal with the consequences of his son's behavior and pushed the issue off the table of his consciousness. *The kid has a mother. Let her deal with it.*

Grant opened the gate on the next stall and said good morning to the horse. They exchanged sounds while he quickly examined this horse, decided he was sound, then attached the lead. He followed the same path as he had with Annie's Way, walking the gelding into the paddock, detaching the lead, watching him walk over to the feeder before he turned his back, walked out of the paddock and closed the gate. The activity shifted his thoughts to another problem.

Elaine Tabor, the young neighbor with whom he'd had a casual affair for several years, was showing signs of being too demanding. She wasn't satisfied with expensive gifts and occasional sex. She was talking about a future with him. She threatened to tell Emma about their affair, although he wasn't really worried about that. Emma would just laugh it off. He also had the more sophisticated Adrienne Knowles to satisfy, a relationship that cost him time as well as money. Adrienne might be able to wreck his career if he didn't keep her happy.

In spite of these worries, he'd recently noticed a young woman who sat in front of the library to read at lunchtime. She sat on the wooden bench surrounded by old boxwoods that shielded her from view from the street, and a magnolia tree provided a canopy. She was a storybook heroine, with long black hair and slender legs. He'd noticed over several weeks that she wore black leggings with everything: skirts, shorts, dresses. There was just an inch of skin at her ankle that showed between her leggings and the tops of her red leather sneakers. He found this small sliver of skin overwhelmingly seductive. He had started going to the library to browse through the DVD collection to have an excuse to pass her as she sat on the bench. He imagined himself stroking the skin at her ankles.

Yesterday, he was standing on the library steps, preparing to approach her when a homeless guy sat down on the bench next to her. Grant watched their interaction. *She's kind. She doesn't flinch, flee, or tell the guy to go away, however, she doesn't give him anything but a smile, either.* Wodehouse knew the guy by sight, Warren somebody. Sometimes he let Warren use the bathroom in his office to wash up, although his admin Ann Roberts objected. Ann would go through the bathroom with bleach spray afterward. Grant also gave the guy a fiver now and then so he could get a square meal at Grandma's Diner. *There but for the grace of God*, Grant told himself.

Mostly to make an impression on the girl, Grant walked over to the bench and said hi to Warren, who greeted him as his long lost friend, which had a positive effect on the girl. Grant could see she was impressed that Warren was cordially familiar with him. Then the conversation got around to where Warren was sleeping these days.

"You know, where I can, Mr. Wodehouse," Warren said, trying to justify his need.

The guy was humble, never complained, nor asked for anything. On the spur of the moment, and more to impress the girl than to help Warren, Grant told Warren that he could sleep in the Wodehouse barn whenever he needed shelter from the elements. "The farm is just up on Ridge Road, about ten miles outside town," Grant told Warren, thinking that it was too far away for the guy to walk, "at 2145. Just walk back to the barn and go in the hayloft. There's running water in the barn and heat."

"I'll remember that, sir," Warren said, shook his hand, thanked him many times, waved, and walked away. Grant sat down on the bench with the girl.

"That was nice of you, but maybe a little risky, don't you think?"

"Sometimes you have to take risks in life," he said to her, looking straight into her large gray eyes, feeling his edges were disappearing. Her lower lip was pink and plump. *What it would feel like if I sucked it into my mouth?*

"Gotta go," the girl said, standing up as if responding to a bell. "See ya." She waved and walked away. She did not look back.

Grant felt an empty ache in his belly, as if his innards had been removed. He hadn't expected that the girl would simply snub him. Maybe he was losing his touch. He was getting old. He was sixty. Maybe that was it. Maybe he wasn't sexy anymore. He called Emma on his cell phone. "Let's go for a drive," he said when she answered. "I have an urge to stroke your thigh."

Emma laughed and said she would meet him at the car. He felt restored. Life was as it should be. Grant was king of his world until the next morning when all hell broke loose in his barn.

CHAPTER 3

8:30 a.m.:

Lagarde walked from the barn over to Emma Wodehouse, introduced himself and asked if he could talk with her back at the house. He took a quick look at the new widow as they trudged up the long slope toward the house. She was dressed in beige corduroy pants, with a white cable cardigan sweater over a T-shirt, rubber barn boots and was wearing small gold hoop earrings. Her salt and pepper hair was cut short yet still looked feminine, and accentuated her warm brown eyes. She took long strides as she walked back to the house. Limber and fit, she wasn't fifty yet. Was she Grant Wodehouse's trophy wife? She probably didn't even need a boot up from a block to mount a horse. Sergeant Black was right. He'd have to be careful that her attractiveness didn't keep him from seeing her clearly. *It couldn't hurt to look,* he mused, smiling to himself.

A year past sixty, the lawman had the look of a gentleman farmer rather than a detective. His faded blue eyes had seen too much, but they could still make a woman give him a second look when he wanted. Hoping to coast toward retirement, he'd discovered that he wanted only a

few things in his life: to do his job well with the least difficulty, to ride his horse, and to love someone—that last
desire proving more of a mystery as the years passed than
any murder he investigated. As Black knew well, love
was Lagarde's weak spot. The running joke between
them was that every woman they met was a potential
danger to Lagarde's sanity. He shook himself a little to
clear his head of everything but the case at hand.

"I'm sorry to have to ask you questions at this time,
Mrs. Wodehouse, but it will speed up our investigation if
you can talk with me now," he explained as they walked.

Emma nodded. "It's okay. I understand."

"Can you tell me exactly what happened this morning,
including whether there were any early phone calls or
anyone who came to the door, anything out of the ordinary that happened before Mr. Wodehouse went out to
the barn?"

Emma walked up the four steps to the back porch,
opened the back door of the house, slid her boots off inside the door and walked into the kitchen in her socks.
She touched the glass pot in the coffee maker on the
counter with her finger, pulled a gray ceramic mug out of
the glass front cabinet above the counter and poured herself a cup of steaming coffee.

She didn't ask Lagarde if he wanted one, didn't ask
him to sit down, either. She turned around to face him,
leaning back against the kitchen counter with her arms
crossed over her chest, her mug of hot coffee in one
hand—a weapon pointed at him. She looked at Lagarde
for an excessive amount of time before she spoke.
Lagarde thought she might be using his own trick of being silent against him. Being quiet, he had found in years
of interviewing, often forced his subjects to tell him
things they never should have revealed if they wanted to
retain their Fifth Amendment right against self-

incrimination. Emma was so calm that he had to keep reminding himself that she had just found her husband impaled and covered in blood. "We were happy here." Her statement wasn't a prologue to her history, she just seemed to be uttering her internal observation out loud, making a comparison between what was true for her the moment before the murder and now after it.

Then she was silent again.

While he waited for her to speak, Lagarde looked around the room. She had obviously remodeled the kitchen in the old stone house. The counters were glossy black granite, the appliances high-end stainless steel. Handmade oak cupboards and shelving painted cream white provided ample space for dishes and food. There was also a butler's pantry with additional storage space between the kitchen and the large dining room. The double refrigerator in the kitchen had glass doors and a built in wine cooler. A large oblong oak table with six oak chairs sat under a wide bay window looking out toward a garden, patio, and the woods beyond. Two wingback chairs upholstered in a cheery plaid flanked what appeared to be a working woodstove. There were no photographs of grandchildren in the pool that could be seen from the window near the table, no snapshots of any member of the family on the refrigerator. The kitchen was functional and impersonal. It could have been the centerpiece of a well-provisioned model home. They were comfortable here. Perhaps that's what Emma meant by 'happy.'

"Nothing unusual happened this morning," she said finally. "I mean, before. We woke up at our normal time, around 6:00. I got up shortly before Grant did, brushed my teeth, threw some clothes on, came downstairs and started the coffee. Grant came down, put on his boots and went out to the barn to let the horses out. It was a perfectly normal morning. Well, except that..." she paused and corrected herself. "No, actually, it was perfectly normal, within expected parameters." She glared at him as if to dare him to question her idea of normalcy, as if saying it was normal would instantly restore sanity to the madness of murder.

She put her coffee mug down on the counter, walked over to the sink and looked out the kitchen window facing the barn. She continued with her back to him, "When Grant had been gone about forty minutes, I called down there—we have an intercom system set up between the house and the barn—to see what was keeping him. I was distracted and burned his eggs. His phone rang, but I didn't answer it. I guess I felt impatient that he hadn't finished up with the horses yet. Normally it doesn't take him more than twenty minutes to get the horses out. He lets them out one at a time, you know."

Lagarde nodded to indicate he was familiar with the process for letting horses out of their stalls. *You never wanted to put yourself in the way of a small stampede of energetic horses, even when you were an old hand at managing them.* He also understood that in the face of death it was nearly impossible to put one thought next to another one, much less in a logical timeline. Thoughts were like horses in that way, they could trample you underfoot if you didn't control them. Emma was doing remarkably well for a sudden widow. She turned back to face him.

"What distracted you?" Lagarde asked.

She shook her hand, palm toward him, as if to stop the words coming toward her. She would proceed in her own direction, at her own pace. "Sometimes Grant stops to joke with the kids we hired to muck out the stalls and help put the horses out, but half an hour is the most this chore ever takes. He's not a lingerer. When he didn't pick up on the intercom, I knew something was wrong. I walked down to the barn and called his name. I could see all the horses were out already. It was very quiet in there. I looked in all the stalls and the tack room. I thought he might have had a heart attack and was lying in a stall. He's the age where a heart attack might happen out of the blue. I turned around to leave the barn, to look for him outside, when I saw him, there, on the wall by the door."

She gasped, covered her eyes with her hand, as if to prevent seeing him pinned to the wall again. It was too late for that. She would never forget that image. The photograph her mind took of her husband with the pitchfork sticking out of his chest, blood splatter everywhere, his eyes and mouth open as if to scream, his face gray, would come back to her again and again when she didn't expect it. Her entire body shook.

"Why don't you sit down, Mrs. Wodehouse," Lagarde said, who had already decided she was either a very good actress or she had not committed the murder.

She shook her head no then gave him that palm out hand gesture again. He could see her consciously trying to steady herself. "I'm better off standing. There's a lot to do. I need to start calling people, plan the funeral, tasks I would rather not have to do. I can't crumble." She put a shaking hand over her mouth and looked away from him. She quaked from the effort of pulling herself together.

"I have a few more questions, but I can come back later today or tomorrow if that would be better for you."

He opened the small notebook he kept in his jacket pocket and started making notes, something he did while his mind was taking in his subject's tone, gesture, posture and facial expressions, none of which made it into words on paper but filled out the picture in his mind of what had happened and who his suspect might be.

She gathered her wits. "No, let's get just it over with."

"When you discovered the body, did you notice anything else out of the usual in the barn?"

"No, I could only see his body. I was in a tunnel, surrounded in darkness, with all the light on him. I don't know what else was there. I had to turn on the lights, it seemed so dark."

"Did you touch him in any way, or touch the weapon?" Lagarde hated asking this question because it forced her to look into her memory again, but he needed to know.

"No, no I didn't touch him." Emma drew her hands up to her chest, one over the other, as if the idea of touching his dead body was repugnant. "God help me. I was afraid to touch him." She put her hands over her face for a minute, recovered, and said, "I couldn't move or talk. For a while I couldn't even make a sound, and then I could only scream."

"Okay. We're done with the hard questions. How old was your husband?"

"Sixty, he just turned sixty." Emma sighed and turned her head to look out the window over the sink. "We had his birthday celebration this past Saturday. Everyone came."

"Was he still working?"

"Oh, yes, of course. I don't think he ever planned to stop working. He's a real estate lawyer. It's not hard work. Lots of closings, consultations and representation for developers, estate trusts, stuff like that. He had many clients, made good money."

"How old are you?"

"What does that have to do with anything?" she snapped at him. She calmed herself and said, "I'm fifty-five."

"When were you married?" Lagarde asked, thinking she looked very good for fifty-five-years-old.

"God, you guys, you worm your way into everything. Okay, I'm his third wife. Are you satisfied now? We've been married for ten years, ten happy years. Marrying Grant was the best decision I ever made."

Lagarde noted that she was not talking about love and devotion, but had focused on happiness—an experience that could mean different things to different people—and decision making, a function of reason rather than feelings. Perhaps she didn't love her husband in the traditional way that women were expected to love their partners. Although, maybe she knew something about marriage that Lagarde didn't know—that love wasn't enough if you wanted to be happy. Marriage required grit and patience.

That much he knew, even if he could never achieve it. But Emma seemed to be saying she hadn't married for love and was happy. He'd have to muddle that out at another time.

"Are his previous wives out of the way?"

He was never comfortable asking this question either, but the fact of her being wife number three meant there were two wives out there who had possible motives to murder the man, if necessary by proxy.

She laughed, a harsh sound, a bark. "You mean are they getting enough alimony to leave us alone? The first one is dead, cancer. The second one is remarried, so no alimony, but she does call from time to time when she's drunk and feeling nostalgic. He hangs up on her."

"So you don't think wife number two has any motive to want Mr. Wodehouse dead?"

"Rhonda want him dead? No. She wants him to fuck her again." She looked straight at Lagarde. "You're surprised by my language? I'm not a shrinking violet."

Lagarde didn't blink. Violent images brought out violent language in people who were usually restrained.

"Does Mr. Wodehouse have any children from the first two marriages?"

"Yes, two children. His daughter, Rebecca, from the first marriage, is in her mid-thirties. She lives in Phoenix. She has a husband and children. Seems happy. We see her on some holidays and vacations. His son, from the second marriage, Kyle, is in boarding school in Mercersville, Pennsylvania. Not a brilliant student, a little wild, but okay. He's seventeen and a senior. We see him when he wants to see us. He's an adolescent so he despises us, but he's not homicidal, I don't think. We're very generous with both of Grant's children. If you're looking for motive, it's better for them if Grant is alive. I'm the only beneficiary of Grant's estate in the will."

"Do you and Mr. Wodehouse have any children?"

"No. We married too late. We didn't want to adopt."

Lagarde detected a slight quiver of her lips when she spoke. Thinking there might be more to that story, he went on. "What do you do for a living, Mrs. Wodehouse?"

"I'm a lawyer. I specialize in divorces." Her eyes flashed. "I can give you my card…"

Lagarde thought he saw a twinkle, or maybe that was a warning in her eye. *Interesting woman to be making a joke at this moment…or maybe that wasn't a joke. Maybe she was always trolling for new clients.* "Are you successful?"

If she was capable of this level of calm functioning immediately after her husband was killed, Lagarde was thankful he had never encountered her across the table at any of his four divorces. His last marriage, a quick rebound relationship with the pleasant but flighty office receptionist Joyce, after his failed bid to win Beverly's heart, lasted only six months and still cost him a bundle. Lagarde had realized that he was a man who needed to be with a woman. He had now learned that he should never, ever marry someone he met at work because when the marriage was over, he would still have to see her every day.

There was another mystery he couldn't solve: even when the woman ended the relationship, she still held a grudge against you forever, for failing to keep her. Lagarde turned his attention back to Emma.

"I'm known as the dragon lady. I take care of my clients, leave no stone unturned, if you know what I mean."

Lagarde raised his eyebrows and was relieved none of the previous Mrs. Lagardes had found Emma in the telephone directory. "Were you married before you met Mr. Wodehouse?"

"Jesus." She nodded her head, yes. "Divorced."

Lagarde nodded. "Did you have any children from that marriage?"

"I have a son, William. He's thirty. He's been at Harvard for the last seven years getting his doctorate in something obscure related to Buddhism that no one will ever care about. He says he's done with that now, but it remains to be seen what will happen."

Lagarde noted her frustration with her son and moved on. "Do you think either your son or your ex-husband have a grievance against Mr. Wodehouse?"

"No," she said curtly then looked down at the floor. "Grant has been very generous with my son, and Harry doesn't give a damn what I do. He married his hair stylist."

Lagarde noted that she managed to disparage the woman who replaced her without saying anything bad about her. Perhaps it was her ex-husband she was disparaging by commenting on his new partner's profession. It was also possible that Emma was a snob. "What was your previous married name?"

"Emma Thornton, Mrs. Harry Thornton, of Shepherdstown." She grimaced.

No love lost there. "What were you going to do after breakfast?"

"We were going for a ride. I love riding in the morning, something about the clean air and a strong animal between my legs. We each ride one horse every day, so they all get exercised several times a week. We turn the horses out into the pasture after our ride and pitch some hay into the feeders and fill up the water trough. The neighbor kids help us with that."

Emma turned her back to him again and looked out the window. "Then we would have come inside, stripped off our clothes, had sex, showered, dressed and gone into the office. Is that enough detail for you? We have an office in Charles Town. We didn't have any early appointments. We have, *had* a good life." She put her hand over her mouth, as if she had said too much and wanted to stop any more words from escaping. She was shaking again.

Lagarde thought she might be overdoing the happy wife bit. "Can you think of anyone who wanted your husband dead?"

Mrs. Wodehouse looked out of the kitchen window for a long time. Lagarde waited. He didn't know if she was wracking her brain for a potential suspect or counting them.

"Ask his partner, Eugene Waters. They were arguing over the split of the executor proceeds from a large estate. But really, no, I can't think of anyone who would benefit from his death. Certainly not me."

"We'll need access to Mr. Wodehouse's office in town. Is there someone there who can let us in?"

"Yes, of course. Ann Roberts, our office administrator, can let you in. She'll be in by nine. She's very competent. I should probably call her…" Emma's voice trailed off, following her train of thought out of the window to the barn she was staring at again.

"Thanks. Did Mr. Wodehouse have an office here in the house? We'll want to have a look in it, and his files. And if he used a cell phone, we'll want to take a look at that. It might help us to find his killer."

"Yes, fine. His office is right off the living room." She looked around the kitchen and waved in the general direction of Grant's office. "His cell phone is on the table near the back door." She pointed to the cell phone but didn't move toward it.

Lagarde picked up the phone with a glove and put it in an evidence bag. "We'll return it to you when we're done."

She shrugged, saying, "I don't need it."

"Thanks again for your time. I'll be back in touch with you if I have more questions. You can call me anytime if you think of something pertinent or want to ask me any questions." He fished in the pocket of his jacket, pulled out his business card and handed it to her. "There will be a forensics team at the barn and maybe in your house all day today. They will need DNA samples and your fingerprints to match against the ones we find in the barn."

She nodded her assent. "By the way," she said as if she was almost beyond caring, "there's a horse missing. I don't see Paul in the paddock or the field. Is that important to your investigation?"

CHAPTER 4

John Knowles was a man possessed. He needed a plan and he couldn't think. He had four extended-release OxyContin pills left in his jacket pocket and those would barely get him through the day. His usual dealer, who worked part-time as a custodian at the local hospital, had disappeared, maybe been picked up by the police, maybe been nudged out by someone meaner with better business sense who knew he could get more money for that scarce and highly coveted product.

Feeling more anxious by the minute, Knowles had been waiting an hour for his dealer on the corner across from Ranson's three-story Victorian gingerbread-garnished town hall where he normally hooked up, opposite a little restaurant that was constantly changing hands. He patted his jacket just to make sure the money was still there. It was, a large reassuring lump snuggled down in his inside pocket. He patted it again. The gesture was pleasing to him. At least one thing had gone well this morning. He had gotten out to the Wodehouse farm before light, taken what he wanted, and gotten out of there. No one was the wiser. Now if the dealer would come

along, his day would be made. Out loud, he said, "Oh,
come on, man, show up already."

Standing on the corner this long was waving a flag to
the police, "Come and get me." He'd tried walking off,
stepped off the sidewalk and stepped back on. He
couldn't bring himself to leave. His dealer might show up
the minute he turned his back. In his mind, he ran through
other spots where he might get hooked up. Without a car,
he was limited to locations he could reach on foot: the
park, behind the elementary school, in the alley next to
the municipal court building, this very spot he was standing on.

Knowles had already tried the hospital emergency
room on three different days, in case hospital staff kept
track of his attempts. He faked excruciating leg pain,
writhing and groaning, telling them his pain was a nine
on a scale of one to ten. It wasn't really faking, he told
himself. He was in pain. It was a nine. But the answer
was always no.

"Can't find anything wrong with you, sir," the nurse
practitioner said. That meant no prescription for narcotics
of any kind. At this point, all the emergency docs in town
knew his name. He wasn't getting anything.

"This is drug-seeking behavior, Mr. Knowles," one of
the nurses told him sternly. "We frown on that." She
closed her thin lips in a thin line and looked him in the
eye. It seemed to Knowles that she had practiced that
look a lot.

Okay, been there, done that, burned that bridge.

All this thinking didn't help. He needed action. His
urgency had gotten him out to the Wodehouse farm. He
had searched the tack room in the barn in record time and
found Grant's money stash. Now he had the money but
his dealer was missing.

Life is a crock of shit.

He paced back and forth on the corner, trying to figure out what to do next. The Jefferson Pharmacy was just a few blocks from where he stood but he'd need a weapon to get them to give him what he wanted. The hospital, across the street from the pharmacy, would be the ideal source. They had all the oxy he needed there. He suspected the hospital was the source of his dealer's stash. Knowles just had to figure out how to get his own hands on it.

He wondered if he could walk in through the visitors' entrance of the hospital, wander through the corridors pretending he was looking for the bathroom and walk around until he discovered the dispensary for admitted patients. There *had* to be an in-house pharmacy. They probably locked drugs up so that people like him couldn't just walk in and take what they needed. The entire world was organized against him. He might have to bribe a nurse or watch until the pharmacist got lazy and didn't lock the dispensary door behind him when he left to take a pee break.

Knowles ran his hands through his sandy colored hair, rubbed his whiskered face, rolled his head around on his shoulders and jammed his hands into his jacket pockets, a crazy man. He could see his bleary-eyed reflection in the large plate-glass windows of the restaurant across the street.

For sure, the waitress inside, who had no customers, was sitting at the counter watching him through the window, with her cell phone in her hand. It was only a matter of time until she called the police.

He could hear that conversation in his head. '*Yeah (gum snap, gum snap), he's been out there an hour...Yeah an hour, walkin' up 'n down, up 'n down, nowhere to go 'n all day to do it...Yep, yep, he's for sure homeless by the rags he's wearin'. Spookin' my custom-*

ers.' He had to think of something before police showed
up and told him to move along.

Knowles knew his family wouldn't help him nor
would he get any sympathy from his ex-wife. His teenage
children would say, "Oh, hi, Dad. I don't have any money," and hang up on him when he called. They knew now
that thirty seconds into the pleasant chatter, he was going
to ask them to lend him money he would never repay. It
didn't bother Knowles that he was asking his children for
money. It only bothered him that they wouldn't *give* it to
him.

His so-called friends didn't return his calls. He'd been
sleeping on the cement floor of the pool house in Jefferson Memorial Park in Charles Town while his family
slept soundly in that lovely McMansion with a view of
the Shenandoah River he bought when he was riding
high. There was something fundamentally unfair about
that. Oh, sure, everybody loved him when he was the
bank's vice president and asset fund manager. He and his
wife were invited to all the classy parties. His kids went
to a fancy private school in Maryland. He had been on a
first name basis with the state politicians and the US Sen-
ator to whose party he had given big campaign bucks.

And then just because he happened to use client funds
to pay off a few stock bets of his own that just didn't
work out, he was done. It was over. Everybody just
turned their backs on him. Important people crossed the
street to avoid being seen talking to him. If he happened
to corner an old friend, that so-called friend would say,
"Oh, hey, John, haven't seen you in a dog's age. Gotta
run," the whole time looking at the ground, over his
shoulder, across the street, anywhere but in his eyes, as if
they were afraid that bad luck was contagious and they
would catch it from him.

"You're lucky the bank covered up your mess and

didn't have you charged with criminal co-mingling of funds." No help from his wife, nada, even though she was the beneficiary of the client money he'd stolen successfully without getting caught before. Instead, she screamed at him, "You could have gone to prison!" and stomped out of the house on her three-inch high Louboutin heels, got in her expensive car and drove off, leaving him to pull out his hair alone. There were days now when he thought he'd have been better off going to prison.

But he didn't really blame himself. He blamed Grant Wodehouse for the end of his life as he knew it. He hated Wodehouse, who, as Knowles saw it, was the direct cause of his destruction. It was Wodehouse who had sucked him into living high on the hog, who made him think he needed more and more money. It was Wodehouse who invited him on that fancy Tahiti cruise where he could stare all day at Emma's amazing tits and get away with it, who took him to Ireland to golf, and invited him on a ski vacation in Aspen. That was where the accident happened that changed his life. He slammed into a tree going downhill at thirty-miles-an-hour, grinning to beat the band one second, crushed and senseless the next.

He woke up in a hospital bed with a concussion and multiple injuries, but the worst was his leg, broken in multiple places. His wife, Adrienne, said, "It's a miracle you lived," with a kind of wistfulness that made him think that she wished he had died and she'd gotten the million dollars in life insurance he'd set up for her and the kids. Some days, even he wished he'd died. It gave him some pleasure to think that now that he wasn't paying the premiums. If Adrienne had let the policy lapse when he did die, she'd get nothing.

The doctors had saved his leg. After a year of physical therapy, he could walk without a cane, but the pain had been and still was excruciating, causing him to consume the prescribed Oxycodone like candy. After a while, he couldn't get through the day without the oxy. By midday, coming down from his morning pill, he'd feel anxious. He couldn't make any decisions or made very bad ones. He feared everyone at the bank was after his piece of the pie or was looking over his shoulder, second guessing him, poaching his clients. When he tried tapering off the meds, he couldn't sleep, couldn't eat because he felt nauseous, and every muscle in his body ached. He was a wreck. His wife told him to go back to the doctor, something was still wrong with him. The fact that his wife could care less for him at that stage should have alerted him that something was up. He just didn't see it. He should have realized that while he was caressing Emma's beautiful ass aboard that lovely yacht in Tahiti, Grant was providing similar services for his wife, Adrienne—only Wodehouse didn't stop when the trip was over.

About six months after he had been released from the hospital, still walking with a cane, Knowles had spotted his wife and Wodehouse at the gas station on the corner of Washington and West Streets. He was stopped for the red light, a closed car dealership on one side of him, tire store on the other, a drive-through drug store in front of him to the left and the cheap gas station to the right. The buildings suddenly loomed up above him so that he was in a tunnel that blinded him to everything but the sight of his wife and old friend. He didn't know if they met on purpose or by accident, but while he waited in his car for the light to change, he watched his beautiful wife get out of her silver Audi, walk up to Wodehouse who was pumping gas into his black Mercedes, pull his head down to hers and kiss him with great passion, no inhibitions, right there in broad daylight in front of everyone. It took all Knowles's self-control not to crash his car right into her. No, he drove on, feeling fury embed itself in his cells like a replicating virus until it had taken over his entire body. After that moment, he couldn't do anything right. His life went to hell. He was spending four hundred dollars a week on his happy pills, then a thousand, then two thousand. It didn't help that Wodehouse loaned him fifteen thousand dollars until he could pull himself together. Knowles sensed Grant was throwing his good deed in his face, but he still took the money. What else could he do? With his wife's lifestyle and his prescription drug habit, that money was only enough for a month.

Knowles coasted for a while, lying on the sofa in the family room watching ESPN all day, blissfully unaware of everything going on around him as long as he could pop those little pills that made him imagine he was back on the yacht in Tahiti, rocked gently on the waves.

He got away with this behavior for nearly a year, until his wife threw him out of the house and started divorce proceedings against him. He thought it was ironic that she hired Emma to represent her in the divorce. *Didn't Emma know about Adrienne's affair with her husband? Wouldn't it have come out in deposition at some point?* Nevertheless, together they cleaned him out. When they were done, there wasn't a single piece of real property that he still owned. He was lucky they'd left him his car, his Rolex, and the clothes on his back. Emma told him they were being kind.

Knowles turned around in circles a few more times and decided he'd have better luck stealing pills from the hospital where security seemed lax to him and there were lots of people wandering around, another lost visitor looking for the cafeteria. He had about four hundred dollars in his pocket, which he would have happily handed over to a dealer for twenty pills, but there was no dealer to give the money to. He patted his pocket again just to make sure the bundle of bills was still there. There was an upside: if he could steal the pills, he'd have the money for ten nights at the North Hill motel where he could get a room for thirty-nine dollars a night. There would be a bed, television, his own toilet, and no one would roust him from sleep at six in the morning to throw him out. Heaven, and he didn't even have to die to get there.

He crossed the street and walked the two blocks to the hospital. This is a good plan, he told himself on the way. He'd be indoors while he waited for his opportunity to dash into the dispensary and steal the pills, *and* he could use a bathroom *with* toilet paper. *Strange how toilet paper seems such a luxury.* It never occurred to Knowles, in his crazed state, that the hospital had security cameras everywhere or that, if he was caught, the authorities would want to know where he got all that cash.

CHAPTER 5

9:10 a.m.:

Emma lost her composure almost as soon as Detective Lagarde walked out of her house. She barely made it to a kitchen chair. With shaking fingers, she pulled a cigarette from the pack on the kitchen table and put it in her mouth. It took her five clicks to get the lighter to work.

"Stupid, fucking, stupid, shitty piece of crap," she muttered around the cigarette clamped between her lips. Cigarette finally lit, she took a deep drag, sat back in her chair, and exhaled. "Son-of-a-bitch! *Son-of-a-bitch*! How could this happen now, when things were going so well?"

It didn't matter to her that what she was saying made no sense. She was simply making sounds, angry sounds that matched the howling in her head—steam escaping from a boiling kettle. She realized she was talking out loud, got up from her chair, and walked around the first floor of her lovely home.

They had gotten the historic home and its adjoining two-hundred acres cheap during the 2008 Great Recession when no one was buying property in West Virginia's Eastern Panhandle. The price had dropped from one and a half million to $600,000 and they jumped on it. They had loved fixing it up.

She still enjoyed the number of rooms she had to wander around in: a sitting room, a living room, a dining room in which they could seat twenty guests, a library they used as a den where they watched television, Grant's large office with built in mahogany shelving and storage. There was also the large kitchen, a mudroom right off the back porch, a butler's pantry, the solarium that led to a stone patio next to a beautifully landscaped pool designed to replicate a natural pond they had installed. Her office was also on the first floor in what had been the housekeeper's suite, with its own bathroom.

She had decorated each room with care over several years, no prepackaged feeling of a designer's hand, which always appeared to have been pulled out of plastic bags. Each of her rooms was unique in its furniture, arrangement and fabric patterns, but all of them shared the palette of dove grey, cream white, deep brown and goldfinch yellow colors she had chosen. There was a fireplace in every room, and large multi-paned windows were draped with brocade or velvet which she swapped out in summer for linen. She bought local artists' work—large multimedia pieces, oils, and water colors—so that visitors to her home always thought she was an art patron. Actually, she bought paintings with colors that went with her color scheme, and she bought local art because it was dirt cheap compared to New York prices. And, she had to admit, some of the work was beautiful. She bought what appealed to her, regardless of style. And really, what else mattered? This was her home. She only had herself to please.

Emma completed her circuit of the first floor. No intruders yet. No one had overheard her outburst. She would have to struggle to maintain decorum when the forensic techs were crawling all over her house, because she was sure they weren't going to stick to Grant's office. If not the techs, then the investigators would pick apart their entire lives until every little bit of dirty laundry was laid out for everyone to see. And then there would be the reporters of these stupid local papers, each looking for their own particular slant. There were aspects of her life with Grant that she intended to keep very private. Her anger flared. "What a mess you made, you stupid son of a bitch," she shouted at the walls.

She realized it was foolish to blame her husband for getting killed, but she was overwhelmed by feelings she couldn't control. She had to blame someone. He was dead, certainly couldn't defend himself. She walked over to their wedding photograph in a silver frame on an imported inlaid wood chest placed under one of the large windows in the living room. The chest was framed by the sweep of stage curtain drapes pulled back from the window. In the photo, she was glowing in a pearl gray Donna Karan suit and he was handsome in his very expensive Armani. In a way, he had been Prince Charming to her Rapunzel—he had rescued her from the tower of exurban boredom in a way that getting a law degree at the University of Baltimore, setting up a practice, or even cheating on her first husband hadn't done.

Worth a fortune? If people only knew. Their whole existence was a façade. They borrowed from one bank to pay back another, flipped credit cards, flipped houses, placed large bets on stock tips and got out early as soon as the stock rose ten points. They didn't need to go over to that blue-collar casino in Charles Town to gamble. They were doing it with their lives. If a stock tanked or land value bottomed out, they were out hundreds of thousands of dollars. Late in the recession, after they realized the local economy was not going to bounce back quickly or as robustly as it did in New York City, they lost their shirts in a real estate development scheme. You couldn't buy low and sell high if nobody was buying, but Grant was addicted to doing business that way and nothing she could say would stop him.

"Don't worry, honey," he would say, "we'll come out ahead. You'll see."

He'd been right. They had now recouped their losses, but the uneasy feeling in the pit of her stomach that risky transactions gave her continued. She was sure Grant was engaged in a new scheme that would not be good for her financial health. Three years ago she had started sheltering her income from him. She set up her own law practice as a separate LLC and put aside a substantial portion of her income and assets in a living trust for which she was the grantor and trustee, of which only she and her son William were beneficiaries. She had convinced Grant to put the deed to the historic house in her name to shield it from business vicissitudes and that property was now included in the trust. It seemed the only logical thing to do. If his financial house of cards tumbled down now that he was dead, she would be okay. Emotionally, she wasn't so sure, although she had tried to insulate herself against a long winter of loss. It seemed that she might have been wrong. Emma walked back into the kitchen and stubbed out her cigarette in the ashtray on the table.

Grant had also taught her about the upside of risk-taking. Sometimes the risk of a big bet was worth it. When they won, the world was their playground. Once they had chartered a yacht that came with captain and crew and taken friends to Tahiti. The sex on that trip was amazing. They engaged in a little spouse swapping and frankly she was just as eager to try something new as Grant was. They shared arousing details afterward. She and Grant still talked themselves into the sack by telling each other stories about that trip. Given her age, she had doubted she would ever have another adventure like that one. Today, for the first time, she doubted that she would ever want another one. It took her by surprise, her sense of endless loss. She'd been cavalier about sex with other people, thinking herself sophisticated in her attitudes about marital fidelity. And although she had never been jealous, and had dabbled herself in couplings with strangers, Grant's death, at this moment, was the end of love and intimacy.

She kept trying to get her mind to focus on the fact that she had to get on with things, but her mind was a slippery character and wanted to go where it wanted to go. Her mind wanted to linger on odd details: the eggs that had stuck in the pan, the eggs she scraped into the trash before she went out to look for Grant. *Grant had gotten a call on his cell phone at eleven o'clock last night, had walked away from me to answer, and didn't tell me about it afterward. He was looking right at me from the spot he was nailed to on the barn wall, as if he were trying to tell me something. If I hadn't been distracted, I would have known something was wrong sooner when he didn't come up from the barn. Could I have stopped his murder if I'd walked down to the barn earlier, or would I also be dead?* She had always thought of her marriage to Grant as pragmatic, the smart choice of a smart woman. She hadn't expected to feel grief when he died. She was stunned by the array of emotions shooting through her. There was nowhere to go in this maze that didn't lead to pain.

Emma knew she had to call Grant's son and daughter, at least them and Grant's idiot partner. She should probably call their accountant, too. Her sister, her closest friends, she could text with the news. The idea of making these calls was too high a wall to jump, typing the words

"Grant is dead" too much effort for the muscles in her fingers. She sat down at the table again and lit another cigarette. *It doesn't matter when I call the children. Grant will still be dead, no matter what, for the next thirty years of my existence—if I live that long—he will always be dead.*

CHAPTER 6

9:10 a.m.:

Lagarde ambled from the house back down toward the paddock with a list of more people to interview and no good clues. It was early in the investigation, the time when everyone and anyone was a suspect. The boys who'd had the wits to call nine-one-one were now sitting on the top paddock fence rail talking to Sgt. Black. They seemed to be glad to hang out and tell him everything they knew instead of going to school. It was possible the kids had seen, heard or were aware of more than they thought. Black was right to try and tease that information out of them.

"Hey, guys," Lagarde said, walking up to them. "Is there a horse missing?"

"Oh, yeah," said the taller boy with sandy blond hair hanging over his eyes. "Paul's missing. They usually keep him in the pasture if the mares are in the paddock. He's a good sized horse, a stallion. Mr. Wodehouse was going to geld him this year. Sometimes he jumps the fence and takes a trot around. He usually comes back."

"Did you notice if anything else is missing from the barn?"

"We didn't really get a good look in there," the shorter kid said. "We were coming over to help with the horses and heard Mrs. Wodehouse screaming. She was inside the barn, sort of bent over holding her stomach, pointing at Mr. Wodehouse, and making these really weird noises between the screams. We saw Mr. Wodehouse dead and all. It creeped us out. We ran out of there. Al called the police."

He had close-cropped brown hair and blue eyes. *The boys didn't look like brothers, but they could have different fathers.* Family lines snaked all over, something Lagarde knew from his own life. You couldn't tell anything by appearances.

"Let's go back in the barn and you guys can take a look around." The body had already been loaded into the ME's van. There was nothing left in the barn to frighten them except the memory of what they'd seen, well that and a little blood. "Just make sure you stand where I tell you and don't move around."

As they walked toward the barn, the kids were as excited as if they were getting free tickets to a Redskins football game. Now that their initial repulsion had receded, their curiosity had taken over. "I'm definitely Skyping about this as soon as I get home" the taller one whispered to his brother.

"Get anything useful from the witnesses?" Lagarde asked Black as they walked into the barn.

"The boys like it here," Black explained, "no bad vibes between the dead guy and the missus, no scenes in recent memory of any threats from anyone else that they witnessed. They said the horses are well fed and cared for. There's plenty of hay and feed delivered on time. The farrier and vet get called when they're needed, and no worry that they know of about money. Wodehouse was giving them fifty bucks each a week to muck stalls and groom the horses. Sometimes he took them along on events, paying them extra for that. He let them walk the horses alone, but not ride them alone. He was giving them riding lessons. He trusted them to take care of the horses on their own if he and Mrs. Wodehouse were away. The boys are pretty proud of that."

"Sounds irresponsible to me," Lagarde muttered. "How come the boys aren't in school?"

"In-school service day." When Lagarde looked blank, Black explained, "You know, for teacher training. Kids get out of school for the day." To Lagarde's continued blank stare, Black clarified, "No school today."

Lagarde nodded. "Was the mother of the toddler also the boys' mother?"

"No, she's Mrs. Tabor, the neighbor on the other side. The kids live in the house to the west of this one. The tall one is Albert, fourteen. He's the one who made the call, around 7:30, he says. I'll check that with dispatch. The short one is Marv, ten-years-old. Last name is Le Gore. Their mother's a nurse, works those twelve-hour shifts four days a week at Winchester Hospital, about forty minutes away in Virginia, so she's gone by six-thirty a.m. and comes home in the evening after they get back from school. They said she's glad they have something 'wholesome' to occupy them. They both put air quotes around the word wholesome. There doesn't appear to be a father at their home, at least one the boys talk about."

"What did Mrs. Tabor have to say?"

"Elaine Tabor, twenty-six. She was pretty shaken. She kept weeping and talking about what a great guy Grant was, how helpful he was, how she could always count on him. I got the idea that there was more between them than simple neighborly kindness. Her husband drives long-haul truck, so he's gone weeks at a time and she's alone with her baby girl, three-years-old. If I was Mr. Tabor, I might want to get a paternity test on that baby."

"You're leaping, man. There's no evidence for that kind of speculation."

"Think about it, sir, she's running over here in a nightgown so flimsy you can see her thighs and what-not through the fabric with only a sweater thrown on for modesty in the early morning when she *knows* Wodehouse is out here messing with the horses. There's a long leather couch in the tack room, nice fleece blanket hanging off the back of it. Somebody sleeps, or does whatever, there. We should get the blanket to forensics, test for DNA. I'll tell them to check out the sofa also."

Lagarde had raised his eyebrows at Black's use of the term *what-not and said,* "Is that an anatomically correct term?"

He looked back in the direction of the road, noting he couldn't see either the Tabor home or Ridge Road from the barn. The woods surrounding the property were too dense with broadleaf evergreens, holly and rhododendron, to see more than a few feet from the verge. "Well, if you're right about Mrs. Tabor and Wodehouse, that gives them motive. Maybe they were in it together." It was well-known detective lore that the most obvious murder suspect was someone the victim knew, often intimately, although Lagarde never let the obvious stop him from theorizing otherwise.

They walked into the barn and Lagarde told the boys not to touch anything but to stand still and look around. The boys shook their heads and said they didn't see anything unusual, except the blood. They walked into the tack room. Taking their assignment very seriously, the boys stood in one spot and turned in a circle. One of the boys raised his hand, as if he was in class.

"Yeah?"

"There's a saddle missing," Albert said. "And the

small lock box—see over there," he pointed to a small metal box on top of the old wooden chest, "it wasn't ever locked, and it was kept in the top drawer of that chest. Now it's open and empty. Mr. Wodehouse kept cash for hay and feed deliveries, the money for me and Marv and other stuff that had to be paid for right away out here so he wouldn't have to run up to the house, or if he was gone when a delivery came, he would text me and I'd run over and pay them."

"How much money did he keep in the box?"

"Sometimes a couple hundred. It depended. Marv and me took our pay out of the box every week."

Lagarde was struck by how trusting Wodehouse was. He kept a wad of cash in his barn and expected these boys to take only what they'd earned. Maybe Wodehouse was a fool, or very careless. Maybe he had way too much money to worry about a few hundred bucks. But the missing money might mean Lagarde's original hunch was right, there was someone in the barn when Wodehouse walked into it, maybe hiding in the hayloft or the tack room, someone who knew about the lock box and the cash in it who surprised Wodehouse right after he had let the horses out.

That someone killed him, took the money, saddled up a horse and rode off sounded momentarily like he'd time-traveled to a previous century. Whoever this guy was, and Lagarde was convinced the murderer was a man, they had him on horse stealing if nothing else. They just had to find a horse thief.

He looked over at Black, who was already on his cell phone calling in a description of the horse as Marv was telling it to him. Lagarde had a moment of severe cognitive dissonance. Horse thieves and cell phones simply didn't go together. Anyone who had ever watched Sesame Street knew that.

"Make sure the forensic guys bag the lock box for prints too," he told Black.

There were only a few small problems with his theory: if all the perp wanted to do was steal money and a horse, why didn't he do it before Wodehouse came down to the barn. That would have been a lot easier. The barn wasn't locked. Even if the thief was surprised in the process of stealing the money, why wouldn't he just run away? Maybe the perp came to do the murder and the theft was simply a matter of opportunity. The other problem with this theory was this: somehow the perp had enough time to steal the money and the horse before Mrs. Wodehouse came down to the barn. *Not unless the barn and everyone in it fell into a time warp at just the right moment. I am missing something important in this timeline.*

Lagarde walked out of the barn and Black and the boys followed him. He took another visual inventory of the property. From the barn, he could see a Jeep, a Lexus and a Mercedes parked in a circle around a tree to the right of the house. A Dodge Ram pick-up truck was parked near the upper level hayloft entrance to the barn. *These folks certainly have a lot of vehicles.* Nearby, a horse trailer sat on the grass by the side of a gravel lane that led from the main road to the barn. A thief could have taken any of these vehicles to leave the farm. *Why take a horse?* Lagarde told Black to get an inventory of all the family vehicles from Mrs. Wodehouse just in case one was missing.

"Larry, get the forensics techs to check the horse trailer also. Maybe the perp hid in it. Come to think of it, maybe he's still in it." Lagarde ran up the slight hill toward the horse trailer. He noticed footprints pressed into the long grass going downhill and stepped to the right of them, motioning to the others to stay clear of the area. *Man-sized, sneaker tracks*, he noted, mentally storing the information away. *Not Wodehouse's. He was wearing boots.*

A little winded by his brief exertion, Lagarde un-hitched the back of the horse trailer and looked in. No perp, and no signs that anything had been in the trailer for a while. He let out a deep sigh. It was never that easy. He revised his developing scenario. The thief might have been sleeping in the tack room after walking to the farm in the middle of the night. He might have waited for Wodehouse to come down to the barn. Lagarde walked toward the pickup truck and looked in the window with-out touching anything. The keys were in the ignition. So why didn't the perp just take the truck to make his geta-way instead of going through the trouble of saddling a horse?

His theory of the crime wasn't going to hold. The guy had his own transportation or he walked away. Neverthe-less, they'd have to check out the truck and see if there were prints, food wrappers or discarded items, maybe even gum chewed by someone who was not Emma or Grant. It was never a simple task to gather all the evi-dence. It had to be done one item at a time. It was time consuming and Lagarde was always annoyed when fo-rensics' findings contradicted his hunches. Regardless, his job was the same. He'd have to run down every pos-sible suspect, check their alibis and connect the dots. He was putting together a puzzle for which *all* the pieces were currently blank. If Black was right about Elaine Ta-bor's relationship to the dead guy, the group of suspects might include a cuckolded husband or an outraged wife.

Now that he thought of it, he and Black should drop by the Tabor's house before they left the neighborhood to ask a few more questions about her relationship with Wodehouse.

Lagarde walked into the hayloft and looked around. Black and the boys followed him. "Is Paul easy to ride?" Lagarde asked the boys.

"No way. He's touchy. He'll buck you off if he doesn't like you, and even sometimes if he does, just for fun. It's a game to him. Mr. Wodehouse has a tough time with him. He mainly keeps him for breeding. Paul's a great jumper. Won a lot of ribbons in steeple chase racing, but he's no good for dressage. He won't do patterns or behave well enough. Oh, and he bites other horses."

The kid sounded pretty knowledgeable to Lagarde. That was the way you learned about managing horses, by hanging around them, helping out. Albert reminded Lagarde of himself when he was young.

"Yeah," Marv said, knowing this fact from experience, "that's a horse you don't want to walk behind."

"One last thing, guys, before we let you go today, did Mr. Wodehouse ever let anyone sleep up here in the hayloft or in the tack room?"

The boys looked at each other then looked down at their feet, moved a few stalks of straw with the toes of their shoes, then looked back at Lagarde. "Well, I don't know if he lets them," Albert said, "but some homeless guys know their way here. They sleep in the hayloft sometimes, just over night, on their way to somewhere else."

"Do the Wodehouses know about this activity in their barn?" Black queried.

"If they do, they never said anything to us about it. Not our business, anyways. We don't say anything to them."

Black gave the boys a high five each and sent them back to their house. "Fingerprints are going to be a mess," he said woefully.

"The boys certainly expanded our perp pool," Lagarde

added, knowing what lay ahead, scanning the floor for anything.

His head snapped, zeroing-in on what he spotted, something gleaming under the hay. As the sun rose, it picked out the edge of something metallic that now flashed, catching his eye. Lagarde strode over, donning a latex glove he'd pulled from his pocket, and picked it up. A brass compass, not cheap, perhaps antique. The cover was scratched as if it had been pulled in and out of a tight pocket frequently over many years. The back of the compass was engraved: *For my wonderful Warren, to help you find your way. Love always, Mom. June, 2004.*

"Check this out, Larry. Our perp might be a mama's boy who lost his way." He held out his find to the sergeant.

Black walked over and pulled a small clear evidence bag from his pocket. He opened the top and Lagarde slid the compass inside. "Man, too many metaphors and puns for me," Black said, writing details of what they found, when and where on the bag.

"See if you can find out where 'Mom' got this and for whom." Black kept writing, adding to his ever-growing to-do list. "Get any fingerprints on it. And check with the sheriff, see if the Wodehouses ever reported intruders camping in their barn."

Black nodded as if he hadn't thought of doing exactly that on his own.

"Oh, while you're at it, have the tech guys check out Wodehouse's phone for anything useful." Lagarde pulled the bagged cell phone from his pocket and handed it to Black, who wrote on the bag immediately where he'd gotten the item and when. "He left it in the house," he said with raised eyebrows and a slight tilt of the head. "Be good if we knew the last person he talked to."

Lagarde looked around the hayloft once more to see if

it would cough up anymore of its hidden treasures. "Let's move on to Mrs. Tabor."

Black nodded in agreement. "Maybe the forensic techs will find something more useful up here than a compass."

CHAPTER 7

9:10 a.m.:

Elaine Tabor pulled on a pair of skinny jeans and a cotton turtleneck sweater. It was easy for her to get dressed—she didn't wear underwear or makeup. She ran a brush through her blonde hair and lifted it up into a ponytail, controlling a small tremor when she looked at herself in the mirror. Grant would never again tell her how pretty she was. Right now, she didn't care how she looked. And if she had, she didn't have time to do anything about it. The one thing she had learned about being a mother was that there was very little "me time" in her life. She looked at herself again in the mirror to assess whether she looked sad, but her daughter, Molly, was already pulling at her leg. She'd have to settle for *thinking* she was pretty. At least that's what her mother always told her, "You have a beautiful face. You'll go far, baby doll."

Molly wanted to show Elaine something in the living room. Elaine figured it was something on the television. One of the Muppets on the show Molly watched in the morning must be doing something clever. She remembered from her childhood Mr. Rogers telling her from his perch on her television screen to go ask her mommy what some word meant. She would go running to her mother, who was always in the kitchen, screaming the word at the top of her lungs as if it was the most important mission on earth.

Her mother would put her cigarette in the ashtray, put Elaine on her lap, smooth her hair, and say, "Let's see, a 'companion' is a friend who's always glad to see you, baby doll." Then she would give Elaine a squeeze and a kiss on her cheek. Such care was what she loved about her mother, in addition to always having the right answer.

Elaine wished now that she had listened better when her mother suggested that she not get involved with Grant. She had been so excited about him, thinking that he would divorce Emma and marry her, take her away from the tedium of her life, take her to fancy hotels in Hawaii and expensive shops in New York City. She had watched all the *Sex in the City* episodes on television and it was easy to imagine herself in designer jeans, stiletto heels, a little mink jacket and really expensive diamond jewelry strutting down Fifth Avenue.

Her fantasies of a future life with Grant excited her so much she felt she might burst if she didn't tell someone. His name was always in her mouth, about to be spoken. Sometimes she just said it out loud to herself, "Grant Wodehouse, Grant Wodehouse," to release the tension. She wrote it over and over on the pad in the kitchen, but then she balled up the pages and threw them away because she didn't want her husband to find them. She certainly couldn't tell any of her friends. They were terrible gossips.

She had confided in her mother, who didn't approve of the affair at all, saying, "Baby doll, you gotta stop this foolin' around or it'll come back to bite you."

Mom never understood. Don't I deserve something

better than this old doublewide? Now, I'm never getting away from here. Grant had a way of dropping by mid-day when his wife was in court or meeting with clients. He would walk in the front door of Elaine's house without knocking, stride up to Elaine, take her face in his hands and kiss her passionately. The kiss always took her breath away. Within seconds his hands would be in her pants, under her shirt and she would be walking backward toward her bedroom or the bathroom, anywhere there was a door she could close so Molly wouldn't see what happened next. Sometimes they didn't make it to the bedroom. She loved it when he backed her up against the wall and buried himself in her. She wanted to suck him into her body, to breathe him in. Their couplings were over in a matter of minutes. He would wash up, kiss her, put five hundred or a thousand dollars under a plate on the table in the kitchen and go out again, leaving her smiling.

"He's buying your services, honey," her mother had said.

She resented her mother's blunt description of Grant's behavior. "He's not, Mom. He's helping me out. He knows Ron isn't making a lot of money and I have needs."

"What needs are those? The needs between your legs?"

"C'mon, Mom, you know I'm saving money so Molly can go to private school and have pretty clothes and riding lessons in a few years."

"What does your girl need a private school for? Public school was good enough for you. What kind of hoity-toity ideas is this guy putting in your head, girl? You need to think straight and get him out of your life. Ron's a good guy and you're gonna lose him if you keep on."

"Oh, Mom, you don't understand. Grant is so kind to

me." As hard as it was, she resisted the urge to bite her fingernails while talking to her mother.

"He's kind to his dick. Nothing but trouble's gonna to come to you from this."

Elaine supposed her mother would be relieved Grant was dead. "Good riddance," she would say. *Maybe I should call Mom and tell her.* Wiping that thought from her mind, Elaine sat down on the floor with her daughter and started putting one little wooden block on top of another.

"Look, here's an A," she said to Molly and handed the block to her daughter. Molly put the A, red side on top, on the block on the floor, picked up another block and handed it to her mother.

Elaine had close to fifteen thousand dollars in the bank, enough to get her own place if she wanted. The question was, did she want that? *Now that Grant is dead, why not stay with Ron? He is a good man.* She agreed with her mother about that. *Good looking in his own way, with his red hair and beard, and he's a hard worker.* But then she remembered he could drink a six pack a night when he was home, which worried her a bit, *and* sometimes he backhanded her when she got "uppity," as he called it, but he made a decent living. Now that she had that little nest egg set aside, maybe she wouldn't be so irritated with his little ways. It wasn't hard to pick up his clothes off the floor, empty his ash trays, and cook him his fried chicken with macaroni and cheese. He never asked her to go to work, didn't cheat on her, at least as far as she knew, and she didn't mind his frequent absence. It gave her a lot of time to herself. *With the money I've saved, maybe I could fix up our house, buy a few clothes for myself and Molly, and still have savings in the bank.* It made her feel respectable to have savings.

She had gotten to this comfortable place in her consid-

eration of her future when someone knocked on her front
door. She unfolded herself from the floor, walked to the
door and opened it without looking to see who was there.
Molly followed her.

"Oh, come on in, Detective," Elaine said to Sergeant
Black, recognizing him from earlier that morning, then
looking past him to Lagarde. Black had talked with her
briefly and gotten her name, where she lived and why she
was there. She held the storm door open. Molly clung to
her mother's leg and looked up at the men.

"Want a cookie?" Molly asked the two men.

"Not right now, honey," Black said, rubbing her head.
"We need to talk to your mommy." He turned to Elaine.
"This is Lieutenant Sam Lagarde. He's the lead detective
on the Grant Wodehouse case."

Elaine nodded in Lagarde's direction. "This is Molly.
Please have a seat." She pointed to the sofa and chairs in
the living room.

They made their way around the litter of toys on the
floor and sat down—Lagarde and Black in each of the
chairs, Elaine and Molly on the sofa. The TV was still on
and puppets were counting to ten. Molly picked up the
chant toward the end. "Eight, nine, ten," she screeched
then grinned at Lagarde for approval.

"Good job," he said to her.

Taking in the surroundings, Lagarde noted the trailer
was decorated in what he considered "standard American," solid pieces of furniture clad in wear-hard fabrics
and patterns, designed to hide dirt and go together, and
could be found in every strip mall furniture store. The
narrow, plastic blinds, stained from age, covered each
window and were accentuated by panel drapes. The doublewide, situated on a cement foundation, was roomy for
a family of three but lacked any frills. He'd noticed on
the way over, the driveway wasn't paved. Loose gravel

brought them to the doorstep, and the only protection for the vehicles was an aluminum canopy off to one side of the drive, under which her car sat. They kept the trashcans beneath the shelter, along with an assortment of tools in a large, open Rubbermaid box.

After evaluating the interior, Lagarde assumed that the organization outside was Mr. Tabor's doing. Inside, Elaine Tabor had absolutely no housekeeping system and no intention of developing one. A clothing, toys, magazines and food wrapper bomb had exploded in all directions in the living room and Elaine, he noticed, simply stepped around the mess.

The house appeared to be on a half-acre of land, set back from the road about two hundred feet, screened on three sides from its neighbors by dense woods, which adjoined the Wodehouse farm. This land must have been part of the main farm's frontage and sold off by the previous owner even before the Wodehouses bought the farm. It was possible Mr. Tabor's parents gave him the land.

There was no zoning in Jefferson County, unlike neighboring Loudon County, Virginia. Mansions and shacks co-existed side by side here and no one thought anything of it. A man's property was his to do with what he pleased, for the most part, in West Virginia. In Lagarde's estimation, Elaine Tabor's husband had tried to provide the best habitat he could for his wife.

"Do you work?" Lagarde asked, focusing his attention on Elaine. He started interviews in the middle and worked his way outward to the easy and hard questions. It was a method that kept people off guard. They couldn't anticipate what he was going to ask next and prepare their answers.

"Oh, no, Ron doesn't want me to work. He says I'm too pretty to go out in public on my own." She giggled and tossed her ponytail. "I was Miss Jefferson County in 2008. Anyway, what would I do?" She smiled somewhat apologetically and shrugged.

So he's a jealous man. "Is your husband gone a lot?"

"Yeah, maybe three weeks out of four. He drives long haul across the country from Baltimore to San Diego. Sometimes he does the run to Florida. He contracts with several of the trucking companies. 'Never drive an empty truck,' he says." She pulled Molly onto her lap and started braiding the child's soft blonde hair. "It gets lonely here sometimes," she said to Molly's head, "but I have my friends and my mother nearby."

"Does Mr. Tabor own his truck?" Black asked.

"Oh, yes, he just bought it last year. A Cascadia Evolution. It's very fancy." She beamed proudly at them and Lagarde instantly understood her allure. "It has a bed in it and a microwave and even a TV. Ron can use the bathroom at the truck stops and sleep in the truck. Saves lots of money, he says. He leased a truck for a long time, but he said that was a losing proposition, giving back money to the trucking company that they should be paying him." She rolled her finger in her ponytail. "Yeah, he was pretty pleased with himself when he got that truck. He got the down payment from Grant."

"Do you know Grant Wodehouse pretty well?"

Elaine blushed to the roots of her blonde hair. "I do," she replied, refusing to make eye contact.

"How would you describe your relationship with him?"

Her long eyelashes brushed her pink cheeks as she stared at the floor. "We're close."

"How close?"

"Well, we're neighbors and all."

"Are you friendlier than neighbors?" Black asked.

"Why do you need to know that?" Elaine raised her

large blue eyes and looked at him as if asking him to help her do something difficult.

"This is a murder investigation. Everything about Grant's life is going to be examined. If you tell us everything you know, you might help us catch the killer."

"You don't have to tell my husband what I'm saying, do you?" she asked in a hushed voice, looking over her shoulder around the room as if Ron Tabor was standing in the hall leading to the bedrooms.

"No, ma'am, not unless it's relevant to the case."

"Well…we're lovers." She smiled and blushed again, appearing not to see either man for a second. "Grant was going to divorce his wife and marry me," she said in a rush then looked up at them as if to dare them to tell her differently. "He said he wanted to dress me up, take me out, and show me off to all his friends."

"How long has the affair been going on?"

"About four years. It started when I couldn't get my car started one morning, the day I had to take my mom to the doctor." She explained, hoping they would be sympathetic. "I ran over to his house, asking for help. He drove me back here and jumped my car for me. After that, he'd just drop around whenever he had time to see how I was doing. Sometimes he brought me groceries. Once he bought me a leather jacket with fur inside. It's really soft. He took me over to the garage once to get tires for my car. Nothing big that Ron would notice."

A man might not notice his wife's new jacket, but how could a man not see that his wife's car had new tires and there was no credit card bill to be paid for the four-hundred-fifty dollar purchase?

Elaine paused to put Molly's finished braids into a single purple ruffled band she slipped off her wrist onto the child's hair. She kissed the top of the child's head. The tike climbed off her lap and sat on the floor with her blocks. Brightly colored puppets danced on the television screen in the background. Lagarde assumed that the TV was on pretty much all day in the Tabor house, not so much to be watched as company for Elaine Tabor.

"But you were having sex with Grant?" Black said, looking over at Lagarde to score the point.

"Oh, yes. After a while, it just seemed the natural thing to do." It was a matter-of-fact statement, not defensive in the least. "I mean, I loved him and all." She looked around her living room. "He's very good to me. He bought me that painting, on the wall by the dining table, of the people in red jackets riding horses with the dogs all around them." She pointed to the oil painting. "It already had the frame on it when he gave it to me. Isn't it beautiful?"

This woman is so naïve—or very calculating, Lagarde thought as he examined the painting for a minute, nodding. "Does your husband know that you are having an affair with Mr. Wodehouse?"

"Oh, no, not at all," she answered quickly. "When Ron's home, he's all I do. He takes up all my time. I'm always home when he calls me from the road. He's not worried at all."

"That must be a relief to you. What did you tell your husband about the painting?"

"I told him I got it at the big flea market down at Harpers Ferry, where I could find such things, probably." She nodded as if to confirm that her statement was accurate, her ponytail bouncing with affirmation.

Elaine Tabor thought nothing of lying to her husband, a fact that made Lagarde wince a little. "Is Molly Grant Wodehouse's child?" he asked point blank.

"*Oh, my gosh!*" she exclaimed, putting her finger to the corner of her mouth. "How could you even ask a question like that? Of course she's not. She's Ron's daughter, through and through."

Lagarde nodded. Black made a note in his notebook.

"Do you go over to the Wodehouse barn a lot," Black kept up the questioning.

"Not really—only sometimes—when I really want him and can't wait for him to drop by."

"Like this morning?" It was a long shot, but Black had to ask, if only to knock down his theory.

"Yes, well...I did want him this morning. I woke up wanting him, and we don't take very long, so I thought we could just have a quickie and Emma would never know. I couldn't imagine this—I mean, that he would get killed." She paused to blot the edges of her eyes with her fingertips. "I never thought that would happen."

It seemed to Lagarde that she was less shaken than she should be. She was either very shallow or Wodehouse's death hadn't sunk in yet.

"So, did you see Grant this morning before he died?" Lagarde prodded.

"I did, for maybe ten minutes, well maybe a little more, right when he got down to the barn."

"And he was alive?" Lagarde had to confirm this.

"Oh, very much so." She smiled at the memory.

"What time was that?" Black asked, taking notes as fast as he could write.

"Gee, around 6:40 this morning, I guess."

"And you had sex with him?" Lagarde had to know.

"Yes, in one of the empty stalls. It was very exciting," she said, looking away from them. "He wrapped my wrists up with the leather leads and—" She paused, her face suffused by a rosy glow.

"And he was alive when you left the barn?" *I can't believe this woman.*

"Yes, he was bringing out a horse. He said he wished

he could see me ride him naked, like Lady Godiva. He was laughing."

"What did you do with Molly while you were in the barn?" Black's voice had the edge of someone deeply irritated by the woman's complete self-absorption.

"I left her here in her crib. She's safe here. I gave her a banana to eat," she said, as if leaving her child alone was a normal, acceptable thing to do. "I wasn't gone long."

"What made you come back to the Wodehouse property later, then?" Black was losing his patience. *Poor little girl.*

"I don't know. I just got this funny feeling that Grant needed me, so I grabbed Molly and started to head over. When I got outside, I heard someone screaming and screaming, so I ran to see what was happening." She shuddered and put her hands on her cheeks.

"What time was that, do you remember?" Black was looking at the previous notes to confirm what she was about to say.

"That would have been around 7:30. I had enough time to walk back to my house after being with Grant, get Molly up and dressed, and run back. But I don't know for sure since I didn't look at the clock."

"Did you see anyone in the barn or near it when you went down there the first time this morning?" Lagarde was trying to test her memory, although it was probably still cloudy from the exotic sex. "Did you notice anything out of the ordinary?" While he gave her time to process the question, he was silently calculating that the murder must have been around 7:20. Black, too, was marking down the times in his notebook.

"I was pretty focused on being with Grant. I don't think I saw anything but the open barn door and Grant inside."

"So you just walked into the barn in your nightgown

and you and Grant had sex immediately?" Lagarde wanted to nail down his timeline.

She nodded, looking down at her child as if to protect
her from this conversation. "We had this kind of whoosh
moment, you know what I mean? Like you smack together hard and the breath goes out of you and…it's all hot
and all, you know?"

"Are you aware that the barn can be seen from the
kitchen window in the house?"

"Oh…"

*Is she really that stupid? Or is she totally controlled
by her sexual urges? Could she have wanted Emma to be
watching from the kitchen when she walked into the barn
in her nightgown?* Nothing goosed an existing wife into a
divorce faster than flaunting an affair right under her
nose. He should know. "When you left the barn the first
time, did you happen to see any activity around the barn,
anyone out of the ordinary walking around?"

"No, but I wasn't looking. I was just thinking about
running back to my house and getting cleaned up."

"Do you know if homeless people sometimes stay in
the Wodehouse barn?" Black asked, bringing the conversation around.

Elaine's face went completely blank. *Is that her thinking expression?*

Her mouth opened in a pretty O and she shrugged.
"Not that I know of. Grant never said anything about
them. Are you saying there were homeless people in the
barn watching me and Grant this morning?" Her voice
rose and her eyes welled up.

"We're checking on that." Black answered in a way,
he hoped, would make her think, to realize she should be
embarrassed and ashamed.

Elaine had not shed a single tear about her lover's
death, only about the prospect of being spied on. He

made a brief note to himself on his pad. This young woman was fairly calculating. Her affair with Wodehouse was not for the romance.

Lagarde stood up, thanked Elaine for her cooperation and candor, said they might want to talk with her again, and walked to the door. He told her the forensic techs would be by shortly to get her fingerprints and a DNA sample. She nodded her assent.

He turned back at the door. "Oh, one more thing, when do you expect your husband back?"

"Tonight, maybe tomorrow. He'll call me later today and let me know for sure. He always lets me know so I can cook him his favorite dinner."

Black also paused at the door. "Goodbye, ma'am, take care of that cute daughter. Might be a good idea to lock up." He left the house with Lagarde.

Elaine picked up her daughter and watched while the detectives got into their vehicle and pulled out of her driveway. She closed the front door and turned the deadbolt, something she never did. All at once, she had a very uneasy feeling, as if she was being watched, picturing some homeless person lurking in the woods behind her house. There was some comfort in knowing that the police were next door and that folks would be coming over soon to take her fingerprints. At least for a few minutes, she wouldn't be alone. Knowing that didn't allay her uneasiness, however. She locked the back door in the kitchen then went from window to window looking out, checking that the small levers meant to keep the windows closed were in the locked position. There was nothing to see from her windows except the dense woods behind the house and the lawn leading down to the winding road in front. No traffic on the road. She picked up her cell phone and called her mother. She suddenly felt very vulnerable in her little house on the edge of the woods.

CHAPTER 8

9:20 a.m.:

Paul, the horse, was found along Route 480 in Kearneysville ten miles from his home, trotting at a comfortable clip, seemingly on his way to Shepherdstown with occasional stops to munch the succulent green grass on the large lawns of houses along the road. Fortunately, the driver who spotted him knew a few things about horses and happened to have an apple in her car.

She positioned herself ahead of him by fifty feet and stood with her arms out from her sides, apple in her left hand. As the horse walked right up to her and took the apple in his teeth, she grabbed his bridle with her right hand. While the horse was distracted eating the apple, she patted his long neck and located the reins which had been knotted and pulled back over the pommel, as if the rider had tried to put the horse into cruise control. *The horse must have bucked him off.* She held onto the bridle while she called the police, one-handing her cell phone. The yellow lab in her car went crazy barking at this demonstration of her care for another animal, or maybe it was just that the dog wanted to get out of the car and take a good sniff of the interloper. Whatever the reason, by the time animal protection rolled up with a horse trailer, the woman was a bit frazzled. The horse was a handful.

"Took you long enough," she snapped at the officer.

"Thanks, ma'am," the female officer said. "We've been looking for him."

"He's saddled," the woman said as if the officer was blind. "The rider must have fallen off somewhere. He might be hurt."

"Yes, ma'am. We're looking for the rider also. I don't suppose you saw anyone chasing the horse?"

"If he's a rider, he's knows better than to chase a horse," she said, showing her exasperation at the amount of time this good deed was subtracting from her day.

"Yes, ma'am. Well, we've got him now. You can move along. Thanks for your help."

The woman looked dubiously at the officer, as if she doubted her ability to load the horse into the trailer alone, then she walked back to her car. She spoke quietly to her dog for a minute, sat down in the driver's seat, and closed the door. She waited until the officer drove off and then made a call on her cell phone.

"Emma. Emma, I just found your horse…Paul…You know that beautiful jumper that Grant always brags about? He was just trotting down Route 480 like it was the most normal thing for him to do in the morning…I'm on my way to the vets, that's why I'm out this early, and I spotted him…Animal control came and got him. I figured they would be faster. You know, he's saddled. Grant might have come off somewhere and be hurt, or he tied him up and…"

She listened to the phone for a few seconds.

"Oh, God, Emma, I'm so sorry! Oh my God, how horrible! Can I do anything for you?"

She listened then clicked the end-call button on her

phone. She reached over and scratched her dog behind her ears. "Wow, Beauty," she said to the dog, "Grant Wodehouse is dead. He was killed in his barn with a pitchfork." She shook her head, put her car into drive, dialed a friend on her cell, then headed to the vets. By noon, everyone who had ever met Wodehouse, in any capacity, in the three historic Jefferson County towns, knew that he had died in the most gruesome fashion.

CHAPTER 9

10:15 a.m.:

Kyle Wodehouse crouched low in the woods behind Elaine Tabor's house. He had briefly watched the direction the woman in the filmy nightgown walked, after she swatted his father on the ass with one of the crops she'd swiped off the rack then went skipping out of the barn. Once she'd gotten ten feet into the woods, he'd lost track of her. Later, he'd walked in the direction he assumed she'd gone, pretty sure that the doublewide on the road near his father's house was the woman's home. From behind the bushes, several yards back from the cleared lawn around the house, he'd seen two policemen pull up to her house in their car and go in. They were inside for a while. About a half an hour after they left, two more cops rolled up and went in the house.

Kyle sat on the ground and leaned against the wide trunk of an oak, exhausted. No, not just exhausted, completely drained of all energy. It was as if his blood had thinned. He was nauseated and dizzy. All he wanted to do was sleep. He had been awake for more than twenty-four hours. It was hard to believe. He hadn't needed a rest. He woke up yesterday at 8 a.m., rolled out of bed, pulled on his school uniform of chinos, blue button down shirt, navy blazer and tie and ran to his first class at 8:30, another boring hour and a half of history in which they were once again learning about the American Revolution. If he heard about Thomas Paine and *Common Sense* one more time he was going to vomit.

"What fundamental rights were the revolutionaries struggling for against Britain's King George III?" the teacher asked, as if anyone in the world cared about this old stuff.

Kyle doodled squares within squares in the margins of his notebook. All of that crap, the entire American Revolution, had nothing to do with him. If anyone applied common sense to education, he wouldn't be cooped up inside four walls for six hours a day. As far as Kyle could tell, teenagers had no rights, particularly not the fundamental one of self-expression. There was no situation in which they were allowed to say what they thought. It was as if the American Revolution didn't happen for them.

He'd spent two hours in the dean's office last week, eyes on his knees, enduring the sound of the guy's grating voice endlessly repeating the same thing. "You can't act out here. You can't disrupt the class. You can't just do anything you please." The dean leaned over and shook his finger at Kyle. It struck Kyle that a shaken finger was about the most impotent weapon ever devised. The guy's halitosis, on the other hand, was lethal.

Kyle was bored with being reprimanded. He'd seen this act many times before. "I'm trying, sir," he'd said. That was the truth. It took all of his concentration to simply sit still in class. He was bored beyond belief.

Yesterday, he'd managed to stay in his seat until the bell rang and history class was over. He stopped at the water fountain, between classes, and took another of the pills that were supposed to help him concentrate. The school nurse had explained to him that the atomoxetine prescription would help him focus on his schoolwork. He was supposed to take only one a day, but if one didn't work, he figured he should take two, or three for that matter. Anyway, nobody seemed to care what he was doing as long as he was quiet and didn't get into any more trouble.

His mother only called him to whine about how much she missed his father. He had finally said, "Mom, it's been more than ten years since you got divorced. Get over it." That didn't work with his mother. She hung up on him, but she always called back. Who else was she going to complain to? She *never* asked Kyle how *he* was doing.

He loved his mother in a half-hearted kind of way, as if he knew it was the right thing to do but resented having to do it. He also despised her. She was weak, drank too much, and was unpredictable at night. From the time he was five, he never called for her if he awoke shuddering from a nightmare. She was not a ministering angel. Instead, it sometimes seemed to him that a many-headed monster had replaced his mother—one that staggered, said hateful things, told him to stop whining and go to sleep if he knew what was good for him.

His father had been the reliable one, a comfortable deep rumble of sound in the middle of the night, a hand to hold when he needed one, and then he was gone, leaving Kyle alone to deal with his mother. Seeing his father for eight hours on a Saturday or even over a weekend was not the same as having him in his life. Kyle never recovered from that empty feeling in his stomach that developed the minute his father told him he was divorcing his mother, or the sense that, at seven, he was left alone in the world to fend for himself.

He hadn't seen his father since early August when

Emma arranged for everyone to go to the beach together. That vacation hadn't been too bad. He liked his half-sister, Rebecca and her husband, and her kids were okay. They knew how to have fun. Emma's son William was a doofus, as far as Kyle could tell. They had nothing in common. William read all day, except when he was sitting in a lotus position chanting under his breath. The most interesting thing about William was that he could stand on his head. On the other hand, William had figured out a way to live off his mother without ever having to do a day's work. Kyle didn't count teaching religion 101 to an auditorium of bored freshmen or grading their exams and essays as work. It was a sweet deal. He needed to find out how to swing that kind of arrangement himself. Why shouldn't he have the same perks as William?

His second class yesterday was French. He slouched in his seat at the back of the room. The collar of his shirt irritated him. He loosened his tie and unbuttoned the top button of his shirt. He was glad they sat alphabetically and that W wound up in the last row. It was the sixth week of classes and he still didn't understand a word the teacher was saying.

She insisted on speaking only French in class. She was young, blonde and wore sweaters, jeans and boots to class. For several weeks Kyle watched her out of the same visceral compulsion that made him watch every female in his vicinity. When she wrote on the blackboard, her entire body swaying with each long mark of the chalk, he sometimes had to put his textbook in his lap to hide his erection. She pushed her lips together when she spoke, almost as if she was going to kiss him with each word, but the sounds that issued from those lips were incomprehensible.

When she called on him, he would shrug and say, "*Oui, oui, Madame, je vous entende mais je ne parle pas français*," in his fully American accent. "Yes, yes, ma'am, I hear you but I don't speak French," was the only thing he had pieced together using Google translation that made any sense to him. The class laughed, more at her than at him. The teacher's face turned red and she threw him out of the room, pointing to the door and yelling in a mixture of French and English, "Out, out! *Vite, vite! Petite monster, sortez!* Get out!"

He had expected her to learn that she shouldn't call on him, but she persisted, as if it was her job to humiliate him instead of to teach him a new language. Yesterday morning was the wrong day to pick on him.

She started her humiliation trolling with, "*Monsieur* Wodehouse," said in the middle of a long monologue that rolled by his ears like the sound of the ocean, her entire face forming itself into the deep vowels and heavily weighted consonants of her native tongue. Everyone in the class turned to look at him. He had been minding his own business, wasn't fidgeting, well, maybe his heel was bouncing on the floor in a way that Emma called his motor running. His knee might have been knocking against the bottom of the desk, but he wasn't bothering the teacher as far as he could make out. Now she was picking on him out of the blue when she knew he hadn't a clue what she was talking about.

Kyle found himself standing abruptly. He hadn't intended to stand, but there he was. He picked up the textbook, raised his arm and threw the book at the teacher. He had a flash of understanding where that colloquialism might have come from. It fell with a splat many feet from her, but she started to yell at him in French, her arms waving as if they might carry her into flight, a blonde dragon circling the ceiling, lashing him with her tongue. With a flip of his hand, he knocked his desk over. The noise of the desktop hitting the floor made his classmates jump up and back away toward the walls, their faces white, their mouths open in terror. *I have no friends here.* He grabbed his backpack and stomped out of the classroom, slamming the door behind him.

Out in the corridor, Kyle strode toward the double door exit, slamming his backpack against the walls as he went. He wanted something bigger, noisier, more effective than slamming his backpack against something. He wanted to hurt someone. Somehow he needed to correct the imbalance he felt. He was always in the wrong, always made to feel small, insignificant, foolish. He kicked the door a few times before he went out. The sound reverberated down the corridor. He ran across the quad imagining ramming his fist down that teacher's mouth. By now, she would have called the Dean's office. They'd have school security out looking for him in their little electric golf carts. *Do they have any idea how stupid they look putting around in those vehicles, swaggering because they carry Tasers and Billy clubs, things they could never use on the rich kids who go to this school?*

Running was good. It came easily to him, the speed of his legs matching the speed of his brain. He ran until he was off school property and then another mile because it felt good. His plan was to hang out in Mercersville's four-block wide downtown for a while, let everyone cool down, and then he'd go back to the dorm. What could they do? His dad would just pay them more money and they would shut up.

It was a good plan until a townie smoking a cigarette, hanging out on the corner in front of the deli mouthed off to him. Kyle was just minding his own business, walking through town, when this slacker in a dirty gray hoodie, T-shirt, jeans and a Pittsburgh Pirates baseball cap said, "Hey, rich kid, whatcha doin' here? You lost? Ain't you s'posed to be in your little class right now?"

That was all that Kyle could take. This nobody, this little shit who would never amount to anything, was ridiculing him. Blood rushed to Kyle's face, boiled, prickled his skin. His fists clenched. If he didn't do something the top of his head would explode. He rammed his fist into the kid's face, moving so fast he surprised the kid and himself.

The kid backed up. He put his hands up, palms flat toward Kyle. He didn't want to fight. "No, no, man, sorry. I'm outta here."

But Kyle grabbed him by his sweatshirt and yanked him back, hitting him again and again with his fist. He just kept hitting the kid in the face until the boy dropped to the sidewalk. Kyle's knuckles were split. He was breathing hard.

But he felt deeply satisfied. He dragged the semi-conscious boy into the alley next to the deli where they kept their trash dumpster. He pulled off the kid's clothes and baseball cap, rolled them up and shoved them in his back pack. Then he ran again, this time back toward the campus to his car.

In the campus parking lot, he yanked off the uniform all the good little soldiers at his school wore, threw his clothes in back seat of the Audi 3, and put on the townie's grungier duds. Luckily, they were the about same size. He felt immediately better out of the restraints of the so-called civilized uniform of the upper class school boy. Uniforms were one of the ways students were suppressed. They weren't allowed to express their individuality. It was too dangerous. The one book he had read, *The Catcher in the Rye*, had it right. All those adults were hypocrites, the teachers, administrators, parents, teaching them the principles of the American Revolution but caging them in a system of rules that was anything but free. He needed to be free from all of them, and for that, he

needed money, a lot more money than his father gave
him as an allowance.

And he needed it right now.

He got in his car, put his head back against the head-
rest, and rested for a few minutes. What was the best approach to get money out of his father? It was usually his
mother who asked for the money. He didn't need his
mother to intervene. He had to talk to his father face-to-
face. He had to have this conversation at a time when his
father was normally relaxed and in a good mood. That
wouldn't be in the middle of a workday, and his father
probably had some social event planned for the evening.
Good ol' Dad always had somewhere to go in the evening
and intruding on that would be a big mistake. Any delays
would be annoying and he did not wish to experience his
father's wrath. *In the mornings, when Dad takes care of
his horses, that's the best time.* So he'd just take his time
getting from Mercersville, PA to his father's house in
West Virginia. No need to break any speeding laws or
call attention to himself.

Kyle's stomach reminded him he was hungry. *A few
burgers and fries sound good.* His first stop had to be a
restaurant, but not in *this* town. He needed someplace
bigger where no one would know him and no one was
looking for him. He cranked-up the car, typed Carlisle
into the GPS—his first stop, after which he'd work his
way south on Route 81—then pulled out into traffic, trying to be as inconspicuous as possible.

The plan worked beautifully, until he got to his father's barn just after sunrise this morning, when he saw
his father tying up a naked woman in a horse stall. For a
minute he thought he was dreaming. The scene was right
out of an X-rated movie he watched sometimes on his
laptop, with the sound off, in the middle of the night. His
eyes were riveted by his father's rutting, the grunting and

moaning, the woman's giggles, the way she threw back her head and opened her mouth. He could not help throwing-up in the stall where he was hiding. They were so loud, they never heard him. He pushed bedding straw over the vomit with his foot, his head swimming dizzily. He stared mesmerized as his father slapped the woman on the butt the way he would a horse when telling it to giddy-up, and laughed as she reciprocated by snatching a crop and whopping his ass back as she walked out of the barn. Kyle peered around the wall of the stall, following his dad with his eyes, as he led each horse out one-by-one. He stopped with the last one, Paul, whom he saddled for a ride. Kyle had to bide his time, wait for the right moment to approach his father.

Out of the blue, Kyle felt the fury from the day before take over his body. He couldn't resist it, remembered the satisfaction he got from beating that townie senseless. Fury was good for him, made him strong. He was ready to deal with his father as soon as he was done with the horses. His only problem was that later he couldn't find the money in the barn where his dad normally kept it, although he searched everywhere. Maybe his father gave it to the woman before she left. *I need that money and I am going to get it.*

Now, he had to be patient. There were police everywhere, around the barn and up at the house, but he wasn't worried about that. No longer able to plan anything, he was being carried along by forces greater than himself. *The right moment will come, and when it does, I will know what to do.*

He had the leather leads he'd taken from the barn wrapped around his hands as a reminder of what he had seen, and his father's fancy hunting knife that he'd found lying on top of the chest in the tack room tucked into his waistband. The game plan was to tell that little whore to drop dead and take back the money his father must have given her. *Just wait until the cops are all gone. I have all the time in the world.*

Watching the woman's house, thinking about what he might do to her, his eyelids grew heavy. He closed his eyes. *Just for a minute,* he told himself, and fell asleep, his back against the old oak tree. *Plenty of time to do what I have to do.*

CHAPTER 10

Eugene Waters, Grant's partner for the last ten years, was on the phone with a bank officer when Ann Roberts, office administrator for Wodehouse & Waters, let him know that Emma had been trying to get through to him. He groaned and rolled his eyes.

Ann stood in the doorway to his office, her hand on the doorjamb. "She's on the phone right now." She tapped her finger against the doorjamb as if counting out the seconds it was taking him to respond.

Ann had told Eugene about Grant's murder when he walked into the office at nine that morning, flat out as if she was a weather reporter. "Grant's been killed. With a pitchfork. In the barn."

He stopped at her desk for a moment or two, silent, waiting to see what she expected of him.

She'd continued, "Poor Emma," as if to demonstrate how Eugene was supposed to behave. She explained she had heard about Grant's death from the mayor when she stopped at the café on Main Street to get her coffee before coming into the office. "It's all over town."

Eugene scowled and walked to his office. There was

no love lost between him and his partner's wife. They were polite to each other during obligatory social occasions and accidental encounters, but otherwise they avoided each other like the plague. Emma made it clear to Eugene that she despised him because he lured Grant into questionable practices. She didn't mince words. After verbal encounters with her, Eugene always felt eviscerated by a thousand paper cuts across his gut.

Eugene didn't like Emma, but wanted to fuck her in every possible position in every possible location until he was blind, and that, he knew, would never happen since she *despised* him. It didn't help that his own wife knew about his obsession. The tension made inhabiting the same offices difficult, to say the least. He was frankly relieved that Emma wouldn't be in the office for a few days. Maybe she would take a month off. He suppressed his glee at the idea of having the office to himself. *Will the Wodehouses pay their share of the office rent if they aren't here anymore?*

Eugene mopped his perspiring forehead with his handkerchief, adjusted his large frame in what seemed to be an ever-shrinking leather executive chair, put his hand over the receiver and barked at Ann, "Tell her I'll call her back. I'm in the middle of something."

Ann didn't try to disguise her surprise. "You mean, you're doing something that's more serious than your partner being killed?"

He was, in fact, in the middle of something very tricky: he had committed a little bank fraud that, if national real estate sales didn't pick up, was going to cost him millions in fines and maybe land him in prison. Eugene's latest questionable venture, one that Emma tried desperately to keep Grant from joining, might just sink him into such deep trouble no amount of legal double talk could solve the problem. If Grant hadn't been miraculously extricated from the mess by being unceremoniously killed early this morning, he would have been implicated also. Eugene thought Grant might have gotten the easier way out.

"Tell her something nice," he said, failing to think of any of the right words on his own. He waved his hand as if Ann would magically disappear at the gesture.

She did.

In a few minutes, he heard the low murmur of Ann's voice on the phone organizing friends to bring food to Emma for the next several days. *That's nice, but I bet Emma would rather be left alone.* At least Ann understood him well enough to leave him out of her condolence plans.

Although Grant hadn't been paying a lot of attention to Eugene's scheme, he *had* been happy to take his cut of the three million dollars they had netted so far. Of course, Eugene hadn't spelled out the source of the million-dollar dividend when he handed the check to Grant a few days ago, but there was a note in the memo field identifying Gold Coast Properties as the source of the money. All Grant had to do was remember which real estate venture that was. To prove that Grant was involved in the fraud, Eugene needed the canceled check. It would be just Eugene's luck if Grant died before he deposited the check.

Quietly panicking for three months, he'd finally decided this morning that he had to tell Grant the deal had gone south. He called Grant on his way out to breakfast, but Grant hadn't picked-up. Now he understood why. At least he didn't have to have that awkward conversation. He tried to remember what he'd said in the message he left. Something innocuous, probably, about needing to talk. He hated giving Grant the upper hand.

He ran his finger around his too-tight shirt collar and loosened his blue tie a bit. It seemed very hot for October. Then Eugene had a realization, a light breaking through the clouds after a storm: Grant was dead. Eugene could almost hear the trumpet sounding, "tah-dah!" He could say the fraud was all Grant's idea, the whole thing. Grant's signature was on all the documents along with Eugene's. Well, maybe Emma could dispute his assertion that Grant was the culprit, but she'd be preoccupied with the funeral and grieving. She wouldn't be paying attention to business. He had a nagging feeling that Grant would have said that dead partner or not, Eugene was still liable for his own acts, but that couldn't stop him from trying to get away with it. *I did not murder anyone*, Eugene consoled himself. *Blaming Grant is the perfect solution.*

The weight of responsibility shifted. A relieved Eugene called Emma back to say in his most concerned voice, "Emma, I am so sorry Grant died in this terrible way." The statement was true. Eugene wasn't sorry Grant was dead, only that the method was so messy.

Happily, Emma dispatched him in a few sentences, waiving any and all help from him for the funeral, which would be delayed because the police had said they would keep the body for a few days to run additional forensic tests and do an autopsy. She did, however, ask him to be a pallbearer when the time came. More for show, she said, than because he gave a damn about her husband.

He readily agreed and could afford to take the high road. In a few weeks, he would turn state's evidence and make a deal with the federal prosecutor about the bank fraud, would be the long-suffering partner of a scheming devil. It would be all over the papers. Everyone who went to Grant's funeral would have new gossip to spread—and it might bring that cold bitch down a peg or two also. Eugene mopped his face again and squared his body in the chair, ready for whatever the day would bring.

Ann Roberts was on her fourth call to set up food delivery at the Wodehouse residence. "Hi, Sally. Have you heard about Grant Wodehouse?" So far, everyone she'd called already knew that Grant had been killed that morning. "I'm setting up a food chain—" she was cut short by Sally who was way ahead of her with a list of what she'd be able to bring over to the Wodehouse farm and when.

Up to now, no one had said no. Most people were curious about how Emma was taking Grant's death. Some people were genuinely moved. It didn't matter to Ann what their motives were. She wanted to make sure Emma was taken care of, which had been her job for many years. It was hard to go cold turkey on something that had been going on for so long.

Ann always admitted to being a creature of habit, not because it was good, but because it made her life easier. She kept her hair cropped short, used only mascara and lipstick, bought well-made clothes with simple lines online, a luxury afforded by the generous salary the Wodehouse-Waters partnership paid her. She wore ballet flats in the spring and fall, boots with a low heel in winter, and Crocs sandals in the summer. She rose at six in the morning and was in bed alone by ten at night. She cleaned her house on Saturday and washed clothes and shopped for food on Sunday. Sometimes she longed for a spa day, but she never planned it.

With two children to bring up on her own, structure, schedule and rules helped her get through the day. She had made a safe place for her children, even if it was a cage to her. Her kids knew that on school days she would wake them at 6:30 a.m., kissing their cheeks, shaking their shoulders, saying good morning. If they weren't out of bed in ten minutes, they knew she'd be back, pulling off the quilt and making louder noises. Dinner was at 6:30 in the evening, no electronic devices at the table,

napkin on your lap. The kids took out the trash, helped
clean up their rooms and set the table. They knew that
their mother loved them because she told them every day,
but also by her close attention when they told her about
their days in minute detail.

She dialed the next person on her list. "Carol?"

She wished that her employers were as good at learning routines as her children. They weren't. Receptionists,
typists, paralegals came and went in complete frustration
in that office, but she was always there. She could be
counted on to have the information her bosses realized
they needed at the moment they needed it. She knew their
patterns, how they operated and what was important to
them. She brought order to their chaos and kept their se-
crets.

She put a check next to Carol's name and wrote
"meatloaf."

Ann liked Emma. Her own affair with Grant was over
long before Emma Thornton, a gorgeous fairytale ice
queen, came on the scene. Ann had been young, a recent
college graduate, split from her first lover and very vulnerable when Grant seduced her twelve years before. She
hadn't understood at the beginning of the affair that he
thought of her as dessert, some delectable morsel he consumed when he saw it and then forgot about completely.
He was irresistible. Sometimes in the shower or driving,
Ann still had flashes of searing sex with Grant, the feeling of his hands on her body, images of his face above
her, the moment of skin touching skin. He experimented
using various surfaces in the office—desks, conference
tables, the counter in the office kitchen—for what she had
come to think of as terrorist sex: sudden, unexpected, and
explosive. The affair lasted three months. Her marriage,
although brief, had weaned her from Grant and the flash-
backs diminished over the years. Grant did pay well, she

always reminded herself. As far as she was concerned, he owed her.

She was not keen on the previous Mrs. Wodehouse, Rhonda, who still called and whined on the phone to her about losing Grant to "that woman." As far as Ann was concerned, Emma was a much better fit for Grant than Rhonda. Emma didn't care about Grant's dalliances. She focused on what was important to her: her own career, her growing fortune and her creature comforts, which included her own interludes with various men Emma referred to as "fast food" or "vacations from reality." Ann doubted that Grant knew about Emma's sexual indulgences. On the other hand, Emma's lack of jealousy was probably the reason she and Grant were still married after ten years. Ann knew Grant hadn't stopped his own extracurricular activities. She was the one who screened Grant's phone calls from both the discarded and the newly amorous women in his life. And she knew that Emma knew about them as well.

Emma was the opposite of Rhonda, who spent her afternoons with a bottle of vodka and her memories. Rhonda called Grant daily about the trouble their son, Kyle, was in. In some twisted way, Ann thought Rhonda wanted Kyle to be in trouble so that she'd have a reason to call Grant. For the last two years, Grant had been paying big bucks for the teenager to go to a boarding school in Pennsylvania that took difficult children. The school was filled with kids whose parents had gotten them out from under charges of drug use, shoplifting, driving while intoxicated and, in Kyle's case, accidental vehicular manslaughter. Ann wasn't sure the private school environment was doing Kyle any good, but it wasn't her concern. Ann was good at clearing anything off her desk she didn't think of as her own problem.

This morning, Rhonda called Grant at the office to say

that she needed a few thousand dollars extra to pay for reparations from a little spree that Kyle and his friends went on in the small town where his school was located. Although Ann attempted to stop her, Rhonda explained in detail what the money was for. "Boys will be boys," she said to Ann.

It fell to Ann to tell Rhonda that Grant was dead. She told her as simply as possible: "I'm sorry, Rhonda, but Grant died this morning." Ann didn't have a chance to provide any further details.

"No, no, no, no, oh God, no!" Rhonda screamed then hyperventilated as if she were standing in the room with the dead body of her ex-husband. When she caught her breath, she began to sob uncontrollably.

Ann heard a clunk of the phone receiver being put down on a hard surface. She heard the chink, chink of Rhonda filling a glass with ice then the slosh of liquid poured from a bottle into the glass. Ann thought she understood Rhonda's agony: her access to Grant's money was now finally cut off.

"What am I going to do now, how am I going to live?" Rhonda said into the phone. She dissolved again in sobs. "What will happen to Kyle?" she whimpered.

Ann waited a few minutes to see if Rhonda was going to ask anything that she could actually answer. When she realized the woman was going to endlessly repeat herself, she said, "I have other calls to make, Rhonda. I'll let you know what the funeral arrangements are." She hung up the phone before Rhonda could object.

Ann shook her head. Some people just did not know how to move on with their lives. Did she? She got up from her desk and walked into the small office kitchen. She fixed herself another cup of coffee and thought about what Emma might do now. She watched the cream make a white spiral in the dark coffee as she poured. This sudden death was different from a divorce. It would be a shock for Emma, whose whole life would be unwillingly overturned. Ann weighed how much she wanted to get involved in helping Emma over the next few months. If she was honest with herself, she didn't want to help at all. Maybe she was ready for a change also. She knew Eugene was in deep trouble. She was glad she had insisted that she would have nothing to do with Gold Coast Properties. There was no question it was time to move on. She just had to find the next opportunity.

Eugene buzzed her. "Would you bring in my list of appointments for today?"

Ann brought him the piece of paper on which his schedule was printed. It annoyed her that he couldn't be bothered to use the technology tools they had purchased to organize their work. She handed him the schedule and pointed out that there was a new addition to his afternoon: the police were coming ASAP to talk with him about Grant's murder.

"A Sergeant Black called earlier. The police want to talk to us about Grant. They need background information, although they'll probably ask for our alibis for this morning. At least, that's what I'm guessing," she speculated.

"Why this morning? What are you talking about? This morning I was having breakfast in Grandma's diner with Henry Washington," Eugene sputtered. "He was hitting me up for a contribution for that wreck of a historic house his organization is trying to buy."

"This morning was when Grant was killed," Ann said, as if explaining to a toddler that grass was green and the sky was blue. "You're an obvious suspect. No love lost, fighting about Gold Coast Properties, pending fraud charges, and all that. Right?"

"What? Me a suspect? That's ridiculous. I might have

hated the guy but I can't even effectively kill flies," Eugene protested.

"Yes, you," she said incredulously. "Did you save your receipt from the breakfast? It'll be date and time stamped, even better if you paid by credit card."

"Yeah, somewhere here," Eugene said, searching in his jacket pockets, his shirt pocket, then opening his wallet and fishing through it. He pulled the receipt out of the wallet, looked at it then held it aloft, triumphantly shaking it. "See, here it is. Proof I didn't kill that bastard."

"You might want to tone it down a bit for the interview," Ann advised. "The detectives may take your resentment of Grant for motive." She walked out of Eugene's office and back to her own desk. It didn't occur to her that Eugene could have hired someone to kill Grant.

Who would have killed Grant? She didn't feel grief over her employer's death. It was more of a sense of forgetting something and not knowing what it was she'd forgotten, as if there was a task she'd left undone, one that she hadn't written down on her to-do list. The absence of grief left her at loose ends. She was waiting to remember the missing thread.

Grant interacted with many people every day. Most clients liked him, even if he was soulless, because he was ruthless on their behalf. He gave out money as lollipops to children, to every good cause, and even handed out five dollar bills to homeless people on the street, saying five dollars was the equivalent of a quarter during the depression. He never told his children he had hit his limit, and even set up 529 education accounts for Ann's two children as part of her compensation package so they would have a starter fund for college.

Who could want him dead?

She tried to imagine herself driving a pitchfork into his body. It was a horrible way to die. She didn't think it would have been a quick death. He would have had time to scream. *Did his life flash before his eyes, like people said it did?*

Did he see me in one of those flashes? Stop it! Don't think about that! She didn't have time for sentimental nonsense. *Did Emma hear her husband scream?*

CHAPTER 11

11:00 a.m.:

Lagarde had an itchy feeling, something he had seen that his memory had recorded but that he wasn't paying attention to. That old saying "you don't know what you don't know" annoyed him. Lagarde thought what he didn't know was a stone wall he would run into head on if he didn't keep his eyes open. He was always on high alert, had to scratch his itches. It might be one of his failings, but he was who he was.

He filled Black in on his interview with Emma over a cup of coffee in the office. The best way he knew to figure out what was bothering him was to talk it through with his partner.

"Are we missing something obvious?" he asked Black as they took the back road from Kearneysville to Wodehouse's Charles Town office. They had filed the initial paperwork for the Wodehouse murder and dropped off the compass Lagarde found in the hayloft and Wodehouse's cell phone for processing. "I have this weird feeling that there was something right in our faces and we missed it this morning, something big, important, that we should have seen."

Black glanced over at his partner. It was his turn to drive while Lagarde went through his notes. The first part of the trip would be through hilly farmland with large open pastures and fields. There would be fewer S turns, but this was still a two-lane road with rises high enough to conceal a vehicle charging toward him in the oncoming lane. He kept his eyes on the road while he speculated out loud. "Let's see, a guy goes out to his barn in the early morning to let out his horses. His wife gets up to make them breakfast. She can see the barn from her kitchen window, which means she can see who approaches the barn at the stable level. But, she can't see if someone drives or walks up to the barn from the other side, the entrance to the upper level hayloft. So, while she's making coffee and frying up eggs, or boiling them or whatever she does with them—and, wait a minute, where were the eggs she said she called down to the barn to tell him were getting cold? Why didn't you see them on the table? Did she dump them in the trash before she went down to the barn to find him, or before we got there? Or were they metaphorical?"

Lagarde looked at him. Black never ceased to surprise him. "Right! Problem number one with what I observed at the house and what we were told: metaphorical eggs. So, was Emma lying about the course of events this morning, or the timing of those events, or omitting something? Or all of the above?"

"Yeah, if she was lying about the eggs, what else was she lying about?"

"Exactly, but I think there's more."

"Okay," Black continued his analysis, "Elaine Tabor runs from her house through the woods down to the barn in her boots and nightie, right past the kitchen window from where anyone standing in the kitchen could see her, but Emma doesn't. Elaine goes into the barn. She gets tied up by Grant, they do their thing in less than ten minutes, which might be a record because it's got to take at least half a minute to unzip and drop his pants. She comes sauntering out of the barn when they're done, again, right in front of the kitchen window, while he's letting out the horses. Emma doesn't see her leave the barn, either. In fact, Grant has time to lead four horses out of the barn before he's skewered. So that puts his murder around 7:10 a.m. And then the killer makes a clean escape on a horse and no one sees him flee. None of them, not Elaine, Emma or the boys see anyone else on the property. So that means Emma must have been distracted from looking out the window by something or someone else for quite a while."

"She did say she was distracted, but she wouldn't say by what. I didn't press her hard enough on that. We'll have to re-interview her."

Black paused to pay close attention to the road for a minute then went back to following the story that was evolving in his head. "The boys show up around 7:30, right after Emma Wodehouse finds her husband..." He paused then continued once they were on a straight-away, "and they don't see anyone either. And a horse that's been saddled is already gone. Let's assume that Wodehouse saddled the horse in preparation for his ride after breakfast but never got around to saddling the horse for Emma. But that only makes sense if her story about going riding that morning is true. It's got to take at least, what, ten minutes to saddle a horse. Don't you have to clean the horse first?"

Lagarde nodded. "Yes, at least brush off the dirt. Tell me again, why didn't the kids have to be in school? Doesn't the bus pick them up earlier than 7:30?"

"In-school service day, remember? No school for them. Usually they do their horse chores in the afternoon." Black went back to his speculation about the murder. "But if Wodehouse had to brush off his horse before he saddled him, when did he have time to do that? He's at the barn at, say, 6:35, Elaine drops by at 6:40, then they mess around until 6:50...let's give 'em another ten minutes slack, at which point Wodehouse goes back to taking care of his horses. So, say he gets all of them out in the paddock by 7:10, he saddles his horse, and then he's surprised by the killer, who now has only ten minutes to kill Grant and disappear before Emma shows up."

They had reached Ranson city limits. Black slowed to a stop at the first traffic light. Ranson, the opposite of Charles Town, was not trying for quaint and historic. Every kind of business from commercial to light industrial that could locate right on the main drag did so. In quick progression there was a Moose Lodge, a lumber warehouse, a gentleman's club, a used car dealer, doughnut shop, garden shop, cleaners, and the innumerable small business dreams of people who hated working for someone else. This, as far as Lagarde was concerned, was the real America. The history of American enterprise was baked in, no one needed to worry about preserving it.

"What's also odd is that Emma Wodehouse doesn't see the horse bolt out of the barn with or without a rider, nor does she see Elaine go into or come out of the barn. Either the *whole* timeline is off or Emma's involved in the murder. The best suspects in terms of opportunity are Elaine and Emma. Both of them have a motive: Emma because her husband is cheating on her and Elaine because he's not leaving his wife. Both have easy access. The weapon's right there in the barn. What if Emma does see Elaine go into the barn? Emma runs down there to confront them. They get into a huge argument. Both women grab the pitchfork, tussle with it, and accidentally stab Grant then freak out." He looked over at Lagarde and grinned. "Or, maybe they killed him together for spite."

"Or, while the killer is attacking Grant in the barn, someone came to the house and deliberately distracted Emma, someone she doesn't want to tell us about because she's protecting him. This co-conspirator, like, say, the guy with the compass, drives up to the hayloft, comes down to the stable by the stairs and runs-through Wodehouse while he's distracted by Elaine. Maybe there were two people working together, but not the women. And Elaine is lying about not seeing anyone and not knowing anything because she's afraid she'll be killed."

"You're thinking Elaine's husband did it, with an accomplice? Why would Ron Tabor have a compass engraved with Warren's name on it?"

"Crap," Lagarde agreed. "You're right. Maybe there *was* a homeless guy in the hayloft, which might mean we've got a witness. Regardless, Tabor's definitely on the list of probable suspects. He must know his wife is fooling around on him with Wodehouse. No man would mistake a set of tires and a five hundred dollar painting for simple kindness. He leaves his truck up on the road to the hayloft and walks down to the barn. He's got plenty of woods for cover. Maybe he just thinks he'll have a talk with Wodehouse, warn him off. He walks in through the hayloft, hears his wife below in the stable, runs down the stairs, sees her putting it out for Wodehouse and starts yelling. Wodehouse freezes. Tabor grabs the pitchfork because it's the closest thing to a weapon that comes to hand. They exchange words. Something Woodhouse says tips Tabor into insanity and he stabs him. When he realizes what he's done, he runs back the way he came, leaving his wife to make up whatever story she can to cover for him."

"So what does the accomplice do? And why don't the Le Gore boys see Tabor when he's running back toward his truck? He would've been going in the direction of their house."

"I can't figure that part out." Lagarde shook his head and looked out of the car window as if hoping the answer was hiding behind a storefront window.

"I think we better find Tabor and question him," Black suggested. "But that version of events doesn't account for the missing horse and money. Did the accomplice take the money and split by riding on the horse?" He laughed at the image this idea brought to mind, pausing to swerve around a foolish groundhog that had waddled into the road. "Is Elaine cold hearted enough to have taken the cash after Wodehouse was dead, knowing that would be the last few hundred bucks she'd ever get from him? Well, if your theory is right, Tabor's prints will be on the pitchfork shaft because he didn't expect to kill Wodehouse and didn't wear gloves to avoid leaving his prints on the weapon."

"Right. Although if I'm correct, Elaine Tabor is one amazing actress and she doesn't seem to be that smart. And you're right, this version of events doesn't solve the missing horse or money. Tabor wouldn't have known about the lock box and he wouldn't have had time to stop in the tack room and find it."

Black nodded. "Elaine might have known about the money. Would she have told her husband about it?" He shook his head. "Nah, doubtful. She was keeping the affair a secret. Telling her husband that Grant kept money in the barn would open up a million questions, even for a guy who was half asleep at the wheel."

"The problem with this case is that we've got a whole damn pound cake worth of crumbs to deal with and no idea what they lead to," Lagarde stated.

Black raised his eyebrows at the metaphor and parked their vehicle in a "Police Vehicles Only" spot on George Street by the new municipal court house in Charles Town and he and Lagarde walked two blocks on wide sidewalks that abutted three-story brick buildings to the offices of Wodehouse and Waters on Washington Street.

Laid out in 1786, Charles Town was having a twenty-first-century identity crisis. City government was working to prevent the city's demise, but, in Lagarde's estimation, small town extinction was part of global economic change, the first life form to fail under international treaties that governed where goods would be produced and sold. Tattoo parlors and thrift shops replacing boutiques were just the first sign. It was only a geologic minute until stores were boarded up and the town died. Although, if he kept this logic going, it was only another geologic minute until the entire human race disappeared in a mass extinction. They were surely due. Lagarde looked around and shook his head. In the immediate time horizon, despite the beauty of the area, West Virginia's towns would very soon be home only to the retired and the very poor. Everyone else would move away.

"What are we getting from Wodehouse's partner and staff?" Black wanted to know before they opened the street level door to the office.

"A definitive lead on a suspect," Lagarde offered. "I hope."

Lagarde's first take on the Wodehouse & Waters office was that they didn't spend a lot of money on a designer. The office was in what used to be a retail space, with a large display window at the front of the building. The lawyer's names were painted in gold script on the window, the office hours on the door window. The furniture inside was old, but not antique. Chairs in the waiting room had a previous, exhausting life and were undoubtedly picked up second-hand from the shop across the street called Needful Things. That thrift shop also featured an old-fashioned luncheonette that served a tuna salad sandwich that wouldn't kill you, in Lagarde's non-foodie estimation.

The office's plaster walls had been stripped down to the original brick. Emma Wodehouse must have overseen the tasteful remodeling. There were stunning photographs of iconic scenes all over Jefferson County, featuring views of the rivers, quaint downtowns and mountains. Perhaps the ambiance this partnership was going for was approachable—walk in off the street and find a lawyer. Maybe that was good marketing, Lagarde decided, or maybe the quiet seediness of the office hid something less benign, like failure.

Lagarde and Black were shown into a windowless conference room with a long shiny black table that could comfortably fit twelve. Lagarde thought the office administrator might not want police officers in the reception area, sending the wrong message to potential clients. They sat in the modern open-weave swivel chairs and waited.

Lagarde was admiring the photographs in the conference room when Eugene Waters waddled in—cheeks red, forehead wet with perspiration, tie stained with egg, hands shaking. He hoped the man wasn't going to have a heart attack right in front of them. Either Waters was greatly moved by his partner's unexpected death or he was guilty as sin about something. Lagarde stood and offered his hand. Waters ignored the hand, walked to the other side of the table, and sat down.

Duly noted. Lagarde sat back down and introduced himself. "Mr. Waters, I'm Detective Sam Lagarde. This is Sergeant Lawrence Black." He showed his credentials and slid a business card across the table to Waters.

"We're here to ask you some questions about your partner, Grant Wodehouse, who was killed this morning in his barn."

Eugene Waters waved away Lagarde's ID and badge. "Yes, yes, I know about that," he muttered. "Horrible thing, horrible."

Lagarde noted that Waters's cheeks got redder and his head wobbled a bit. Even though Emma said that Waters and her husband were having heated disagreements, there was no way this guy was in the kind of shape necessary to run at Wodehouse with a pitchfork and jab it through his body. He couldn't even imagine Waters walking from his car to the Wodehouse barn. Nevertheless, he needed to check the guy off his list of possible suspects. Out of an odd sense of charity, he hoped Waters had a good alibi.

"Where were you this morning between 7:00 and 7:30 a.m.?" Lagarde asked watching Black take out his notepad. There was no point in beating around the bush. Waters wouldn't be able to make a full circuit.

Waters pointed with his thumb at the wall behind him. "I was having breakfast with Mr. Washington at Grandma's diner just up the street." He produced a small restaurant receipt, which Black took from him, examined, then handed back after noting the date and time. Black nodded at Lagarde.

Lagarde went on questioning. "Have there been any threatening calls, or difficulties in your practice, anyone who was very angry at Mr. Wodehouse that you know about?"

Waters turned redder.

So there is *something going on in the office.*

"Well, we were in the middle of a set of real estate transactions that haven't been going too well." He pulled a handkerchief from his jacket pocket and mopped his face. "I expect that we may be investigated soon by the FDIC or some other government entity. But it was all Grant's doing. His idea. Totally his plan." Waters made sure he pinpointed the blame. He was breathing hard.

"Were there other people besides you and Mr. Wodehouse involved in this transaction?" Lagarde looked him dead in the eyes. Waters was definitely demonstrating the "protest too much" defense.

"Oh, yes, we have twenty-five investors, each of whom put in upward of fifty-thousand dollars, and we have a consortium of banks supporting the venture. The deal's worth twenty million."

"I'm confused, Mr. Waters. You seem fairly proud of this deal, the number of investors and its monetary value."

"Oh, well, yes and no," Waters spluttered, mopping his face again, sweating profusely. "There might have been some papers filed that didn't state the absolute facts, all Grant's doing of course. I had nothing to do with it, other than my name being on the application papers."

"So are you saying that someone involved in this real estate deal might have killed Grant Wodehouse because they discovered their investment is a fraud? Do your investors know the deal is a fraud?"

"No, well, yes, no maybe..." Waters trailed off, looked around the room at all the miscellaneous photographs, refusing to make any other eye contact, then put the handkerchief over his mouth, mumbling, "It's not all a fraud. I bought the houses. The assets are there. Just, nothing's selling right now."

Black looked over at Lagarde and shrugged. "How about giving us the names of your investors and we'll check out their alibis?"

"Yes, yes, I—I'll have Ann print that out for you," Waters stuttered, shaking his head yes.

More breadcrumbs. We have too damn many leads. He had lost all patience with Waters. Lagarde tried one more time to get useful information from the lawyer. "Is there someone who has recently threatened Grant Wodehouse that you know of? Is there anyone you have seen with your own eyes, overheard on the telephone or in person, or who threatened him in a letter, email or note?"

"Well, Knowles hated Grant's guts, but everyone knows that," Waters said, seeming to relax now that they were no longer talking about his real estate deal.

"Who is that?"

"John Knowles," Waters impatiently spit out as if Lagarde were very slow on the uptake. "He was the local bank vice president, headed up their investment branch. Did very well for a while. I'd say he was one of the one-percenters in this state. But he's a total junkie now, hooked on prescription drugs and so on. Hates Grant with a passion, not least because his ex-wife Adrienne was having an affair with Grant."

Black wrote the name in his notebook. "Where can we find Mr. Knowles?"

"Oh, he's homeless, so he could be anywhere." Waters waved his hand in the general direction of outdoors. "He used to hang around outside our office here. Sometimes he wore a big cardboard sign: 'Wodehouse Lies.' Grant used to give him money, thousands of dollars. He felt sorry for him."

This is the best lead we've had so far. "Thank you, Mr. Waters. We don't need anything more from you right now, although we may be back in touch. Would you let your admin know we'd like to speak with her also?" Lagarde stood to indicate the interview was over.

Waters looked as if he had survived a tsunami by hanging onto the roof of his house with his bare fingers as the thirty-foot wave went over his head.

He was obviously not the partner who went to court for their clients. He walked out of the conference room, dabbing at his forehead and wiping his neck with his handkerchief.

Lagarde and Black waited a few minutes until Ann Roberts came in and seated herself next to the senior detective, swiveling in her chair to face him.

He had a moment to realize he had not fully comprehended how attractive this woman was when she showed them to the conference room earlier.

"You wanted to ask me some questions, Detective," she said, leaning forward slightly, handing him a printed list of shareholder names for Gold Coast Properties, LLC and their contact information. "Here's the prospectus also, in case you need more information about the venture." She put an elegant looking portfolio on the conference table next to him.

Black looked over at Lagarde and raised his eyebrows. He knew what Black was saying, "Be careful, man, she's an attractive woman, your weakness."

Ann was indeed a beauty with large hazel eyes, golden skin, short curly hair the color of honey and long legs that seemed to keep going. *Way too young for me,* Lagarde reminded himself, if he had learned anything from his past experience.

"Yes, Miss, or is it Mrs. Roberts?"

"It's Ms.," Ann said, but she smiled at him as if to mitigate the sting of the correction.

"How long have you been the office administrator here?" Black asked.

Ann turned her hypnotic eyes with their gold-flecked irises toward Black. Lagarde watched Black blush. *Now who needs to be careful?*

"I've been with Grant Wodehouse twelve years, right out of school," she answered matter-of-factly. "I've been his admin since he was married to Rhonda and before he partnered with Eugene."

Lagarde noticed that she was parceling out the information they needed in small packets. "Just for the record, can you tell us what you were doing between 6:30 and 7:30 this morning?"

"Yes, I was getting my two children up, fed and ready to go to the babysitter. There's no school today, but we follow our regular schedule. Their bus usually arrives at 7:30. They both go to Paige Jackson elementary."

Lagarde saw Black write that down, thinking they could cross Ms. Roberts off their suspect list, but his experience with the Cromwell murder had taught him that women, particularly beautiful women, could be just as effective at murder as men.

"What do you know about John Knowles?" Lagarde asked.

"John and Adrienne Knowles were friends of the Wodehouses for a number of years. John got hooked on Oxycodone after a skiing accident then co-mingled funds at the bank, lost his job in disgrace, and was divorced by his wife. Emma handled the divorce. The man has nothing left but the clothes on his back."

Lagarde marveled at her ability to condense a man's history into so few sentences. "When did all this happen?"

"The divorce was final last year. He's been homeless for two years, I guess."

"Did Grant try to help him?"

"He did. He gave him money, but John ran through that pretty quickly. I think John's habit costs him two-thousand dollars a week now. It's very sad."

"Did you witness any altercations between Grant Wodehouse and John Knowles, or see any correspondence, or overhear any conversations between them in which Knowles threatened him?" Black asked.

Ann turned and looked at Black who smiled at her, trying to make her more at ease. She looked down at her hands for a few seconds. "I don't think John is a killer," she said looking first at Black and then back at Lagarde, "but I did hear John yelling at Grant that it was 'all his fault.' But he was incoherent, probably in withdrawal and desperate for his fix."

Lagarde nodded. "Did you try to help John Knowles?"

"I tried to get him to commit himself to long-term rehab, but he wouldn't go. He loves his pills. They might be the only thing he loves," she said, shaking her head.

"Did you have a personal relationship with Knowles?" Lagarde's line of questioning took a turn.

"No." She knew where he was going with it. "I just feel bad for him. He was flying high for a while. To crash to such lows, it's a little terrifying for everyone, isn't it? It shows you what can happen in life if you don't stay in control."

Lagarde glanced at Black. *The guy was in love!* Black was leaning forward on his elbows, totally absorbed in watching Ann's face. Lagarde doubted if Black had heard anything the woman said. "Do you have any other questions, Larry?" he said, just to see his partner startle when he said his name.

"Uh, no, not right now," Black said, looking directly at Ann, "but I might have some later, if you don't mind." He handed her his card and watched her tuck it into her palm.

"Is there anyone else who might have wanted Grant Wodehouse dead, Ms. Roberts?" Lagarde had to prod.

Ann sat back in her chair and closed her eyes for a second. "Except for Eugene?" She laughed briefly. "Not that I know of, but it couldn't hurt to talk with his second wife, Rhonda Morewood. She might know of some folks who weren't happy with Grant."

Black flipped over a page in the little pad. "Does she live in the area?"

"She lives in Burkittsville, just over the Potomac River, in Maryland. Her son, Kyle, is at boarding school in Pennsylvania. Grant pays the tuition and puts Kyle's allowance in a bank account he can draw on with a debit card. Apparently Kyle's in trouble again. Rhonda called this morning." She stood, insinuating the interview was over.

Lagarde gathered up the prospectus and list of investors, and, in one fluid motion, he and Black stood and followed Ann out of the conference room to the front of the office where her desk was. Lagarde noticed there were white lilies in a glass vase on her desk. No card. It was hard to believe this woman didn't have a husband, live-in partner or boyfriend.

Ann saw Lagarde looking at the flowers. "I buy them for myself. They make me happy."

Lagarde looked at Black. *This woman is self-sufficient,* he tried to make his face convey. *That isn't good for romance.* It was the best warning he had to offer, but he knew Black wouldn't take the hint. Lagarde had just a glimmer of self-realization, perhaps caused by the light reflecting from the glass vase. *I guess women have to be a little needy to be receptive to romantic overtures.* He'd have to check his white knight impulses from now on.

Ann wrote down the contact information for Rhonda Morewood and Kyle Wodehouse on a piece of paper that had her own name and contact information at the top and handed it to Black. Black held the piece of paper as if he expected to frame it.

Contact complete, Lagarde thought. In a month, he would ask Black if he was dating the beautiful Ms. Roberts. Meanwhile, they needed to find Ron Tabor, John Knowles, Rhonda Morewood and Kyle Wodehouse. The list just kept getting longer. Lagarde thanked Ann Roberts and walked out of the office. Black lingered to shake her hand.

CHAPTER 12

1:00 p.m.:

Kyle Wodehouse woke with a start. His mouth was dry. *How long have I been asleep?* He looked at his watch. It was after noon. He'd been dead to the world for almost six hours. He shook himself and looked around. There was blood on the jeans and sweatshirt he'd stolen from the townie. He needed a change of clothes. He tried to remember if Emma kept some of his clothes at the house. *Maybe she did.* She always put him in the same bedroom on the third floor and whatever he left there after he'd visited his father and stepmother, she would wash, fold, and put in the dresser drawer in that bedroom.

Then he remembered he had wanted to do something before he fell asleep, something about that woman his old man banged early this morning. He tried to get his head to clear by closing his eyes and opening them a few times. It seemed to him that everything was blurry. His pills were in the backpack in his car. He had forgotten all about that. He'd have to move it. He was unbelievably thirsty. He had to something to drink—water, juice, anything. That woman probably had beer in her house.

He stood up, shook off the leaves, took off the base-ball cap and ran his hands through his hair. He put the cap back on, checked that the knife he had taken from the barn was still in his waistband, and then headed toward the trailer. He considered going up to the front door and knocking since he was her neighbor, sort of, but she didn't know him from Adam. Maybe she'd just open the door, anyway. Halfway to the front of the house, he changed his mind. *She doesn't know me. What's the point? She'd never open the door.* There were other ways to get into a house. He was an old hand at climbing out of the window in his mother's, going carousing for the night, and climbing back in when he got home early in the morning. He knew how to do this.

He walked along the back of the house to check the windows. The dwelling was a one-level doublewide with a crawl space underneath it. He guessed these windows in the back were for bedrooms, the small one a bathroom. He could reach the windowsill of any of the bedroom windows without standing on anything. Creeping up to the window at the left end of the house, he pulled the knife out of its scabbard and inserted the tip under the bottom of the screen, yanking it off the window and toss-ing it onto the ground. He slid the knife along the edge of the window and switched the lock to the open position. Pushing the window up, he stuck the knife back in his belt and, with his hands on the sill, jumped up and somer-saulted into the bedroom. His foot caught the lamp near-est the window and it crashed to the floor.

A woman called out, "Who's there?"

She sounded scared. He liked that. He stood up and waited for her behind the bedroom door. She was talking to someone. He heard them scurrying around.

Elaine ran into the room holding a crop over her head as if that was the kind of weapon that would work on someone who had broken into her house. He leaped at her, wrenched the crop out of her hand, and threw it on her dresser. He grabbed her arm and twisted it behind her back, pushing her down toward the bed.

She screamed, "Molly, stay in your room, stay in your room!"

Kyle figured she had gone nuts from fear. He hadn't seen her with any Molly when she was in the barn. Her fear was all right with him. It fed the fury that engulfed him again. The more afraid she was, the stronger he felt. The more she struggled, the more aroused he became. Her fear was as good as sex.

"You like fucking my father, don't you?" he whispered in her ear, his face close to hers.

"What, what are you talking about?" she screamed at him. "Who are you?" She wriggled, trying to get free. "Let go of me right now."

"I'm going to show you who I am, you dumb whore."

He wrapped her wrists and ankles with the leads he had taken from the barn and tied her to her bed posts. When he pulled the knife out of his belt, she started screaming. It was a wonder no one could hear her. Her screams pierced his mind like a blade. He had to balance that sound. As he cut her clothes off her and surveyed her naked body, for a second, he thought about trying out the goods his father enjoyed so much. And then the thought revolted him. She revolted him. The last thing he wanted was for his skin to touch hers. She was disgusting and dirty. He could smell her, smell the sex with his father *on* her. The knife was in his hand. He plunged it into her body up to the hilt. It was completely satisfying. He did it again and again.

When she was inert, not a twitch from a finger or leg, he stopped. His clothes were a mess. His hands and arms were soaked in blood. His face felt sticky. He wiped the knife on her pillow then peered around the room. The closet door was open and men's clothes hung from the bar. He jumped off the bed, pulled off his sneakers, stripped off the bloody clothes he had borrowed from the boy he beat senseless yesterday, and opened one drawer after another in the dresser, leaving bloody fingerprints everywhere.

He didn't care. He didn't think that he was leaving a trail of evidence. His actions seemed perfectly logical to him. He saw clean jeans, T-shirts, socks, and plaid shirts in the drawers. He found a gold chain with a diamond-studded heart the woman had hidden under her bras. Naked, he walked into the bathroom carrying his knife, turned on the tap at the sink and washed his hands, arms, face, head and the weapon with the dead woman's soap. He looked in the mirror. *Clean enough.* He used her towels to dry off and dropped them on the floor.

Kyle went back into the bedroom and put on the clean clothes he found in the drawers, as well as a pair of work boots near the dresser. Grabbing the gold chain from the drawer, he stuffed it into the jeans' pocket. He contemplated getting a snack from the kitchen, but something told him it was time to move his car before someone saw it where he'd left it up the road. He grabbed a bottle of water from the fridge, went back to the bedroom where Elaine Tabor's mutilated body lay on her bed, stepped over the mess of bloody clothes on the floor, and went out the window he'd come in.

Beyond leaving the woman's house and moving his car, he had no plan at all.

CHAPTER 13

10:00 a.m.:

Warren Lyles had run as far as he could. He was so hungry he could feel the front of his stomach flat against his spine. He was out of breath not only from running but from sobbing. What he had seen, he couldn't shake the images of. He got as far as Summit Point, a good ten miles from the Wodehouse farm, and collapsed on the wooden bench outside the library, his head in his hands.

He had slept in the Wodehouse barn loft last night, Grant Wodehouse had told him he could, and was awakened by sounds that he didn't understand at first, yelping and giggling and grunting. He'd roused himself from the comfortable bed he'd made in the hay by placing the one really useful possession he had, a sleeping bag, on top of it, and listened for a while. Cozy in his little nest, he slept soundly. *Maybe pigs got into the barn from a neighboring farm.*

The horses were stamping and snorting. There were swallows cavorting in the eaves. It was a wonder he had slept through all that noise. He rolled over, pulled himself out of his sleeping bag, and crawled cautiously on his hands and knees to the edge of the loft so he could look down at the horse stalls.

The stall door nearest to the foot of the stairs leading down from the hayloft was open. He saw a woman naked except for her rubber boots, tied at the wrists by leather leads to the wall in one of the stalls. Her head was thrown back, mouth open. Wodehouse, his jeans down around his ankles, gripped the woman's buttocks and slammed himself against her with such force that her head banged against the wooden stall wall. The woman had her legs around Mr. Wodehouse's waist. She was groaning, Wodehouse grunting. In a few seconds, Wodehouse was done and was kissing her face and neck and breasts and she was laughing. He undid the straps around her arms, kissed her wrists, fondled her breasts, picked up her nightgown and handed it to her. She pulled it over her head. Wodehouse pulled up his jeans, zipped up, and buttoned them. They were joking with each other. He gave her a slap on her backside, and as she left, she swiped a crop and hit him on his ass in return as he was leading a horse out of its stall.

For a few minutes, Warren was frozen to the spot. He couldn't believe what he had seen. *Holy shit! Did I just see that? Am I still asleep?* In his five-year marriage, he had never had sex like *that*. He started to gather his things together, pulling on his jeans and sweatshirt, reasoning he could just go out the hayloft door and no one would be the wiser. Wodehouse didn't need to know that Warren had seen them together. That would be too embarrassing for both of them. Warren put on his sneakers and tied them, spun around, and rolled up his sleeping bag. Warren had no idea who the woman was, but he knew it wasn't Mrs. Wodehouse, who was considerably older than the blonde woman he'd seen in the stall. He was ready to leave—his belongings collected, pack and sleeping bag tied together—and had slung the pack onto his back when he heard more strange sounds from the stable below.

He heard Wodehouse yell at someone, "What the hell are you doing? You've done it now! You've gone completely crazy! I always knew you were a worthless piece of shit. I should've cut you off a long time ago."

Warren crawled over to the edge of the hayloft again and looked down. Wodehouse turned his head at the noise, spotted Warren in the hayloft and opened his mouth to say something. At that moment, a man wearing a baseball cap, yelling at the top of his lungs, rushed at Wodehouse with the pitchfork, running with such force that he pushed Wodehouse all the way to the wall, the iron tines of the old pitchfork sliding through Wodehouse's clothes into his body and sticking into the wood of the barn wall. Wodehouse was pinned, still staring at Warren, his mouth opening and closing as if he were trying to scream, but no sound came out of him. Blood sprayed everywhere and bubbled up out of his in his mouth. Warren froze to the spot, unable to move a muscle. He'd had time to see that the murderer had long hair under the baseball cap. He was wearing a gray hoodie, jeans and sneakers. Then Warren's mind was screaming at him, *Get out of here! Get out! Get out!*

The killer turned his head to see where Wodehouse was looking and stared straight at the visage of a terrified Warren. He let go of the pitchfork at the precise moment Warren scrambled to his feet and ran out the hayloft door. Warren fled as if chased by banshees through the pasture, leaping over the fences, and bee-lined for the woods, stopping only when his heart felt it would explode and his legs had turned to Jell-O.

Gasping, images of Wodehouse and the violent sex, the pitchfork, blood, the killer's eyes memorizing what

Warren looked like—hate, such hate—flashed constantly through his mind. All Warren wanted now was to get as far away from West Virginia as possible.

He had gotten his breath back while he sat on the bench in front of the library. He reached into his pocket for the compass his mother had bought him when he became an Eagle Scout. It wasn't there. He searched all his pockets. He went through his sleeping bag and his back pack. Gone. The barn! Warren felt a deep panic as if he had been flung into a foreign universe he had no way to navigate. He was lost.

The killer would have found the compass and know who he was by now. Fear came over him as fast as a hard frost on a field. Panting in short bursts, he scanned the area. He had to get out of the state. But without his compass, how would he know where he was going? He looked all around him. Summit Point. The sign on the library confirmed that. Across the narrow street from the library was an old stone chapel, a church that appeared plucked right out of Agatha Christie's St. Mary Mead where Miss Marple lived. His mother had been a big fan of the Miss Marple shows on TV. Thinking about his mother made him calmer. Immediately across the way going east, he saw a long, winding country road that led uphill to large farms that fanned out on either side of the road. Behind the library in the other direction was a street with a mix of houses seemingly built in the early nineteenth-century. It was a very quiet place. He felt safe here. There was no way the killer would guess that he had run this far.

The library would have maps! I could plot back roads and walk right into Pennsylvania. It's not that far, maybe a day or two hike, if I don't get lost. I can make a copy of the library's map on the photocopier machine.

Grant Wodehouse's gapping mouth, blood running out

and down his neck, flickered across his vision. Warren gulped air and shook his head to rid it of the image. *Oh, God! Mr. Wodehouse is dead! He's been so good to me.* But he couldn't hang around and just wait for the killer to find him, he had to run, had to take care of himself first. Maybe when he was far away from the Panhandle, somewhere safe, he would call the police and tell them what he saw.

CHAPTER 14

12:00 Noon:

Black scrolled through his email, ostensibly to see if a preliminary report from the medical examiner had come, even though it was way too soon. In doing so, he was able to check if, by some miracle, Ann Roberts had sent him a note. It could just be a short note, about anything (he would've been happy if she had sent him her shopping list) to which she would have signed "Ann" at the bottom. *It is not much to ask. The universe could deliver one small miracle couldn't it?* He looked through his inbox. The report had come, but there was no note from the beautiful Ms. Roberts. Feeling considerable disappointment, he opened the report attachment and read the information in the document.

"Hey, Sam," he said, swiveling in his chair to call out to Lagarde, who was getting his fourth cup of coffee of the day from the scummy pot on the filing cabinets near the fax machine. "Take a look at this. I think we might have to adjust our timeline, and maybe we were right and both Emma and Elaine are lying through their teeth."

Lagarde leaned over Black's shoulder to take a look, squinting. *Nope.* He went back to his desk, put down his cup and picked up his new reading glasses. He had gotten the magnifiers cheap at the local pharmacy. No eye exam necessary. He stood in the aisle and tried on various levels of magnification until he could read the small print on the back of the packaging. He hated the glasses, but they did help him read what was on his computer screen *and* the print on written reports. Lagarde didn't bother to check Black's expression when he donned the glasses. He had already taken all the ribbing he was willing to accept about being old enough to wear them.

Every year another physical ability diminished. It was as if he was going backward in a video game. Every time he leaped up to grab a power up, instead of gaining a new superpower, something else went wrong with him. At this rate, they'd have to carry him home on a stretcher from his retirement party. Lagarde leaned closer to the screen.

"So if I'm reading this right, the medical examiner is saying that the blood spray was because some of the tines on the pitchfork pierced Wodehouse's lungs. Most of the bleeding from the heart was internal. Somehow the perp had good enough aim, or just dumb luck, that the weapon wasn't deflected by anything hard or dense like ribs, sternum, costal cartilage or vertebrae. The killer must have struck downward at running speed and pierced the heart in both ventricles and the lungs simultaneously, the ME says." He looked up at Lagarde. "The killer had to have been taller than the victim to get that angle, so that rules out Emma Wodehouse and Elaine Tabor."

Lagarde stood up and ran a hand over his ever-more graying head. "Helluva way to die," he admitted.

"Right. But here's the main point: the ME's saying that Wodehouse would've lived for at least another ten minutes, maybe more, after he was skewered. He didn't die immediately. Basically, he exsanguinated. He would have had time to identify his killer, maybe—if he could talk through all the excruciating pain, *and* if someone had come down to the barn as soon as Emma said she was there. There's a remote possibility that if he had gotten to surgery immediately, he might have lived. Well, maybe not, but either Emma knows who the killer is and she's in cahoots with him, or the whole timeline shifts to the right. Or both." He looked up at Lagarde, who had leaned even closer to the screen to see the text. "I'll print it out for you, man."

Lagarde harrumphed and straightened up. "The ME puts death between 7:00 and 8:00 a.m. give or take, based on body temp when she got there. It's the period after Wodehouse was stabbed that Emma is lying about, if he was actually dead when she found him. Or maybe she found him *after* the time she said. Maybe she waited for her husband to die before screaming for help. The killer had plenty of time to flee the scene on foot."

"I can think of a kinder interpretation," Black said. "She was in such shock when she found him that she couldn't get close enough to touch him to see if he was still alive. Maybe she stood in shock near the body for five to ten minutes without knowing he was still alive before she could even scream. I know it would freak me out."

"That *is* a kind interpretation. We need to take another run at her. And this time, no more Mr. Nice Guys." Lagarde grimaced, doing his best Clint Eastwood imitation.

Black laughed and looked back at his computer screen. "Wait. I've got a note from forensics. They got a pop on the prints on the lock box that had money in it. In addition to the boys and Grant Wodehouse's prints on the box, there are identifiable prints from John Knowles, recently booked for vagrancy." He looked up at Lagarde. "Maybe we caught a break here. John Knowles, the

banker turned homeless druggie who blames Wodehouse
for his downfall, was also in the barn, although it's not
clear just from prints when that was. Could've been days
or weeks ago."

He looked back at the computer screen and read farther into the email. "Nope. Spoke too soon. The prints on
the pitchfork handle are not from Knowles. The forensics
lab guys don't have a match yet for all the prints we got
there. They'll keep working on it." He swiveled around in
his chair to face Lagarde again. "There were several people in that barn this morning. Very busy place."

"Let's find Mr. Knowles," Lagarde punched Black's
shoulder to get him moving, "and see if he has an alibi
for this morning. Maybe he was wearing gloves for the
murder and took them off to count the money in the lock
box."

They both knew that wasn't probable. A killer smart
enough to wear gloves to commit murder wouldn't take
them off while he was still there. The more they learned,
the more it seemed their killer was an amateur, and that
this was his first, maybe his only, murder. They could
only hope for that, and for remorse to set in early. Maybe
they'd get lucky and Knowles would turn himself in and
confess.

"One more piece of information," Black said, reading
from his screen. "The last call to Grant Wodehouse on his
cell phone was from his partner, Eugene Waters, at seven
this morning. That, coupled with his restaurant receipt for
breakfast, pretty much rules out Waters as a suspect if we
had any thought he was the doer. Last night, at 11:00
p.m., there was a call from someone named Hamby that
apparently Mrs. Wodehouse didn't know about or didn't
tell you about. Might be useful if we called Hamby ourselves."

Lagarde raised his eyebrows. At this point, it was no

surprise to either of them that Emma was keeping information from him. "Get a print-out of all the calls to and from that phone for the month," he ordered. "Maybe that will help us focus. But first, let's start with Knowles, who we know threatened Wodehouse and who was in his barn. With a little luck, maybe we'll have our killer. If not, we'll call this Hamby person."

CHAPTER 15

2:00 p.m.:

Honey, I'm home," Ron Tabor announced loudly as he juggled the six pack of beer tucked under one arm, a bouquet of flowers in his left hand and the rucksack of dirty clothes in his right hand while he turned the key in the kitchen door lock. He was already mildly annoyed that the door was locked. He unlocked it with his key, turned the knob, shook his head at the trouble his wife's overly cautious nature was causing him, and walked into his house.

The kitchen was a mess, he noticed, now more annoyed. This is what she did when he wasn't home. He was not impressed. He looked around. There were dirty dishes in the sink and on the kitchen table. Cigarettes, obviously her mother's, overflowed the ashtray on the table. The kitchen floor needed sweeping and mopping. Trash was overflowing the pail in the kitchen, which made no sense since it was only fifty steps to the trashcan outside under the carport. Elaine had left something cooking on the stove that had boiled over and hardened into a mess on the stovetop. *It might have been alphabet soup.* The burner was still on and the residue in the pot was turning black. She was damn lucky it hadn't caught fire already. He restrained himself from yelling, dropped his laundry on the floor, reached over, and turned the burner off.

He took a few deep breaths, the way the rage counselor had taught him. If he had phoned her, the way he always did when he was close to home, she would have cleaned up the house before he got there. He had wanted to surprise her, though, having made the last run from Tallahassee to Baltimore in much less time than he expected, a tailwind behind him, a whole day early. He waited a minute for her to run into the kitchen, into his arms, and plant a big one right on his lips. He loved her enthusiasm. She was his private cheerleader. She even said things like, "Yay, you!" and jumped up and down. But he was getting nothing right now. It steamed him a little. *Where is she?*

Ron could feel his blood pressure rising. Not good. He didn't want to have a blowout with her in the first few minutes of coming home. Then he'd have to endure hours of her sulking. For the last four hundred miles, he had been imagining something quite different with his little pinup girl. He put the beer and the flowers down on the table, shrugged off the lightweight Lands End jacket she'd bought him at Sears, threw it over the back of a chair, and walked into the living room. Molly's toys were scattered around the floor.

He stood in the middle of the living room and listened. He heard muffled sobbing. He ran to his daughter's room. For a minute, he couldn't see where she was. He was frantic, dizzy. Then he saw her. She had crawled under her crib. Her face and tiny body were hidden behind a large stuffed elephant, leaving just a golden fringe of her hair showing. He got down on his knees and gently pulled his child and the toy toward him. She looked up at him, saw his face, let go of her soft toy, and buried her head in his chest. He wiped the snot from her upper lip with his thumb, kissed her forehead, then cradled her and rocked. "Oh, baby, my little Molly, it's okay, baby. I'm here, Daddy's here." He looked around. There wasn't another other sound in the house. *Where the hell had she gone? How could she just leave Molly alone in the house?* He felt that dangerous anger he barely kept in check burrow up from his stomach into his throat, but had to control himself for Molly's sake.

Holding his daughter, Ron walked toward his own bedroom, expecting to find his wife sitting on the bed, painting her toe nails, listening to music on her iPod with ear-buds in her ears. One foot into the small room that had just enough room for him to squeeze between the bed and the closet doors, he froze. First, he saw a pile of bloody clothes on the floor by the dresser, the drawers open, bloody fingerprints on the whitewashed wood. The closet door was open, so was the window, and its screen was missing. He sniffed. *God, it smells like a deer has been butchered.* Then he noticed his wife's bare feet, her toenails done in an electric blue, each foot tied with some kind of leather strap to a newel post on either side of the bed's footboard. He put his hand on his daughter's head and held her face against his chest. Backing out of the room, he turned around in circles in the living room a few times before he got his wits back. His child was still whimpering in his arms, calling for her mother.

He pulled his cell phone out of his back pocket, dialed nine-one-one and yelled when the dispatcher answered, "My wife, my wife, she's dead. She's been killed, stabbed I think, a lot. There's blood everywhere. On the bed, in my bedroom...My wife!...Oh, yeah, Tabor, two-two-five-three Ridge Road, Shenandoah Junction. Come right away. My baby was here through the whole thing...Jesus God, I don't know what she saw. She's a baby. Come right away."

He pushed the cell phone into his pants pocket without ending the call, unlocked the deadbolt on the front door, and walked outside, taking deep gulps of air, as if he had been underwater, holding his breath for longer than his lungs could bear. Holding Molly close, he tried not to cry.

Fifteen minutes later, when the sheriff's deputies and the ambulance with the EMTs got there, he was still cradling his daughter and pacing his yard. Only when a female officer got him to release his hold on Molly and took the child into her arms did he drop to his knees on the ground and start to wail. He couldn't speak for an hour.

CHAPTER 16

7:00 a.m.:

L ook, Mr. Wodehouse," Lionel Hamby said on the phone at eleven the previous night, "the kid is out of control. I just barely got him out on bail for *this* burglary. His list of priors is getting too long."

"Call me Grant. We're colleagues," Grant encouraged the man.

Grant had always congratulated himself on being a good parent, but different from Emma who seemed to luxuriate in having all the kids around her. All those voices talking at once brightened her eyes, brought color to her cheeks. She needed the children in her life, he'd realized. He didn't. He didn't get in his children's way, didn't question their motives. They were free to become whoever they wanted to be. He was always ready to give them a hand up, like giving Rebecca forty thousand dollars for the down payment on her house, or giving Kyle whatever it took to keep him happy. *What could be better than that?* he'd asked himself. He wished his own father had been as generous.

Unfortunately, Kyle was getting a bit out of hand. *Boys will be boys, of course.* Grant himself had sowed some wild oats in his time, might still be sowing them, if he was honest. But he had learned, at least somewhat, how to manage himself. Although, maybe he'd only learned how to cover his tracks. The point of hiring Hamby, a criminal defense lawyer licensed in Pennsylvania, was to help Kyle do that. But cleaning up after the kid was turning out to be a full time job, at least based on Hamby's monthly bill.

Hamby skipped right past the pleasantries. "Mr. Wodehouse, the 'he's a good kid who's just made a few bad choices' defense isn't going to fly anymore. The next offense is going to land the kid in juvenile detention." There were only so many DUIs, misdemeanor drug charges, car crashes, and unprovoked physical attacks on his schoolmates, the lawyer said, that he could negotiate down to probation or community service and then expect to get Kyle's record expunged.

"I'm sure you've got more maneuvers up your sleeve."

Hamby made a sound somewhere between sucking his teeth and spitting out a seed. "If Kyle keeps going the same way, in a year he'll wind up being charged as an adult for something we won't be able to negotiate away, something that will result in a felony on his record that will keep him from going to college or getting a job that pays his rent."

That prediction had sounded fairly ominous to Grant. He hated to think that the fancy school in Pennsylvania couldn't manage Kyle. He parked Kyle there because Rhonda had no idea at all how to deal with him, and her husband had said he would throw the kid out of the house if she didn't do something. He'd thought the school would get Kyle through the next two years and that miraculously the kid would mature and be ready for college.

Grant couldn't understand what had happened to Kyle. The kid had anything he wanted. He wasn't dumb, seemed to be perfectly fine in grammar school. Then overnight, at fourteen years old, he turned into a demon. Grant blamed Rhonda's marriage to that nimrod Arnold Morewood for their problems with Kyle. Morewood was too strict, a martinet, a former Marine who had that total Marine sergeant intimidation routine down pat. Grant had seen him in action. The guy's body stiffened, his arms locked straight at his sides, he leaned slightly forward, his mouth open so wide to bark his orders that Grant pictured him as a python swallowing a hawk. Kyle was the hawk. No kid would react well to that, particularly after years of coddling by Rhonda.

Grant wasn't sure why it was his job to always clean up the messes, but Kyle was his son and somehow it was his duty. In a year and a half since he got his driver's license, Kyle had plowed through two previous cars. In his first car, Kyle crashed into enough cars in one night that both sides of the car, the front, back and top were crushed. Grant never got the whole story, just paid the five hundred dollar ticket for going ninety-five-miles-an-hour on the New Jersey Turnpike and forked out the money for considerable court costs, as well as Hamby's fee. Insurance picked up the rest.

The lawyer said that Kyle was drunk, lost control of the car, rolled it and walked away from the accident without a scratch. The car was totaled. The drivers in the cars he hit weren't so lucky. One died and occupants of another car were injured. Hamby was worth every penny, as far as Grant was concerned. Kyle got out of that jam with three-year's probation instead of being jailed for vehicular manslaughter, because, and here Grant had to laugh at the sophistry of the law, Kyle had been impaired by the amount of alcohol he'd consumed and couldn't have been capable of forming the intent to kill anyone.

"Mr. Wodehouse," Hamby said, as if to deliberately

annoy Grant by not calling him by his first name, "Kyle is an alcoholic. He needs to be in rehab, a good rehab, the kind where you go for two years in the middle of 'Nowhere, Montana.'"

Grant couldn't believe that. Kyle was barely seventeen. "No way is a teenager, certainly not my son, a determined enough drunk to need rehab." Kyle just hadn't been drinking long enough for that. "He'll grow out of it. I did."

Hamby sighed and turned to other matters.

After they finished the call, Grant realized the lawyer was right. Kyle's latest caper, breaking into an empty office, vandalizing it and stealing equipment, was going to cost some real bucks. It made him angry. Grant had been tempted to tell Hamby to let the kid do some time, to learn there were consequences for his actions. But Hamby had already gotten Kyle out on bail. He had called to tell Grant it would cost a few thousand just for that. Grant conceded. Hamby was right. It was time for rehab. A judge might consider the rehabilitation placement in lieu of sending Kyle to juvenile detention. That was better for Kyle's future, for all of them.

As he'd walked down to the barn in the early morning, Grant had just decided to give Hamby a call and tell him to go ahead with this alternate plan. Maybe rehab would save his son. And then he was delightfully distracted by Elaine, looking as if she had just awakened, practically naked and already wet for him, showing up in the barn. The woman would let him do anything to her. Kyle and all his problems simply faded away for a few minutes of bliss. Twenty minutes later, reality cut through Grant's afterglow.

CHAPTER 17

1:30 p.m.:

The luck Lagarde needed was briefly on his side. With a few clicks on his computer and a couple of calls, Black had located John Knowles. He was currently detained in the Jefferson County Sheriff's holding cell in Charles Town pending arraignment in circuit court for winning the low life criminal trifecta: breaking and entering, burglary, and possession of a controlled dangerous substance with intent to distribute. A set of crimes he committed all in the same five minutes, Mr. Knowles was bound to be a guest of the state for at least two years.

Security cameras had captured Knowles lurking in the hallway near the hospital dispensary at ten o'clock in the morning. The normally locked dispensary door was left open by a harried, pregnant nurse who had trouble getting her medications cart and herself through the automatic door. When she hurried away, Knowles grabbed the door before it closed and walked inside as if he belonged there. Another camera tracked him inside the dispensary. He had found Nirvana, pawing through thousands of pillboxes and bottles, locating his drug of choice, popping a few immediately, and filling his pockets. He was so absorbed in the task of cramming as many pills as he could in his pants, jacket and shirt pockets that he was surprised in the act of putting a bottle inside his shirt by the deputy sheriff on loan to the hospital who walked into the dispensary and grabbed Knowles's arms.

As they drove into Charles Town, Black told Lagarde that Knowles explained to the arresting officer that he just needed his fix, just ten or twenty pills would do him fine. He'd put everything else back on the shelves. If the officer could just see his way to turning his back, Knowles said, and letting him walk out of the hospital through the emergency room exit, he would never come back. The officer told this story to everyone he talked to after the arrest, including Black. He thought it was the funniest thing he had heard in a very long time. Knowles explained it was a win-win: no fuss for the officer and a very nice high for him for the next ten days.

Knowles had nearly four hundred bucks on him when they booked him. He also had a wallet stuffed with expired credit cards and a driver's license that he was a year late in renewing. The officer noted in his report that Knowles could use a good shower once he got to the regional jail up in Martinsburg. Otherwise, Knowles didn't give him any trouble, wasn't violent, and didn't resist arrest, but maybe that was because he was already as high as a kite in the five minutes it took the deputy to transport him in his cruiser to the jail.

When Knowles was brought into the interview room at 1:30 p.m. in handcuffs, the first thing he asked for was a glass of water. It was clear to Lagarde and Black from his pallor, sweating, and shaking that only three hours after self-administering his drug of choice, Knowles had entered withdrawal. Black left the room to get a bottle of water for him.

Knowles turned to Lagarde. "Do I know you from somewhere? Did you have an investment account at the bank?"

Lagarde shook his head, no. *Interesting tactic, the perp taking charge of the interview.* He was almost glad that he didn't know this poor sap, because killer or not, Knowles's life was already over, even if he didn't know it. They had found him with enough oxy in every pocket in his clothes to make the charge of possession with intent to distribute stick. That was a felony that would get him at least three years in the state pen. It didn't matter what Knowles said his intention was. The drug charge was by the numbers, and this many pills added up to a felony. Add in the robbery, and he was going to see a lot of time inside. Ann was right. It *was* a long way to fall.

Sweat had soaked through Knowles's shirt collar. His graying brown hair was plastered to his skull. He was gaunt and pale. *Had he eaten anything but pills in the last few weeks?* It was hard to imagine that this guy once thought of himself as a master of the universe.

Knowles put his head down on the table. "Man, my head hurts. This is really bad. Can't you guys get me something to help me out here?"

Black walked back into the room with the water and put it down on the table. Knowles grasped the bottle in his manacled hands and brought the water shakily to his mouth. He drank, a portion of it spilling down his chin onto his shirt, and set the bottle down on the table.

"That's all the help you're going to get from us," Lagarde said, feeling a little guilty about being cruel. "I'm not here about the drug charge. The sheriff has you cold on that crime. They've got you on video. Your best bet there is to plead no contest and do the time. They'll detox you and then you'll have three meals and a bed for a few years. But I might be able to make your time easier for you, if you can help me out. What I'd like to know is if *you* know Grant Wodehouse."

John Knowles's head shot up. He stared at Lagarde open-mouthed for a second. "That lousy bastard, sure I know him, he ruined my life. What about him?"

"Were you at the Wodehouse property this morning, October twelfth?" Lagarde asked, holding his breath. *It couldn't possibly be this easy.*

Knowles shook his head no, but he said, "Yeah, I was there. The bastard owes me for all the hell he put me through."

"What did you do about that? Did you get even with Wodehouse this morning?"

"Yes, I did. You don't know what he's done to me."

"We have some idea. What time were you at the Wodehouse property?"

"I was there before light. I know Grant keeps money in the barn. Only guy I know who would just leave cash lying around like nobody needs it. So I went there, maybe around six this morning, looked around, found this little metal box in the tack room. I open it and there's a few hundred dollars in there. Grant doesn't really need the cash. I do. The sheriff stole that money from me when they brought me here. I need that money back. Grant owed it to me."

"How did you get out to the farm?" Lagarde tried ignoring the whole line of unreason about how a guy who steals money immediately thinks of it as his.

"I hitched a ride from a trucker getting onto Route 9 in Charles Town, up to Shenandoah Junction. He dropped me off right at Ridge and Jones Valley Road and I walked up to the barn. I think the trucker said he wasn't going much farther."

Lagarde and Black glanced at each other. Black jotted something in his notebook. Lagarde assumed it was speculation that Elaine's husband, Ron, might have gotten home very early and been the Good Samaritan who gave Knowles a ride. That would put Ron Tabor, a cuckolded husband if there ever was one, in the vicinity of Wodehouse's barn at the time of the murder.

"Did you see Grant Wodehouse when you were in the barn?" Black asked.

"No, way too early for them. Emma sleeps till it's light, or close to."

Lagarde didn't ask how Knowles would know such an intimate detail about Emma Wodehouse's habits, though he was curious. "So, you went to the barn, stole Grant's money, and then what?"

"Then I left, went looking for my dealer." He looked from one face to the other. *Are these guys too stupid to find their asses with both hands?* "That was the whole point of going there, to get money to pay my dealer for some oxy. If I had found my dealer where he was supposed to be, I wouldn't be here with you being asked these dumb questions." He put his head back down on the table.

Lagarde and Black looked at each other. If Knowles was the killer, he had somehow missed getting any blood spray on his clothes. He certainly didn't have any clothes to change into. His plaid Woolrich jacket, corduroy shirt, T-shirt, and jeans were filthy, but that was it. Whatever money he had put his hands on during the last year, he hadn't used it to buy any clothes for himself. *Does he know he can get free clothes at the community mission? Maybe he's not the kind of homeless guy who talked to anyone else who was in the same situation.* Lagarde couldn't see Knowles standing in line for the one free meal a day served by the Mission or at 7:00 p.m. for a cot in the church for the night, but maybe even the high and mighty needed a warm place to sleep and a free meal sometimes. Knowles would have thought of himself as in a different class from the other people whose bad luck, worse decisions, and miserable choices brought them to society's dead end. He obviously brushed off the advice of anyone who tried to help him, according to Ann Roberts. It was probable Knowles left his marriage with a car, cell phone, laptop, and some expensive jewelry, at least a watch and a wedding ring. He must have sold off all those material possessions, little by little, to get the cash to buy his drugs. When he sold the car, he would have lost his shelter. If Lagarde thought about it too long, he would start to feel sorry for the poor bastard.

"Did you see anyone else at the barn or on the property when you were there?" Black had his own check-list. "Either when you were walking into the barn, while you were there, or when you were leaving?"

"I didn't see anyone but I think there was something in the hayloft moving around. I didn't stop to check what it was though. Could've been a dog or a raccoon, maybe something slightly bigger than that."

Lagarde had one of those brain pings, a small explosion in his head. It reminded him they had forgotten to check on the compass they found in the hayloft. Dogs and raccoons didn't need compasses. They just followed their noses. If he believed Knowles, then between his statement that he'd heard someone in the hayloft and the compass Lagarde had found, there was proof that someone was definitely there early this morning.

"Did you let any of the horses out?" Black checked two questions off and looked directly at the man.

"What? No. Why would I do that? My entire goal was to get the money." He looked up at them a little wild-eyed. "What do you care about a few hundred dollars, anyway?"

"What we care about, Mr. Knowles, is that Grant

Wodehouse was found skewered by a pitchfork in his barn this morning, and you happened to be one of the people who was in that barn who shouldn't have been there right before he died."

John Knowles responded by turning his head and projectile vomiting across the floor. Lagarde and Black simultaneously jumped their chairs backward. Lagarde stood. Black got up from his chair and opened the door.

"We'll catch up with you at regional if we have more questions, Mr. Knowles," Lagarde said, locking eyes with the man.

They walked up the short corridor to the intake area. "He's all yours," Black said to the desk officer. "You'll need a mop. Oh, and send a sample of that mess to Forensics for a DNA match, please."

Even though they half-believed Knowles admission that all he wanted was the money Wodehouse kept in the barn, it wouldn't hurt to have a little science confirm that John Knowles had nothing to do with Grant Wodehouse's death.

"As soon as I'm back in the office I'll check in with forensics to see what news they have."

Lagarde nodded. They'd closed a small gap in what they didn't know, but they still had a long way to go.

CHAPTER 18

6:45 a.m.:

Emma had given her son, William Thornton, a key to the house in Shenandoah Junction when she and Grant first purchased it. She wanted him to think of it as his home, she'd said. Today, he was taking her at her word. Early on the morning of October twelfth, he pulled his Jeep into the driveway behind his mother's Lexus, went up the stone walk with his backpack in his hand, unlocked the front door, and walked in. He found his mother in the kitchen making coffee. Sneaking up behind her, he put his arms around her.

She jumped, whirled around and said, "What the? Holy shit, William, you scared the bejesus out of me. It's quarter till seven in the morning. What the hell are you doing here? Why didn't you call?" Then she grabbed his arms and hugged him then stepped back to look at him.

That wasn't exactly the welcome he'd been hoping for. He'd expected his mother to be tearfully delighted that he'd come home. He hung his head, stuck his hands in his pockets, looked around the kitchen and then out of the window. In the distance, he saw a vaguely familiar young man wearing a Pirate's baseball cap running down the slope from the graveled lane toward the barn's stable entrance. It was dark in the barn and he couldn't see Grant inside from where he stood. William figured the guy was someone Grant had hired to help with the horses. He didn't think it was important enough to comment on. He needed to get his mother on his side. *That* was his overriding concern. His reasons for coming spilled out.

"I've had enough, Mom. I want to stop going to school. I need a change. I need to do something else. I want to come home for a while."

"That's nice," Emma quipped. "Now that I've spent fifty thousand dollars a year for the last ten years, you decide you don't want your doctorate?"

"I can't do it, Mom, I'm not cut out for it. I'm not even close. Even if that bastard approved my dissertation topic, it would be another three years, at least, until I finished. And then what? Search around for some tenure track assistant professorship in hopes that in thirty years I might be a full professor. Frankly, I'll never make back your investment in my lifetime."

"I wish you'd thought of that earlier, when you graduated college. Well, anyway, sit down," Emma said, rubbing his head and caressing his cheek with her hand. "You must be starving. You look like shit. When was the last time you slept or ate anything besides ramen noodles?"

William felt vaguely interrogated, but he knew his mother and this was her way of saying that she cared about him. He could relax now. She would help him.

"I'm really tired. Do you think I could get a nap before we talk?"

"Oh, of course, sweetheart. I don't know what I was thinking. You surprised me. Let's find a room for you and I'll make up the bed."

William followed his mother out of the kitchen, noting

that she was leaving eggs frying in the pan. *Should I let her know the stove is still on? Nah, she knows.* He walked up to the third floor behind her. She pulled sheets and towels from a hall linen closet and brought them into the room. With sheets billowing above the bed, reminding him of sails filling with air as she shook them out, she made up his bed. It gave him comfort just to watch her. William took off his shoes and socks and tossed his pack onto a chair. She gave him a kiss on the cheek, said, "Sleep well. We'll talk later," and left the room, closing the door behind her.

William was exhausted, having driven the 470 miles from Cambridge, Massachusetts only stopping once at some horrible New Jersey Turnpike rest stop to buy what turned out to be ulcer-inducing coffee, get something to eat, and take a piss. He was in a hurry to make sure his mother would change his life since he seemed incapable of doing so on his own. That might involve a lot of cash and his mother had plenty of it.

At thirty, he had been in school since he was three-years-old. He might have been exhausted from that as well. It was slow work getting his Ph.D. in religion at Harvard. So far, every idea he had come up with for his dissertation in early medieval Buddhist spells and rituals had been blown apart by his adviser, who, at this point, William wanted to kill. No amount of meditating could quell the fierce tide of fury he felt toward Dr. Elmer Hodgkins Snodgrass, who was seventy-two and determined to hold onto every vestige of academic power until his death. Snodgrass guarded the gates to academic heaven, and by God, he wasn't going to let in anyone unless he absolutely had to.

William could completely sympathize with other Ph.D. candidates who shot their entire dissertation committee or committed suicide, or both. He'd read a 1998 paper by Alison Schneider he'd found online about all the suicides at Harvard caused by skewed power relationships with advisers. He certainly sympathized. The whole process of completing a dissertation seemed hopeless. Smart people dedicated years of their lives to answering one small question no one in the real world cared squat about. Advisers didn't want you to succeed. If you succeeded, you might usurp their place. You might reveal all the holes in their own work. They might become laughingstocks, or worse, irrelevant in their fields. They were all Freudians under the skin, thinking that their sons wanted to kill them and bed their wives. William Thornton had had enough of the whole lot of them.

At this point, William couldn't remember why he had even started down this road. Maybe he got his bachelor's degree in Classics, Sanskrit, and Religious Studies just to annoy his very down-to-earth mother, who had been hoping William would follow in her footsteps and become a lawyer. Instead of escaping her world of practical matters, he had immersed himself in another that had rules just as rigid, predictable, and demanding as the one he'd hoped to avoid.

William plopped down on the bed, crawled under the quilt, and closed his eyes. He was home at last. This was the spell he had been chanting on the long drive here. In his mind, he saw a whirling dervish beckoning at the opening to a cave. He knew the secret words to say and became that swirling figure—chanting, whirling, and gesturing, drawing mandalas in sand. In his dream, his mother was enough of a goddess to perform a magic ritual of healing for him.

CHAPTER 19

2:30 p.m.:

Halfway back to the office from interviewing John Knowles in the Charles Town jail, Black got a call on his cell phone. Lagarde was driving, deep in his own thoughts about Knowles and how few steps it was from riding high to winding up face down in your own vomit.

"You're not going to believe this," Black said when he clicked off the call. "Elaine Tabor is dead. Found by her husband in her bedroom, stabbed multiple times."

"Found, huh? I wonder...You're right. That's the last thing I expected." He punched the gas and took the next exit off Route 9 and headed back in the opposite direction on Jones Valley road, driving toward Ridge Road. "Let's take a look at the murder scene. Maybe we'll pick up some clues about our first murder."

"Do you think the murders are related? Her husband killed Wodehouse then his wife? Makes sense in a murderous kind of way."

"I think we'll take a look around, talk to the forensic techs, and *then* talk to the husband. We were going to do that anyway. Where do they have Ron Tabor?"

"Crap. I forgot to ask. I'll call Dennis Harbaugh, the deputy sheriff who's on the scene, and check on that."

By the time they arrived back at the Tabor's doublewide trailer, where the front lawn was now overrun with police vehicles, Black knew that Ron Tabor had been taken to his mother-in-law's house. The deputy who was first on the scene said the man was a wreck, there was no blood on him, his shoes or his clothes, and that all he wanted to do was hold his daughter and sob. His mother-in-law had freaked out when they told her about her daughter's death, but she had calmed down and seemed sympathetic toward the husband. "Maybe they will comfort each other," he told Black.

"Just because he's despondent about his wife being dead doesn't mean he didn't do it," Lagarde said, sounding more hardboiled to his own ears than he expected.

Maybe he'd been at this job too long. Dealing with homicides made you crazy, depressed or dead inside. He needed something to lighten his day, and he definitely wasn't going to get to ride his horse this afternoon. That usually did the trick for him, released all the bad thoughts and realigned his soul with the animal's, clear of humanity's unaccountable, endless murderous acts toward each other. Just sitting straight in the saddle, hands on the reins, slow walking his horse made him right with the world.

Lagarde and Black walked through the house to the threshold of the small bedroom where the murder had been committed. The body was already gone. The room was off limits and they didn't want to add hair and dirt from their own clothes or cast off cells from their skin that might contaminate the scene.

Deputy Harbaugh narrated the crime for them. "The intruder gained access to the house through the bedroom window." He pointed to the open window. "It must have been the murderer's intent to surprise the occupants of the house. She, the victim, had the house locked up tight except for this window, apparently. Ron Tabor said he had to use his key to get in the kitchen door, and that the dead bolt had been locked when he went out the front door after finding the body."

"But both doors were unlocked when you got here?" Black asked.

Harbaugh nodded. "The killer might not have known whose house he was going into. She must have heard the noise from the window being opened and him climbing into her room. Looks like she was cooking something, maybe the baby's lunch, when she heard the noise. So she walks around the house and finds the intruder in her room. He probably threatened her with the weapon. Somehow the baby hid in her own room. Lucky thing, too."

"You don't think the child saw what happened?" Lagarde asked.

"God, I hope not," Harbaugh said. "That would scar her for life. The victim was stripped naked, her hands and feet were tied to the bedposts with horse leads. You know, those long leather straps with the clasps on the end that link to a halter, the fancy ones they use for showing. Riders lead their horses with them."

Lagarde nodded impatiently. Black scribbled in his notebook.

"We're guessing he raped her. We'll know for sure pretty soon now," Harbaugh looked at his watch and then continued his narration about the murder. "Then he stabbed her in the throat, heart and stomach over and over. Actually, I think he was trying to rip out her heart and missed his target. Medical Examiner said the weapon was maybe a five-inch hunting knife with a serrated blade and maybe a notched hook for removing bottle caps on the hilt. Apparently there were no hesitation marks. Victim would've died pretty quickly. Would've been a lot of pain. Screaming, probably."

Harbaugh shifted his weight and put his hand on his holster. Lagarde imagined the deputy was thinking about shooting Elaine Tabor's murderer if he caught him. Lagarde didn't think he'd blame him if he did.

"Anyway, the killer then stripped off his clothes and shoes and left them in a pile on the floor. He must have been covered in blood. There's blood residue in the bathroom sink. He washed up in there. He obviously didn't think we could find out anything about him from his clothes. Or maybe he doesn't care if we figure out who did this. *Or* this is his first rodeo and he's not thinking at all, just running on adrenalin. His clothes and shoes were bagged and taken for evidence. The forensics lab will pull blood type off them, just to make sure it's her blood. They'll also check for his DNA from sweat, saliva or semen."

Lagarde nodded and waved his hand around in a circle a few times to let Deputy Harbaugh know he should speed up his narrative.

Harbaugh cleared his throat. "Then the killer must have put on some of Ron Tabor's clothes and a pair of his shoes and gone back out the window the way he came in. Different shoe prints going away from the house than going in by that window. That's all we've been able to reconstruct so far. There are tire marks on the dirt driveway that don't match either her car or the truck her husband was driving, so that might be the perp's car."

"Or ours. We were here interviewing Elaine Tabor at 9:30 a.m." He flipped open his notebook and consulted it. "Yeah, at 9:30 this morning."

Harbaugh shook his head at the immensity of the crime and the difficulty he would have solving it.

Lagarde looked around the room. A beautiful woman with a zest for life and a history of bad decision making had a horrible death in here. The room smelled of blood exposed to air, metallic, rusting iron. There was a considerable amount of blood on the mattress even after the bedding had been stripped off. There was blood spray on the headboard and wall behind the bed. This murderer, if he was the same one who killed Grant Wodehouse, certainly liked to make a mess. Lagarde shook his head, as much to clear it as to express his disbelief at how quickly a life could be snuffed out.

"Got an idea of the time of the murder?" Lagarde asked.

"The ME's quick impression from body temp was that it was between noon and 1:30 this afternoon."

"That was a few hours after we left her. The guy must have been hiding in the woods while we were here. We didn't see any vehicle but hers on the property."

Lagarde thought his partner turned a little gray thinking they had not done a thorough enough search of the grounds. He felt his own stomach sink, knowing they might have been able to prevent this murder if they'd been more observant.

"I'm assuming forensics dusted the closet door and bureau for prints. The perp pulled out clothes. He must've left prints all over the dresser."

Harbaugh nodded. "Right, that's what we thought. There are bloody prints everywhere. Aside from the murderer's, we figure there would only have been the couple's and the child's."

Lagarde thought, but didn't say out loud, *and the next-door neighbor's.* "Did you check the ground around the window outside to see if there are shoe prints confirming your ingress and egress theory, or any other clues?"

"Yeah, we got him coming and going, and we took a

shoe cast that is a possible match to the shoes he left here. So that means, we might have at least partials of his finger prints on his own shoes and the button on the jeans he was wearing that we can match to what we find on the dresser. We should know pretty soon if he's in the system."

"Did you print Ron Tabor?" Black asked.

"Yeah, we got him on the Live Scan machine. I asked the techs to expedite the results, but I don't think he's the guy."

Lagarde looked at Harbaugh as if the man had left half his brain at home. "If he is the guy, do you think it's safe to leave him with his daughter and his mother-in-law?"

Harbaugh shrugged. "We got a deputy over there with them. Nothing's going to happen though. The guy's totally crushed by this."

"I don't suppose the murderer did us the favor of leaving his weapon behind?" Black only hoped.

"If he did, we haven't found it. I just said, ME said the wounds have the appearance of being caused by a hunting knife with some kind of special appliance on it, but she'll have to search her database. She'll have a better idea about it later."

Lagarde shook his head. He'd seen stranger things than a distraught husband kill his child and then himself because he couldn't imagine his life continuing another minute. While he was thinking that, he noticed something odd in the jumble of stuff on the bureau. Elaine Tabor had not been a neat housewife, but this item seemed out of place even in her home, even if she was keeping it as a memento. He pointed out the riding crop to Harbaugh. "Do you think that's hers?"

"Humph. Doubtful. I'll get the guys to bag it. Maybe there's a better print on it than any of the others we have. Doesn't appear to have blood on it. It's a kind of odd piece of equipment to bring to a stabbing murder, though, isn't it?"

"Not if you're coming from a first murder in a horse barn. Your perp might be our killer from the Wodehouse murder this morning, just a few hours before this one. I'll bet the leads the killer tied Elaine Tabor up with came from the Wodehouse barn. If the killer took souvenirs from the barn after he killed Grant Wodehouse, maybe he took another souvenir from this house. My guess is his latest souvenir would be something personal that belonged to his victim."

Harbaugh's eyebrows shot up and took shelter in his hairline. "You're saying he's a serial killer? Hey, this case is all yours. It's not my case, man. That's why I called your sergeant here."

Black looked over at Harbaugh and clapped a hand on the deputy's shoulder. "It's okay, we got it, Dennis. Just make sure we're copied on everything you get from the forensics lab and the medical examiner."

Harbaugh wiped his face with his hand, backed away from the room and walked out the front door of the little home.

"I think we just made Dennis Harbaugh's day," Black said and smiled his grim smile, the one Lagarde always associated with someone who was trying to keep his lunch down.

"Yeah. Let's get out of here. I think we need a break, too." Lagarde headed back to the car.

Sometimes he thought he had already hit his lifetime tolerance level for horrible stuff and couldn't bear to see or hear about another human-caused atrocity. Anyway, they had a lot more forms to fill out back at the barrack office and might as well get started.

Perhaps they could interview Ron Tabor an hour from now. It wouldn't make any difference to his wife.

CHAPTER 20

2:00 p.m.:

It was afternoon before Emma remembered her son William was asleep in the third floor guest room. She forgave herself instantly. Her husband had been murdered this morning. She was rattled, forgetting from one minute to the next what she had started to do. She was a dragonfly, flitting back and forth in the air but not accomplishing anything.

She had not yet given in to the huge, heaving sobs that threatened to break over her but she worried she could not hold them off much longer. The numbness from her initial shock was wearing off and she could see them coming—a three-story-high tsunami forming on the horizon. Once they hit the shore, there would be nothing she could do but hold her breath and hope that she would float to the surface when the grief subsided.

Hours after he died, she was still surprised by her unexpected sorrow. It had never occurred to her that losing Grant would make her feel this way. But until the sobs hit, she was determined to marshal her forces. She had to call the funeral home to schedule pick-up of Grant's body from the morgue whenever the police were done with it.

What she most dreaded was the horrifyingly difficult call to Rebecca to tell her that her father was dead.

She berated herself now that she had sounded wooden and cold on the call. "Rebecca," she said when her step-daughter answered the phone, "your father died this morning."

Emma hadn't engaged in any small talk first or asked after Rebecca's children, nor did she talk about the weather, hadn't even said hello. The three-hour time difference between West Virginia and Arizona did not even occur to her. It seemed like a different day to Emma. Rebecca's family was probably eating breakfast when she called, children around the table, in the middle of pouring orange juice. The call couldn't have been more unexpected.

"What?" Rebecca said. "What do you mean? *My* father? You're saying Daddy is dead? How can that be?"

"He was killed in the barn." Somehow Emma had completely forgotten how to have a conversation, had lost all knowledge of words that might soften the blow.

"Oh my God! Oh my God!"

Emma listened to Rebecca try to swallow her sobs. She knew her stepdaughter was trying to remain calm.

She failed. "I'll call you back later," Rebecca said between gasps and hung up.

Emma sat there with the phone in her hand thinking about all the missed opportunities with Rebecca. Then she gathered herself together and called Ann about the funeral arrangements. She spoke to Grant's idiot partner, Eugene Waters, about being a pallbearer. She was reminded from her few minutes on the phone with Eugene what a complete and utter creep he was. Even his voice made her skin crawl. Of this one thing she was glad: Grant's death gave her ample excuse to sever all ties with Eugene.

Intermittently, Emma tried calling Kyle. Between these calls, she paced the house, watching what the forensic team was doing. They had already come in and instructed her how to put her fingers on the screen of the portable electronic fingerprinting machine. They had gone through Grant's office with a fine-tooth comb, bagging his computer but leaving most of his paper files. It occurred to her to remind them that he was the victim, not the perpetrator and then she just walked out of the room and left them to it. They didn't ask if anyone else was in the house and it didn't occur to her to tell them her son was asleep upstairs on the third floor. *It isn't any of their business anyway*, she told herself when she recalled William's arrival. She walked down to the paddock, leaned against the black, four-rail fence and watched the horses.

Brought up in the city, Emma was terrified by horses the first time Grant had taken her to watch him ride. He was boarding his horse at a friend's farm out on Route 340 in Virginia. She was charmed by the long lane lined with trees, the rolling pastures of grass that surrounded the house and barn, the sight of the horses munching grass and cavorting in their enclosure. But up close to them, she wasn't sure about horses at all. They were huge animals, even if they seemed friendly.

Somehow, under Grant's instruction, she had come to love them. First he introduced her to grooming the horse, long strokes with the curry comb, almost hypnotic in the repetitive movement, then the brush. She learned how to use her hand to stroke the horse Grant was carefully bonding her to, to navigate around her, to talk to her. When she was comfortable with the horse, Grant taught her to lead the older, gentle mare. She and the horse walked around inside the paddock where, if something spooked the horse and she reared, Emma could jump up on the fence and swing her legs over to the safe side. In a few weeks, she was sitting on the horse while Grant walked the animal on a lead, giving her instructions about her seat.

"Sit up straight, straighter—Toes out, heels down. Legs straight. Relax your hands. Elbows at your side," he called to her.

The following week, she sat the horse on her own and walked in the paddock, a giant bestride the earth with a new perspective on the world. That was all it took. She fell in love with horses. She craved her riding time the way runners crave their run.

Her favorite horse, Annie's Way, walked over to Emma at the rail and nuzzled her shoulder. Emma stroked the horse's face and neck. Touch was some small comfort. She reached in her pocket and pulled out cut carrots and offered them in her palm to the horse. The horse kissed her palm. *This is all I have left of Grant.* She choked, breathless at the thought. All the pieces of her life broke apart at that moment, a puzzle she would have to reconstruct. She had no idea where to start or if she could put it back together in any way that made sense.

When the animal control officers returned the runaway horse, Paul, they helped Emma remove the saddle and bridle, put the halter back on the horse and lead him to the pasture.

"He's a handful," one of the officers said, laughing.

"Yes, he's exactly like his owner," Emma said.

Emma was grateful for their help in handling Paul. Her hands were shaking so much that it was difficult to undo the girth. When she removed the bridle, she noticed the reins had been tied together. A stab of grief went through her and she leaned against the horse. Paul nickered and nudged her with his nose. She would have to tell Paul that Grant was dead. She stroked the horse's nose. Maybe he already knew.

Tying the reins was one of Grant's methods for helping him steer the horse one-handed. He must have saddled Paul for their ride this morning. He would have done her horse next. Grant always said he preferred a push button horse, but Paul was anything *but* push-button. Grant liked the horse because he was ornery. At this moment, she cherished the paradox her husband was.

She went back into the house and tried again to call Kyle, the son who gave Grant so much trouble but who Grant loved nonetheless. Trying Kyle's cell phone, she left him a text and an email to call her immediately. She called his school and explained to someone in the Dean's office that his father had died and hung up before the woman on the other end of the line could say anything. Finally, in her desperation to find Kyle, she called Rhonda, who said Ann Roberts had told her about Grant's death.

Rhonda was her usual whiney self. No matter what happened, it was always about her. Rhonda had no room in her small universe for anyone else. After some prodding, Emma realized that Rhonda didn't know where her son Kyle was. He hadn't responded to her calls or texts either.

"He's probably sleeping off a drunk somewhere," Rhonda said.

Emma shuddered at Rhonda's carelessness. Today was not a good day for people to be careless about folks they were supposed to love. She might bite their heads off. She restrained herself with Rhonda simply because she couldn't bear the conversation to go on another minute.

She realized she hadn't eaten all day and went into the kitchen to make herself some toast. Instead of eating, she wound up looking out of the kitchen window at the barn. *How is it possible I didn't see the murderer go into the barn or come out? What the hell was I doing this morning that I was so blind?* Then she remembered William again. William had arrived just at the moment when she would have been looking out the window at the barn, waiting for Grant to be done with his chores. William was the distraction, and William didn't know that Grant was dead.

She felt horrified by the fact that she hadn't awakened him immediately to tell him right after it happened. She had completely forgotten he was there. *Who was the careless one now?* She walked up the stairs to the third floor and knocked on the bedroom door. She heard a muffled, "Yeah?" from inside and opened the door. Her son was still in bed, head on the pillow, one eye open now to look at her. *He's either exhausted or depressed, or both,* she guessed.

"Why don't you get up now, sweetheart?" Emma said. "Take a shower, put on clean clothes, come down and have something to eat. I have to tell you something."

"What? Tell me now," William said, sitting up in the bed and swinging his legs over the side. "You sound on edge."

Emma sat down on the bed, her hands on her knees. She had no idea how this news would affect her son. Grant had been kind and generous with William, but they weren't close, far from close, although Grant wasn't any closer to either of his biological children. She struggled to find the words to tell William what had happened. She had not yet had to say these words face-to-face with anyone, except the police and they didn't count, that Grant was dead, that he had been murdered; that he was never going to walk into this house again, never ride a horse, never put his arms around her and kiss her neck. The words seemed truer said in person. She was afraid she wouldn't be able to get through saying them.

She took a deep breath, looked at her son, and said, "Grant died this morning, maybe right after you arrived, maybe while we were talking." She stopped, put both hands on her face covering her eyes, her entire body shaking.

William sucked in his breath. He jumped out of bed, turned around, sat down close to her, put his arm around her and said, "What? No. God, Mom, that can't be. What do you mean? Did he have a heart attack? Why didn't you wake me?"

Emma shook her head, no. "Somebody killed him—in the barn—stabbed him." Emma shook so hard she was unable to continue talking. She lowered her head.

William tightened his hold on her shoulder and waited. He rocked a little. She was aware of him chanting something under his breath. She looked up and saw his eyes were closed. He was grief-struck. Somehow William having a normal response to Grant's death was a relief. It seemed odd, but his sorrow strengthened her. It was okay to grieve. Her brilliant son had just proved it with his reaction to the news. That realization gave her room to feel the deep sadness that had burrowed into her bones from the moment she found Grant dead. Emma let herself go, sobbing into her hands, then turned and leaned into William's shoulder, making noises she would later think sounded like a crow cawing in anguish. Her son held her and rocked her until her sobs subsided. She pulled away to get a tissue and blow her nose.

When she had control of herself again, Emma said, "Did you see anything, William, when you got here this morning?"

William shook his head. "I don't remember anything out of the ordinary, but I was focused on talking to you about leaving school. And I had just driven a long way, so maybe I wasn't seeing much of anything."

"Think carefully. You might have seen something and just don't have it top of mind."

William got up and walked around the room, he looked out the dormer windows that faced the barn and the woods behind it. "This view always makes me feel as if I've been transported into an earlier century." The horse trailer was next to the graveled lane that led to the hayloft. There were police vehicles everywhere and people in uniform scurrying around collecting samples from the barn, ground and trailer. "Except now." He looked at her in shock. "I remember I saw some guy running down the hill from the hayloft entrance toward the front of the barn where the horse stalls are. A guy wearing a Pirate's baseball cap, with long hair. I figured he was there to help Grant with the horses." William shrugged. "Is that important?"

Emma felt a sensation, an icy spike piercing her spine. "Yes, it's important. We should tell the police while they're here."

By the time she walked down the stairs to the kitchen and began fixing William lunch, she was distracted again by thoughts of what to say at Grant's funeral, who to call at the bank about their accounts, how she was supposed to get a death certificate. She began making a list and completely forgot to tell the police about the guy with long hair and a baseball cap running into the barn, or that her son William had arrived early enough this morning to see him.

CHAPTER 21

3:00 p.m.:

Lagarde and Black got to the house where Deputy Harbaugh had stashed Ron Tabor just at the moment that Tabor's argument with his mother-in-law reached a fevered pitch. Lagarde could hear Tabor's strained voice ten steps away from the blue front door of the stone cottage. He could get very loud, they discovered. *How has Elaine dealt with her husband? Maybe she didn't deal well with anger, but maybe no one does well with anger,* he reminded himself. He had still not crossed Tabor off his list of possible suspects in both murders. Tabor's version of how he arrived home to find his wife stabbed to death, as relayed by Harbaugh, had occurred without any witness but his little girl, and that story was pretty self-serving. *The guy is obviously ready to erupt at the smallest provocation, although, I haven't yet met Tabor's mother-in-law. Maybe she* isn't *a small provocation.*

Black knocked on the door and rang the bell.

They could hear Tabor's mother-in-law yelling, "You stupid sonofabitch, if you'da been home more, she'd never have gotten in this trouble."

Black cringed. "Glad she's not my mother-in-law."

"You're not married, Larry," Lagarde reminded him. "This isn't so bad. It's been a stressful day."

Black grimaced and knocked again. A man he assumed to be Ron Tabor, looking harried and ready to knock someone's block off, yanked open the door. "Yeah?" he said, staring at them.

"I'm Sergeant Larry Black. This is Detective Sam Lagarde." Black paused to show his credentials. "Are you Ron Tabor? Where's the deputy who's supposed to be here with you?"

Tabor shook his head and shrugged. "He went to McDonalds to get everyone food."

Looks passed between Black and Lagarde. That seemed to be a fairly lax interpretation of guarding a suspect.

"Maybe you should be more careful about opening the door without checking who it is when there's a murderer running around," Lagarde said to Tabor. "You and your daughter could still be in danger."

Tabor immediately looked crestfallen, his jaw dropped, he hung his head, tears sprang into his eyes. He lowered his voice and said, "I never could spend more than an hour with Elaine's mom. She gets on my nerves on the best days and *this is not* one of my best days."

Lagarde could hear Tabor's mother-in-law clear her throat in the room behind him. They obviously hadn't learned how to ignore each other for the greater good.

Tabor stepped back from the doorway and let Lagarde and Black walk into the living room of the house where his mother-in-law, Mrs. Cynthia Bailes, had lived since she was a child. Mrs. Bailes was wearing a red sweatshirt that announced in large white lettering, *I Don't Give a Crap What You Think* and a pair of jeans. It must have been what she was wearing when she was informed about her daughter's death. No one, not even the Wicked Witch of the West, would have put it on after learning the news. Lagarde guessed she had completely forgotten what she was wearing, but he took her billboard announcement of her point of view as gospel. She was barefooted. Her short gray hair was permed into a virtual lamb's-wool cap, making her appear to be dressed for winter sports. She might once have been as beautiful as her daughter, but Lagarde's first quick surmise was that Elaine got her looks from her father. Mrs. Bailes held balled up tissues in both hands and periodically dabbed her swollen eyes.

Lagarde introduced himself as Black and he did a quick survey of the house. It was a comfortable home, solid, no frills, akin to Mrs. Bailes herself. In the living room, a blue sectional sofa in which all the seats appeared to recline was arranged in a semi-circle around the television. The sofa and large flat-screen TV were fairly new, perhaps purchased recently with money Elaine had given her mother. Lagarde didn't really need to know where the money for the new furniture came from, and there was no point in asking questions that would make Tabor suffer more than he already was. The man did look wretched, Harbaugh was right about that.

Molly came running from another room to greet them. She seemed to have recovered from the trauma of having her mother killed this morning, but Lagarde reminded himself that children were hard to read. She would miss her mother for the rest of her life, whether she had witnessed the murder or not. The sound of her mother screaming would surely haunt her sleep for years to come. She wrapped her arms around her father's leg and peeked around at Lagarde, who took the child's total trust of her father as an indication that maybe the man wasn't a murderer.

"I member you," Molly said. "You came to our house already."

Lagarde smiled at the child. "Yes, we did come to your house. We saw you this morning." He looked at Elaine's mother. "Mrs. Bailes, could you take Molly in another room while we talk with Mr. Tabor?"

"No way," she said, her voice scraping her sorrow, a razor slicing her heart. "I'm staying right here. I got some questions of my own."

He turned to Black. "Larry, why don't you take Molly into the kitchen and draw with her for a little while. I'll talk to Mr. Tabor and Mrs. Bailes."

Black nodded and held out his hand to the child, which she took as if they were old friends. Lagarde heard him ask Molly if she had paper and crayons. "I have lots of toys in my room," the child said. "I stay with Granny when Mommy goes places." She pulled Black toward her room. "My mommy went away for a long time," Lagarde heard her say when they were nearly out of earshot, "but she still loves me, Granny said."

"This is as good a place as any to talk," Mrs. Bailes said, and sat down in the seat that she probably called hers directly opposite the TV screen. She pulled fresh tissues from the box on the seat next to her and pushed a button so that her seat reclined and closed her eyes. Like Tabor, she looked stunned, shocked beyond her ability to dissemble her grief. Her daughter had been the best thing she had ever done with her life. Lagarde guessed that Elaine had been the whole world for her mother. The thought of life without her daughter was incomprehensible.

"Thank you. Is Mr. Bailes around?"

Cindy Bailes threw her head back and laughed hoarsely, "That mutt hasn't been 'around' for ten years. Drunken lout left me for some floozy he met at the racetrack.

That's all right, though, I got me a piece of his pension and his Social Security, him being a retired teacher and all. I work part-time at Walmart, and I got this house from my mother…and Elaine was always generous with me." Her lips quivered as she picked up an orange throw pillow from the sofa and pressed it to her face.

"Mr. Tabor, why don't you sit down also?" Lagarde indicated a spot a bit away from his mother-in-law. "I need to go over the timeline of when you arrived at home today and some other questions."

Tabor nodded and sat down on the farthest seat from Cindy that he could find. He leaned over, put his elbows on his knees and his face in his hands.

Lagarde looked around for a less comfortable seat, spotted a straight-backed wooden chair in the dining room and brought it over so that he could sit between them. If Tabor was dangerous, getting out of that deep sofa would slow his forward movement. At least that's what Lagarde thought. From his more upright chair, Lagarde would be able to get the jump on him. Black was near enough to hear a scuffle, but Lagarde didn't think Tabor would give him any trouble. The big guy looked as if he had been crushed under the tires of his truck.

"So you got home this morning at what time?" Lagarde asked his first question, watching Tabor carefully.

"No, not this morning, not here, well almost, but really this afternoon," Tabor tried to explain. "I got across the Potomac River Bridge at around 1:30, stopped at the 7-11 to get some beer and flowers for Elaine, then I drove home. I'm pretty sure I got home at around two. I called her when I hit Baltimore just as I always do, but she didn't pick up. I figured she was in the bathroom and couldn't get to the phone." He shook his head as if to settle the broken pieces rattling inside it. "I was just busting to get home. I kept forgetting to call her, racking up the miles under the tires. I figured she'd be happy to see me." He restrained a sob, sat back in the seat, and covered his face with his hands.

Even though people needed to talk about what they saw and what they felt about those observations, Lagarde knew that talking was often excruciating. Information from a witness who was personally affected by a murder was always tainted by their feelings. Even a bystander could get just about everything wrong: height, weight, race, what the perp was wearing, which way he ran, what actually happened and when. Eyewitness testimony to a crime was a coin toss. It was probably accurate only fifty percent of the time, if that. According to the alibi Tabor had just given Lagarde, he could not have committed the murder or seen the perp, who was long gone before Tabor drove up to his house, based on the time of death estimate from the medical examiner. Tabor might have noticed something else in his house or on the grounds that would provide a clue, however. And maybe Lagarde's assumption was wrong, maybe the killer was hiding in the woods waiting to see the response to his handiwork. That would be a long time to hide, though. Lagarde guessed the killer moved on pretty quickly after he killed Elaine. The question was, where did he go? And what was his next move?

"Did you happen to see any unfamiliar vehicles parked on the side of the road near your home, or the Wodehouse property as you drove up to your house?" Lagarde probed.

Tabor took a deep breath, but kept his eyes closed, as if the movie of this morning's drive was running on the screen in his mind. "I did see an Audi parked on the side of the road near the Le Gore's lane, just before the hairpin turn. Never seen it before. The Le Gores never leave their vehicles there. They have about a quarter mile lane

that jigs and jags around before you get up to their house.
You can't see where their lane meets Ridge Road from
their house because of the woods. Besides, I don't think
they can afford an Audi."

"Where is the Le Gore driveway exactly?" Lagarde
asked, leaning forward, taking notes on his pad. He didn't
remember seeing an Audi when he and Black drove up to
the Wodehouse farm.

"It's about three-quarters of a mile west from my
house, half a mile up the road from the Wodehouse property, shorter if you cut through the woods on foot, 'cuz of
the way the road winds." Tabor stopped for a moment as
if he was standing on the road looking at the property and
getting the sight lines right. "The Wodehouse woods go
along Ridge Road all the way up to the property line with
the Le Gores. There's a cut-in that leads from the road to
the Wodehouse barn before you get to the Le Gore's
lane."

He gestured with his left hand to show how the lane
cut in from the main road. "Then the woods wrap around
the Wodehouse's upper field where they pasture the horses and meet up with my property line on the east side of
their house. Those woods around my house are on the
Wodehouse property. You can also get to their barn by
walking through the woods. Along the road, the property
is all posted 'No Hunting, No Trespassing.' I always
doubted that kept anyone out, though."

Lagarde realized that he and Black had driven to the
Wodehouse farm in the morning and then to Tabor's
house this afternoon coming from the other direction on
Ridge Road. He hadn't passed the Le Gore property either time.

Tabor spotting an Audi, not a common vehicle in the
area anyway, near the Le Gore driveway seemed pretty
significant. It would be easy to check if the Le Gores

owned an Audi. He mentally slapped his head for not walking the entire area early in the morning.

Tabor seemed energized by being able to remember something that might help the investigators find his wife's killer. He leaned forward, straining to remember more. "Oh, wait, there was a guy in the driver's seat when I went past the car on my way home. Looked like he was listening to music. His head was bobbing, you know, like he was rockin' out. I didn't really get a good look at him, but I saw the license plate," he said, triumphant that his search of his memory yielded more detail. "I don't remember the numbers, but it was a Pennsylvania plate." He waited, shook his head. "Sorry, that's all I've got."

An out-of-state car, entry-luxury level, pulled off the road near a stranger's driveway was definitely worth checking out on a day when two murders had been committed in houses along that road.

But what kind of killer would just sit in his car without worrying about being discovered? Maybe the Audi and its occupant have nothing to do with my murder investigation. "That's very good, Mr. Tabor." Lagarde switched gears. "Did you know that Grant Wodehouse was killed this morning?"

"What?" Tabor looked up at Lagarde completely blank, as if Lagarde was speaking a different language and for a moment he hadn't understood a word of it. "Oh, man, I know that guy. He's a good guy. He's the one who gave me the money for the down payment for my truck. I was gonna pay him back over a couple years. That was our deal."

Wodehouse apparently spared no expense to get what he wanted, which in this case must have been easy access to Elaine whenever he wanted her. Lagarde had to conclude that Tabor might be a little dense.

"Grant Wodehouse was killed this morning in his barn. Can you establish where you were at seven this morning?"

"At 7:00 a.m., I was about two hours out from checking in my load in Baltimore, on Route 95 somewhere around DC. Got stuck in morning rush hour. Dumb planning on my part." He ran his hand over his face as if poor planning was one of too many mistakes he had made on this day. "I've got the check-in ticket in my truck, at the house. I was there in Baltimore about three hours, filled out some paperwork, contracted for a couple more jobs." A dry sob stopped his breath. He shook his head. "If I hadn't been doing that, I might've gotten here in time to stop her murder."

"We'll need to check your story, Mr. Tabor. Could you write down the name and phone number of the person at the trucking company, or wherever you checked in this morning, and the folks you talked to about the other jobs?" He felt deeply sorry for Tabor. The guy would torture himself with "if only" for the rest of his life.

"Sure." He shook his shoulders, leaned forward, and took Lagarde's pad and pen from his hand. He wrote down the information and handed the pad back.

Lagarde took the pad by its spiral top, pulled out a latex glove from his pocket, folded that around the pad, and put the glove and pad sandwich in his pocket. He now had Tabor's prints, just in case Deputy Harbaugh hadn't gotten a clean set. The next task was to lead Tabor through his arrival, step-by-step in order to extract whatever he might have seen. That, he could tell, was going to prove a little more difficult. "Thanks, we'll check on that. Now if you could remember anything else you saw as you pulled up to your house, when you first got out of your own vehicle at your house, or anything in the house that looked out of place."

While Tabor was silent, eyes closed, waiting for inspiration, Mrs. Bailes slammed the footrest of her recliner down with a sharp bang, stood up, and yelled, "I know who killed my baby doll. I know who it was. You don't have to go through all this interviewing crap." She blotted her eyes. "It was that bitch Emma Wodehouse, that snotty bitch. She was jealous of my girl, so young and pretty."

"What are you talking about, Cindy?" Tabor, instantly angry, yelled at her. "You're not talking sense."

Cindy Bailes looked defiantly at Lagarde and her son-in-law. "I'll talk about the elephant in the room even if you dopes won't. That dried-up bitch Emma Wodehouse was worried my Elaine was going to take her rich husband away from her." She stomped around her living room, put her hands on her hips, and turned around to square off with them.

Hoping to quell an impending blow-up, Lagarde put up his hand like a policeman at a crosswalk, but he was helpless to stop the collision. Tabor leaped up from the sofa much more quickly than Lagarde thought possible. "What the hell are you saying, woman?" he yelled, now furious and unable to control his temper. He reached out to grab her by her shoulders. "You don't know anything about anything."

"I know this, you stupid dolt." Cindy stood square in front of Tabor, glaring at him, daring him to touch her. "Elaine was having sex with that Grant Wodehouse right under your nose and you didn't even know it, and his wife killed my girl because of it."

Tabor was about to lift his mother-in-law off the floor and throw her against the wall. He lunged toward her again. Black rushed into the room and, with Lagarde restrained Tabor, grabbing him by his arms. Together they pulled him back toward the front door of the house.

Molly ran into the living room screaming, "Daddy! Daddy!"

Lagarde took a deep breath. He had known interviewing Tabor here was a bad idea. He should have followed his own instincts. "We'll check out your charge about Emma Wodehouse, Mrs. Bailes," Lagarde said with the intention of instilling calm.

Tabor's shoulders twitched violently.

"Right now, we're going to find another location to talk with Mr. Tabor. Please keep your granddaughter. We will call you if we need to talk with you further."

"Yeah, no problem. Get that moron out of my house!" She slammed the door behind them as they walked Tabor to the back seat of their car.

"We'll talk with you at headquarters," Lagarde emphasized, "as a witness. We're not charging you with a crime at this time. It's just quieter there and you can think."

Tabor nodded his head, sat back in the seat of the vehicle, and looked out of the window. His daughter Molly waved to him from the living room window. He waved back and tried to smile.

The child is his real love. Tabor wouldn't do anything to harm that relationship, which included killing his wife. But it might be a good thing for Wodehouse that he was already dead, now that Tabor knows about his affair with Elaine.

CHAPTER 22

Paul was ready to go. Grant had brushed and saddled him, tied the reins together, put them over the saddle, grabbed the bridle, unhooked the leads anchoring the horse to the grooming area in the barn, and was about to lead the horse out. His plan was to tie Paul up at the antique hitching post near the back porch and then ask Emma which horse she wanted to ride this morning. Her usual horse, Annie's Way, had come up lame and it wasn't a good idea to ride her.

Grant had a moment's regret that he hadn't simply called Emma on the barn phone to ask her before he let all the other horses out, but at that point he was still tingling from his encounter with Elaine and all his brain cells weren't working properly. Elaine could set his head on fire. Now he'd have to catch a horse he'd already put out in the paddock. He was only mildly annoyed with himself since he wouldn't have missed that little interlude with Elaine for anything. The risk of being spotted by Emma from the house had just increased the thrill.

He turned to walk the horse out of the barn and saw his son, Kyle, walking toward him from an empty stall. A baseball cap held down Kyle's mop of blond hair and his blue eyes looked wild.

"What the hell are you doing here?" Grant said without checking the annoyance in his tone. He noted that his son was in a grunge phase, dirty hoodie hanging over ripped jeans, the edge of a repulsively soiled white T-shirt showing above the zipper. "Where are your normal clothes and why aren't you in school?"

"Nice way to greet me, Dad. You haven't seen me in months. How do you know what's normal for me? Aren't you supposed to be glad to see me, give me a hug, all that loving father stuff?"

"Sorry. My bad," Grant instantly relented. He was always confused about how to talk to Kyle, his own disappointment and anger usually trumped his love for him. Somehow he was always wrong with Kyle even when he was right. "But aren't you supposed to be in school? There's no fall break, right?"

"I got tired of school and I need some money for stuff, so I came here," Kyle said, stuffing his fists into his hoodie pockets, taking a wide stance in front of the barn door, blocking Grant's exit. "You're my dad. You're supposed to help me out. I want to go out to Phoenix and visit Rebecca, maybe live out there."

"You mean you need money for that mess you made in Mercersville and visiting Becca's your excuse. I got a call from your attorney, Mr. Hamby, last night. I'll take care of that problem, but I'm not giving you money directly. I'll give it to Hamby. He'll handle all the arrangements." There was no point in telling Kyle right now that he would be going into a rehab facility for at least a year. Grant had heard other parents had their addicted children abducted by strongmen in order to get them to a remote rehabilitation facility against their will. He might have to resort to that with Kyle.

Kyle took his fists out of his pockets and put them on his hips. "No, Dad. I want you to give me money so I can go live somewhere I want to live. I'm not going back to that crap school. They don't teach me anything. I've had it with them."

Grant felt mildly threatened by his son's gesture. He was accustomed to Kyle's tantrums, which he had endured since the boy was a child, but the anger his son was displaying now seemed out of proportion to any insult Grant might have given him. Kyle, he realized, was much larger than he was, almost a foot taller and with the bulk of a football player. The kid's face was red, his pupils were contracted to pinpoints, his body tense as if he were going to spring on an opponent in a wrestling match. Had he graduated from alcohol to cocaine? That could be one reason why he needed more cash. *Maybe Hamby was right, the kid needs to go into rehab.*

"Calm down, Kyle, we'll figure something out. Don't worry about it. Don't I always take care of you?"

The horse shifted feet a few times, a quick dance to indicate he was getting peeved just standing there.

"No, Dad," Kyle said through clenched teeth, "you never take care of me. You just throw money at me and stash me somewhere so you can fool around with your whores."

Grant found himself getting heated. "What the hell are you talking about? Have you ever wanted for anything?" he yelled. One thing Grant hated more than anything else was someone telling him the stone cold truth.

His son hissed at him, "I'm talking about that ho I just saw you pork in that stall right there with your nice wifey up at the house waiting for you."

"You're not making any sense. I don't know what you're talking about," Grant was stalling, thinking desperately how to manage this situation.

"You know exactly what I'm talking about, old man."

Grant realized he wasn't going to be able to slide away from the facts. "You saw that? You were watching us?"

Kyle nodded, his eyes searching the barn for something, his teeth gritted. "You were so absorbed with her you didn't even hear me come into the barn."

"You have no business even being here, Kyle. Now get out of my way. I have things to do and you're not one of them." Grant turned back to leading his horse out of the barn.

"No, Dad, I think this once, you have time for only me!" Kyle yelled. "Kneel down."

"What are you talking about? I'm not kneeling down. I've got a horse to take care of." Grant was still thinking that he could talk his way out of or ignore the strange mood his son was in. "Get in your car and go back to school," he ordered.

There was a sudden creak in the floor boards in the hayloft above them. Paul, whose ears had been pinned back since Kyle walked up on them, spooked, whinnied, rose up on his hind legs and kicked out in front. Grant lost his balance and dropped his hold on the bridle. Kyle jumped to the side and Paul bolted out of the barn door and took off across the field.

Grant was furious. "You see? You see what just happened? It'll take me hours now to find him and get him back in the paddock. You just cost me the whole damn day."

"I'm gonna cost you a lot more than that," Kyle said, lunging to pick up the pitchfork that was leaning on the wall, turning and pointing it at his father.

"What the hell are you doing?" Grant yelled. "You've done it now. You've gone completely crazy. I always knew you were a worthless piece of shit." He instantly regretted the words, but they were out of his mouth and hung in the air, icy daggers pricking his son's thin skin.

Grant circled around so that he was closer to the barn door. He gave up trying to reason with the kid. His plan was now to run for the house. Kyle circled with him, remaining in front of his father, decreasing the distance between them. Grant didn't really believe his son would even nudge him with the pitchfork. Nevertheless, he looked for a weapon near to hand, anything that would help him fend off an assault when he heard another noise from the hayloft. *Did Kyle bring friends with him?*

He looked up and saw the homeless guy, who yesterday he'd thoughtlessly offered a dry place to sleep in order to impress a young woman, staring at him, his mouth open as if he'd seen a ghost or something worse. Grant didn't even have time to ask Warren Lyles what the hell he was doing there in the barn before he felt the tines of the pitchfork pierce his skin. His first scream ripped out of his throat.

CHAPTER 23

8:00 p.m.:

Tabor had revealed nothing else of use about either the murder of Wodehouse or of his own wife, Elaine. After an hour of interviewing him at their headquarters in Kearneysville, with no distractions or interruptions, Lagarde realized that he couldn't charge Tabor with either murder. There was simply no evidence to support a charge. Tabor had substantiated alibis that worked for both murders. He also couldn't keep Tabor in custody, even if a little quiet time might be good for him.

Tabor was completely oblivious to Elaine's affair with Grant Wodehouse. Even in the face of Mrs. Bailes allegations, he couldn't believe that his wife had cheated on him. "No, no, no way," the man said, shaking his head vehemently when Lagarde tested the idea that Tabor knew about his wife and Wodehouse. "There's just no way Elaine would cheat on me. Cindy's off her rocker."

There was no reason to disabuse him, in Lagarde's estimation. Tabor was beyond snapping. He was a man whose emotions had been stretched to transparency. Elaine was his one true love, and now that she was dead, she was perfect. *How can anyone be that blind? But*

*maybe if you were only home one week a month, enough
wool could be pulled over your eyes that you saw only
dimly what was right in front of you.* Tabor called his
brother to pick him up from the state troopers office and
take him to their mother's home. Lagarde guessed Tabor
would consume at least one six-pack in the next few
hours before he passed out from grief and exhaustion.

Black had been busy while Lagarde interviewed Tabor, filling out and filing all their paperwork for the day,
as well as going over more fingerprint results and new
information about the compass Lagarde found in Wodehouse's hayloft.

"Let me hit the head for a minute, Larry," Lagarde
said and walked away. "Order some subs from Brother's
Pizza while you're waiting. It's late and I'm hungry."

Black picked up his cell phone to make the call to the
restaurant and saw an alert that he had an email from Ann
Roberts. He couldn't resist opening it.

"I think you should know what's going on with
Grant's partner, Eugene Waters," the email said. She
suggested meeting with him tomorrow at ten in the morning at her office.

Black flushed, glad Lagarde wasn't there to tease him.
He immediately emailed back, "See you then." Then he
placed the order for their usual: a meatball sub, an Italian
sub, a large order of cheese fries and two cokes. There
was nothing healthy about their diet, and they liked it that
way. Neither of them had wives who might nag about
vegetables, fruit, or too much fat or carbs in their diets.
As far as Black was concerned, the four essential food
groups were sugar, salt, bacon and mayonnaise. As soon
as Lagarde came back to his chair, Black told him about
the meeting he'd set up with Ann.

Lagarde's eyebrows rose, then he grinned at Black.
"Want to go by yourself?"

Black shrugged, as if it didn't matter to him, and said, "Sure, why not? She doesn't seem dangerous."

"That's what you think now, man. Tell me in a month or two if you still think that." Lagarde swiveled around to his computer screen then remembered that Larry had some information for him. He turned back to him. "You said you had a report on fingerprints?"

"Oh, right," Black said, pulling his thoughts away from Ann's hypnotic eyes. "Here's the short version. There are multiple prints on the shaft of the pitchfork. We've ruled out prints from Grant Wodehouse, both of the boys who work in the barn, and Emma Wodehouse, but we have a set of prints from a person unknown."

Lagarde leaned back in his chair and stroked his head with his palm. "Now we're getting somewhere."

"The interesting thing about those prints," Black continued, "is that we have a partial match of the unknown prints on the pitchfork to the prints on the crop you spotted on Elaine Tabor's dresser. Those same prints are on her dresser, closet and on the buttons and cross-trainers her murderer left on the floor of her bedroom. So your speculation that the guy who murdered Grant also killed Elaine seems to track. They're running those prints now through the FBI's fingerprint database, IAFIS."

Lagarde rolled his eyes. He hated the federal government's alphabet soup acronyms.

Black continued, "Since all the police agencies in the tri-state area send the FBI their criminal data, if the guy's ever been printed, even after being hauled in for driving while intoxicated, we might know who he is complete with mug shot and priors before our subs get here. At the latest, we should have a solid ID by tomorrow morning."

"Well that's good news because I'm still really hungry."

"I've got more,"

"So spill it."

"Remember that compass with the engraving you found in the hayloft?"

Lagarde nodded. It struck him as particularly poignant that the person who lost the compass might also have lost his way in life.

"I checked with Feagan's in Charles Town. They do engraving *and* they've been the only jewelry store in town since Main Street was paved. I sent them front and back photos of the compass by email. Turns out they used to do these special brass compasses for Eagle Scout ceremonies. This compass was one of theirs. They still keep paper records going all the way back to 1960 and this order was far more recent than that. Caroline Lyles ordered that engraving for her son Warren's Eagle Scout induction ceremony in 2004."

"Well, good detecting, Sergeant. I don't suppose we have Mr. Lyles's fingerprints on file anywhere, do we?"

"No. We only have the prints on the compass. I asked the tech guys to check local records. They don't match anything we have. They also don't match the prints on the crop or pitchfork. As far as I can tell, Mr. Lyles has never been arrested in this county or state. He might have worked for the state or the federal government, so we might get a hit if his prints are in the civilian database. That'll take a while. He may have lost his way, but he's not a criminal, at least not one that anyone has caught. We'll see if his prints pop up on the national database. So it's possible there was another person in that barn this morning besides Wodehouse, Knowles and the guy who killed Wodehouse. We might have an eyewitness."

"What on earth connects a guy who used to be an Eagle Scout to Grant Wodehouse? We're more in the dark now than we were a few minutes ago. At least with Knowles, Tabor, or Emma, we had motive."

"Tabor's prints are not in the barn, that we collected anyway, in case you're wondering."

Lagarde's desk phone intercom buzzed. He picked up the receiver. "Yeah?" He put down the phone, said "Food's here," and walked out of their office to reception. "I'll pay," he said over his shoulder. "And put out an all-points bulletin for Warren Lyles. Let's get some help finding him. Call him a person of interest in the murder. That'll get more attention from surrounding counties."

When Lagarde returned to the office, Black had already pulled up the BOLO form on his computer and started typing. They didn't have much of a description of Lyles: man in his mid-twenties who lost his compass wasn't going to help any officer driving by someone walking on the street. Black typed, "Warren Lyles, former Eagle Scout, possibly homeless" into the form.

Lagarde held out a cardboard container of cheese fries to Black who grabbed a handful. He crammed a few in his mouth, chewed and swallowed with a sigh of relief. He leaned over the sandwich wrapper now open on his desk and took a bite of his sandwich, pieces of which always fell in his lap or onto his shirt. He sighed again. Then he finished typing and sent out the request for all other police agencies from Winchester, Virginia to Chambersburg, Pennsylvania to be on the lookout for their witness.

The point of finding Lyles was that from the barn hayloft he might have seen Wodehouse murdered early this morning, if that's when he dropped his compass there. And while eyewitnesses were unreliable, the prosecutor preferred to have at least one to shake at a defense attorney. A witness was a big stick he could raise above his head while he did his intimidation dance to get the suspect to plead guilty.

Juries were an iffy proposition. With plea deals, at

least some punishment for the crime was guaranteed.

Lagarde was eager to get the case moving. It was still day one. This was an early break for them. He could feel it. But even with help from other sheriff's departments in finding Lyles, they would still have to find the guy whose fingerprints were on the murder weapon. Both men might be hard to find and they weren't going to find them today, that much was clear. Catching a killer on the same day he committed his crime rarely happened, unless the guy was colossally stupid or got tired and gave himself up. This killer may not have been a brain trust, but he ran. At least Lagarde could comfort himself with knowing they were close on his trail. He took a bite of his meatball sub and automatically wiped off the tomato sauce he knew dribbled onto his chin.

"I'm bushed, man. I'm not doing anything else until I finish eating this mess."

Lagarde was way ahead of him. "When we're done with paperwork here, Larry, we're done for tonight. Whatever else is going to happen today, we've had enough death for one day."

"In that case, I'm out of here now," Black said, shutting down his computer, wrapping up what was left of his sandwich, and heading out the door while Lagarde sat back in his chair and admired the guy's efficient exit.

CHAPTER 24

9:00 p.m.:

Warren Lyles, halfway across the Williamsport Bridge that spanned the Potomac River between West Virginia and Maryland, had a change of heart. The river churned beneath the bridge. A three-quarter moon rose in the sky. His feet stopped moving. *Mom.* He had disappointed her once again. Sitting down on the bridge with his back against the old stone and iron railings, he leaned his head back and rested a bit.

An old Chevy pickup rumbling north on Route 11 across the bridge into Williamsport slowed to a stop. The passenger leaned out the window and called, "Hey, man, need a lift?"

Warren waved his hand and shook his head, no. The truck moved on. Sometimes people were kind, Grant Wodehouse had been, but Warren was wary of kindness right now. It seemed to lead to trouble.

He knew there was a small camp of homeless folks around the canal lock. Hard to know whether they were there tonight, but he might find shelter near the old warehouse the National Park Service converted to a museum. He could check out the situation from the bridge, which took him right over the canal and adjacent park. He'd stopped at this homeless camp before. They were mostly veterans so destroyed by their experiences in Vietnam and Iraq that they couldn't abide living inside any kind of box with anyone. Some of them had elaborate living areas complete with tents, sleeping bags and assorted camping gear. Some had been on the streets for decades, living by their own rules and surviving. Warren didn't think he had their kind of grit, so he stood up and walked on toward the town.

A deputy sheriff's vehicle slowed and then pulled to the side of the road and stopped. He rolled down the window and called out to Warren, "Hey, kid, where you going?"

Warren had learned never to run from the police, even if he was completely innocent. Maybe this was his opportunity. He could tell this officer what he'd seen and then he'd be free of the guilt he'd carried for twenty-five miles. He walked over to the vehicle and leaned in. "Hey, officer, I'm just on a ramble."

"Got any ID, son?" the deputy said.

Warren reached in his back pocket and pulled out his wallet. West Virginia driver's licenses were good for five years, and his hadn't expired yet. He pulled the plastic card out of his wallet and handed it to the officer.

"You're pretty far from home on foot, aren't you?"

"Yes, sir. Wife and I had a spat. She kicked me out." Warren wasn't sure at what point he decided to lie, but there it was.

"Judging from your clothes, that was a while ago."

"Yes, sir, two years." That was the other thing he'd learned being out in the world on his own: only answer the questions you're asked.

The deputy held onto the license for a few more seconds and in the end decided the guy was harmless. He might as well be kind to the kid. No point in calling it in. He handed back Warren's license. "Best find a place to bed down for the night. This a quiet town, but we've got our crazies out here."

"Yes, sir," Warren said, "thank you, sir." He backed away from the vehicle and waited for the deputy to drive away. As he gazed out and over the railing at the canal path park below him, he pondered climbing down there. It was dark. There was no movement below him. *Nah.* He resumed walking into town, thinking about his mother again.

When Warren's mother was dying of stomach cancer, he would sit by her bed while she slept. Every time she woke, she would smile at him and squeeze his hand. But he had seen sorrow in her face, as much as she tried to keep it from him. "You're a good boy, Warren," she'd said to him, but he knew she expected more from him.

All her care for him "hadn't amounted to a hill of beans," as she would say. He was a total loss as a son: jobless, homeless, and a drunk. Even when he wasn't drinking, and that had been two years now, he was thinking about drinking. Some part of his mind, even if he didn't act on it, was scheming to get a drink—was telling itself a story about how it was okay to drink, how everyone else drank, how it was everybody else's fault that he was a drunk. He'd lost his wife and his son due to alcoholism.

His wife threw him out of their pleasant townhouse in Harpers Ferry, not in anger but in complete despair. "I won't let you ruin our lives anymore, Warren," she said to him so quietly he almost missed the point.

He had no place to live. He'd used up all his friends' patience. He wasn't a maintenance drinker. Not him. Once he started drinking, he couldn't stop until he was hauled to the hospital unconscious with alcohol poisoning. He would drink until his stomach rebelled and he passed out in his own vomit wherever he happened to be standing—the kitchen, the bathroom, a street corner, it didn't matter. He would get up in the afternoon when the stupor lifted and start drinking all over again. He longed for the near-death unconsciousness of total inebriation, without a care about the consequences.

In spite of the cancer, he was sure his mother died of a broken heart because of him. She'd worked hard to bring him up the right way: enrolled him in Boy Scouts, went to church every Sunday, even Sunday school, and paid for him to go to community college. When he graduated with his associate's degree, he took the federal test and got a job with the IRS right there in Kearneysville, near his mother's home. There were few demands from that job that he could not immediately fulfill. It made him proud to go into the building with hundreds of other people at the same time in the morning. He felt he was helping to hold up one of the pillars of democracy. He'd met a woman there who, after dating for six months, said yes the first time he asked her to marry him. His mother had beamed at him at the wedding.

And then he discovered tequila at a birthday lunch for one of his office mates and destroyed his life *all by himself.* He had no excuses, had blown through any right he might have had to expect a better life. This homeless existence was his penance. He had no idea how to get back to what other people called normal. Sleeping in the woods and panhandling at intersections was now normal for him.

But maybe with one act, he could redeem himself and become the man his mother brought him up to be…not a hero exactly, but a decent person. A hero, after all, would've tried to stop Wodehouse's murder. Warren couldn't see himself ever doing that. The one man who had been kind to him in the last year was killed right in front of his eyes and he did nothing to stop it. He had not said a word, just ran away, because he was absolutely sure that kid would have killed him if he'd stayed in the barn. There was a look in the boy's eyes that terrified Warren. It was the look of someone who no longer cared what anyone thought about him. He had seen that very same look in his own eyes, once or twice.

He watched the police vehicle stop a quarter mile from him and make a U-turn. If he didn't move on, that cop would pick him up. With no idea what trouble that would bring, he turned around and walked briskly back the way he'd come, south on Route 11 toward Falling Waters in Berkeley County, away from this particular deputy sheriff, who had just called in his sighting of a homeless young man, heard the BOLO description for a person of interest in a murder, and was about to pick Warren up when he realized the young man had disappeared.

I have to stop being afraid all the time. Warren didn't know if what he had seen and heard would help the police catch the killer, but he was pretty sure he was the only one who had witnessed the murder and seen the murderer's face, heard the conversation between Wodehouse and the kid, knew who the killer was. He could describe him. In fact, he would never forget the young man's face. It would haunt his dreams.

It was dark on the West Virginia side of the bridge, as if the state didn't expect people to be out at night and therefore didn't have to provide lights on major roads to navigate by. Even now, with his newfound resolution, his footsteps faltered. He was walking back into trouble. He looked back longingly over his shoulder at what had been his escape. The police vehicle idled on the Maryland side of the bridge, just waiting.

It had taken him a full day to get to this bridge from

the library in Summit Point. It would probably take him more than twelve hours to get back, given his fatigue and the way his feet hurt. He wouldn't make it back to Jefferson County until after nine in the morning. He adjusted his backpack and started walking. He hoped he would make it in time for his witnessing to count, for it to make a difference to his mother.

CHAPTER 25

10:30 pm.:

Although she was exhausted, Emma wasn't asleep. She knew she should sleep, would normally have been asleep by now, but she was still pacing. It seemed to be her new thing, to pound a path through her beautiful home. She had been doing it all day, back and forth through all the rooms as if she was looking for something but had forgotten what it was. For a woman who prized her freedom, her home was now a cage, and yet it was the only place she wanted to be. She dreaded driving away from it, going to her office, going into town. Anything might happen: the house could burn down, she could be killed in a car accident or someone might drown in the pool. Yesterday life was predictable, had a course. Today she realized how fragile, tenuous, and random it was. *I have no desire to go anywhere for a long time.*

Her home was the only place she was safe. She couldn't imagine going back to work, going to the supermarket, going shopping or to the movies or the post office. She was afraid she would break into tears on the road, or standing in front of soup cans in the market, or walking to her desk in the offices she shared with Grant. She worried that something would remind her of him, of something he always said such as, "Buy the bacon with the most fat on it," and she would collapse.

The little mundane things of their everyday life gnawed at her. Grant lived in the soft indentation on his side of their bed, in the metal document clip he had affixed to the bottom of the toothpaste to force her to squeeze the tube from the bottom, in the coffee cup he never washed and left sitting on the desk in his office. She couldn't bear to see those things—evidence of his existence an affront to reality in the face of his total annihilation. She tried reminding herself that this was just day one of her grief. Her feelings would change. The sorrow that filled every molecule of her body would subside. She laughed at herself. *To be replaced with what?* All her good memories of Grant were here in this house: all the photographs of them on their travels, images of them with their arms around each other, glowing, happy just to be together, triumphant in their spectacular luck at having found each other late in life.

It had seemed late in life at the time. Ten years later, facing the prospect of twenty or more years alone, Emma now thought of herself as young when at forty-five-years-old she met Grant at a Chamber of Commerce legislative luncheon. She had been trolling for potential new divorce clients. He, she now understood, had been trolling for a new female conquest. She was instantly enraptured by him. He was charming, intelligent and handsome, all the characteristics on her list of must-haves in a man. Plus, he was funny, daring and rich. Why resist? She was more than willing to have an affair with him. It didn't bother her in the least that he was married. What catapulted their affair into a marriage was that she hadn't cared whether he married her or not.

Some women might call her cold and calculating, but it was the distance she kept between them that intrigued Grant. Elusiveness was what kept him calling and coming back. It was her casual way of shrugging off his failure to show up for scheduled dates that increased the cost of their make-up weekend flings to ever more expensive and exotic places. Somehow she had instinctively understood that Grant always needed to be in pursuit. She made herself hard to get, and *she* got *him*. Emma found herself standing again in front of their wedding photo. Picking it up, she held it at arm's length. *I was beautiful.* She looked into the mirror above the table where the photograph stood. *I am no longer that woman.* She was pale, crushed and deflated, her face unexplainably wrinkled from this morning to now, as if widowhood came with its own mask that instantly dropped down over her face at the moment of Grant's death. Putting down the photograph, she moved on.

At that moment, the front door opened. Looking in its direction, she walked toward it. *I know I locked it. There's a murderer running around, for God's sake.* The police, who seemed completely ineffective to her, hadn't caught him yet. If William hadn't been here with her, she might have been terrified, although she realized that of the two of them, she would have to be the one to defend them if someone broke in.

A few hours before, she found Grant's hunting rifle in the closet in his home office, located the bullets in his desk drawer and loaded five rounds into the chamber before she realized the futility of the gesture. The rifle was still leaning against the built-in cupboard in the kitchen, exactly where she left it when she realized how useless it was. The box of bullets was still in the kitchen junk drawer. She had taken a few shooting lessons, but her greatest concern about using the Remington was that the recoil would knock her off her feet. The gun was really just for show. She'd be better off hitting an assailant in the head with the butt of the rifle than trying to put a bullet into him. In her pacing, she had also made sure that the heavy iron pokers in racks near each of the many fireplaces in the house were removed from their racks and set upright against the side of the fireplaces. She could see herself, if it came to that, running to a fireplace, grabbing a poker and bashing the intruder over the head with it. Somehow that seemed more feasible than shooting him.

When she got to the front door, she found Grant's son standing in the foyer. He was disheveled. His clothes were wrinkled as if he'd been sleeping in his car. Perhaps he had. The puffy down vest was definitely meant for a man twice his size. *What in the world has he been doing?*

"God, Kyle," Emma said walking up to him, hugging him.

His arms remained at his side. He was always a difficult kid to be around—sullen, prone to unexpected outbursts, did not want her to touch him, had never voluntarily hugged her. Being an adolescent hadn't improved him.

"I've been calling you and texting you. I called your school. I called your mother," Emma said.

Kyle rolled his eyes.

"We've all been trying to find you. Where have you been? Come into the kitchen. Have you eaten today? I'll make you some food."

Kyle shook her off and walked ahead of her toward the kitchen. Emma realized he had let himself in with his own key, the same as the one she had given to William and Rebecca. She had been waiting to hear from Rebecca about when she and her family would arrive. She had readied guest rooms for her stepdaughter, and also for

Kyle, even though she didn't know if he'd come and stay at the house or stay with his mother, only a twenty minute drive away in Maryland.

She heard Kyle and William in the kitchen greeting each other in that stiff way they always had, "Hey, bro," back slap, arm punch, neither of them knowing exactly how chummy the other one was willing to be. Sometimes blended families were oil and water, they didn't mix well.

By the time she got to the kitchen, Kyle had the refrigerator door open and was removing containers and baggies of food. "I'll make my own," he said with his back to her.

She watched him pile mashed potatoes, a piece of fried chicken, and a thick slice of meatloaf on a plate and put it in the microwave. He opened the baggie of homemade cornbread, removed a square, and took a bite. She was glad she had the food. Ann was to be thanked for that. Casseroles and baking dishes full of nutritious food and soothing desserts had begun arriving at her house this afternoon, brought by women who simply dropped them off, gave her a hug, and didn't linger. It had never occurred to her that she had friends who would step in and help. They were nicer than she was. *Maybe they were Ann's friends?*

William was sitting at the kitchen table eating his third or fourth homemade brownie. The plastic container was open in front of him and the table was littered with chocolate crumbs. *Did he plan to eat all of them?* It was a good thing she had the boys there. She would have eaten only toast and tea, if she could eat anything. Now her friends' good intentions wouldn't go to waste.

Kyle pulled off the vest and threw it over the back of his chair. He sat down at the table with his plate full of food and started to eat, stuffing huge forkfuls into his mouth, barely chewing and swallowing before bringing the next bite to his mouth. She noticed his hands were filthy, as if he'd been digging in the dirt. There was grime under his fingernails and around the cuticles, and he appeared to be starving.

"Whoa," Emma said, "slow down. The food's not going anywhere. You can have all you want." She noticed she'd dropped instantly into stepmother mode and stopped.

He looked up at her and narrowed his eyes to a squint as if he needed glasses to see her. "I haven't eaten in a while," he said with his mouth full.

Emma felt instantly sorry she had said anything. *His father's dead. He can do pretty much whatever he wants.* She walked over and put a hand on his shoulder. "I guess you heard from your mother."

"Heard what? I haven't talked to my mother."

"Oh, God, Kyle, no one told you?"

It didn't occur to her to ask why, if he didn't know about his father's death, he had come to the house. Grant being dead was the major news headline of the day. Of course, everyone would know it. She sat down in the chair next to Kyle and looked over at William, who had stopped chewing his brownie. Her eyes filled with tears. It had been hard enough to tell William. She put her arm along the back of Kyle's chair.

He leaned away, as usual not wanting her to touch him, then he stood up to put more distance between them. She took a deep breath and closed her eyes. Kyle walked away from the table, leaving his plate of food half eaten. He stood in the doorway facing her, crossing his arms on his chest. "Tell me what?"

Emma looked at him, trying to think how to say the words. After a few seconds of silence, she said, "Your father, honey, your father's dead. Someone killed him this morning." That was as far as she could go for a minute, having struggled to get breath back into her lungs. She had depleted all of her oxygen just saying those few words.

Kyle looked at her oddly, turned his face away, seeming to look into the dining room and then toward Emma's office suite. "Do you have any beer?"

What? Emma thought he hadn't heard her, or wasn't processing the information, which was shocking in itself, hearing it for the first time. *Denial, wasn't that what people felt first?* She tried again. "Kyle, your Dad is dead."

Kyle looked straight at her. "I heard you. I need a drink. Do you have any beer?"

"In the fridge out on the back porch," William said. "I'll get you one." He stood up from the table and walked out the back door, leaving it open. They heard the sound of the refrigerator opening then closing. William came back in with three bottles of Sam Adams, closed the door and handed a bottle of beer to his stepbrother. "There's a case out there in the fridge. Want one, Mom?"

Emma shook her head, no. There was something about this interaction she wasn't getting, male bonding or something. She was glad William reached out to Kyle in such a simple way. Watching them both twist off the bottle caps and take their first swigs, she noticed the difference between them was that William put the bottle down on the table after two swallows, but Kyle drank half the bottle before he lowered it. She knew about Kyle's propensity to get drunk and crash his cars, even suspected that Grant kept Kyle's more egregious behavior from her. *No judging him tonight, though. In fact, I've had enough of this day. I want to go to sleep and wake up in a world where none of this had ever happened.* All of a sudden she felt so tired she wasn't sure she would make it up the steps to her bedroom.

"I'm going to bed, guys." She kissed them both on the

cheek, reminded them to lock the back door and walked out of the room.

She was halfway to the stairs when she remembered she hadn't told Kyle what room he was sleeping in. Walking back toward the kitchen, she saw what registered in her mind as odd. The hunting knife she had bought Grant for his birthday, a fancy carbon steel blade from Cabela's that Grant craved and she had to special order, was tucked into the back of Kyle's pants. She recognized the hilt and the leather scabbard since she'd had Grant's initials embossed on it. The knife had been unnoticeable when Kyle had the vest on. *When did he take it? Where had it been?* She instantly adjusted her thinking, chiding herself. *Of course he can have his father's knife. He should have* something *of Grant's. Grant would want him to have it.*

"Kyle." He wheeled around and stared at her. "I just wanted to tell you I made up a room for you on the third floor, next to William." He looked at her with that new squint. "Good night," she said, turning around, heading back toward the stairs. *It's strange how grief manifests itself in so many different ways.*

Having made it to her bed, she kicked off her shoes, lay down on top of the covers and pulled the cashmere throw over her, lacking the wherewithal to do her customary bedtime routine: brush her teeth, clean her face, put lotion on her hands, change into her usual night clothes, or turn down the bed. She could hear Grant complaining about the fact that she wore more clothes to bed than she did during the day. She smiled. Her response to him had always been that they lived in an old, drafty house and she didn't want to freeze to death in her sleep. It was strange that she could now have this two-sided conversation in her head without his being there.

Not there.

That was something she didn't want to think about. She placed her hand on Grant's side of the bed.

Not there.

Then she remembered she should let Rhonda know where Kyle was. She hated the idea of talking to the woman, but it was the civilized thing to do.

She sat up on the side of the bed, picked up her cell phone and called Rhonda. There was no answer. Rhonda *probably wasn't having any trouble sleeping.* She left a message, "Rhonda, this is Emma. I just wanted to tell you that Kyle is here at my house. He's safe. He looks a little wired and worse for wear, but he's okay. You can call him tomorrow if you want."

She ended the call, put her phone down on the bedside table and looked out of the window. The night sky was clear and littered with stars. The three-quarter moon lit up the barn. For the first time in her life, nature's beauty seemed completely irrelevant. She didn't expect tomorrow to be any better.

CHAPTER 26

October 13, 8:00 a.m.:

Ann rang the bell of the Wodehouse home the morning after her boss was killed. Waiting for Emma to open the door, she took in the grand vista around the property. She hadn't called in advance, but was working from long custom. Emma was always awake and ready to go early in the day. As she stood there, Ann realized that perhaps *nothing* was normal for Emma any longer.

She berated herself for not understanding that, beginning yesterday, Emma's life had a different shape even she, the new widow, hadn't yet discerned. Ann shrugged and looked around again. *I can't be expected to intuit everything all of the time.* From where she was standing, the outward appearance of Emma's world was normal. Fall was in full color. Black urns filled with golden chrysanthemums flanked the front door. Emma must have put them out before Grant died. Ann always thought that this property, with its old stone house, the rolling fields and thick woods surrounding it, was particularly lovely. If she could invent a future for herself, living in this place would be part of it.

After a few minutes of standing on the flagstone threshold, Ann tried the front door knob and found it locked. She knocked on the door again. She looked through the large multi-paned window to the right of the door into the foyer. The house was illuminated only by the morning light coming through the window. The light embraced a spray of red and white flowers in a bowl on a table against the wall. She rang the doorbell again. She had brought Emma breakfast from the café in town, but mostly she just wanted to check on her employer, to see if there was something she should or could be doing for her or the upcoming funeral, and, if possible, if she could do it at Emma's house rather than at the office. In the one day since she had decided to leave their employ, Eugene Waters's idiosyncrasies had exceeded her ability to cope with them. She couldn't stand the man another minute. She wanted out of there, and as quickly as possible. She hoped Emma would allow her to work from one of the Wodehouse home offices until she found a new job somewhere else. It had only occurred to her yesterday that working with Waters compared unfavorably to being tried before a jury in a hostile community. It was worth the risk of annoying Emma to have a conversation with her about changing venues.

Emma must be fast asleep. Maybe she took a sleeping pill to help her rest. She's normally up at six in the morning getting ready to ride, but of course she would change her routine.

Ann felt guilty about having left Emma alone the night her husband died, but she had no alternate child care arrangements for her kids. Bringing them with her to the Wodehouse home when Grant had been murdered there was unthinkable. She knew abstractly that she wasn't responsible for her employers' personal tragedies, yet years of taking care of them made her believe she was somehow the one who was supposed to mop up after them. It was an attitude she had to eliminate.

Ann knocked on the door again. No response. She looked at her watch. Five minutes. She thought about calling then imagined how it would be to be abruptly awakened by a cell phone bleeping. Not good for anyone's blood pressure. She looked to her right at the unpaved extension of the driveway where Grant had made a small graveled parking area around an old oak tree. She saw a Jeep, a Mercedes and a Lexus, in addition to her more modest Honda in the driveway. *I wonder who owns the Jeep. According to the plates, it was registered in Massachusetts. Maybe Emma did have company overnight.* That was a small salve to Ann's conscience. She rang the bell again, shrugged and then walked along the cobbled path to the back of the house.

The barn, marked off with yellow police tape, came into view. The horses appeared to have spent the night outdoors in the fenced pasture. Paul, separated from the mares, pranced around the paddock, his tail held high, snorting and kicking out his back legs. Paul was a handful, she remembered Grant telling her with pride, as if having a willful horse gave its owner macho credentials. With a sudden pang of loss, Ann wondered if Emma would keep the horses. She couldn't imagine Emma handling horse ownership on her own.

She watched a young boy lug a pail of water from the spigot outside the barn out to the trough in the fenced pasture. Hay had been piled in the feeders in both the paddock and the pasture.

Ann was somehow very glad of that, as if that boy making sure the horses were watered and fed was a kindness to Grant himself and not just his animals. Another boy, perhaps a younger brother, carried a pail of water so heavy that his opposite shoulder was almost down to his waist to balance the weight of the water pail hanging from his hand. They were absorbed in their chores and didn't notice her. While she watched the boys, the kitchen door opened.

Ann turned around, expecting Emma. A man stood in the doorway. A few seconds ticked by until she realized it was William, whom she had met a number of times at special dinners or celebrations. She and her children were often included in Thanksgiving dinners at the Wodehouse farm. William was wearing typical academic clothes: tan corduroy pants, blue work shirt and gray sweater vest. He looked as if he had been up late. His eyes were puffy and his face had yet to see a razor. She doubted this was because of grief since she'd witnessed cordiality between Grant and his stepson, but not any deep bond. Perhaps William was sad simply because his mother was sad. Or maybe Ann didn't understand the dynamics of the relationship between Grant and his stepson at all.

"Hi, William. I brought some breakfast, although I didn't know that you were here." She raised the large shopping bag as proof of her statement. "I'm sure there'll be enough. Is your mother awake?"

William was staring at her face as if he was lip reading. "Right," he said finally, as if he had suddenly oriented himself to the language Ann was speaking. "Sorry. Come in." He stepped aside to let Ann into the kitchen. "My brain is somewhere else. I wasn't prepared for visitors at this hour. I heard the bell in the distance, but I was meditating. Don't know what I was thinking keeping you outside. Just deep in my own thoughts." He shrugged, gave a short self-deprecating laugh, took the bag from Ann and led the way into the kitchen.

Emma's usually immaculate kitchen looked as if it had been taken captive by gremlins. Dishes with half eaten food were scattered on the table, empty beer bottles cluttered the island counter. A rifle leaned against the wall by the cupboard.

"Well," Ann said, "let's clear up this mess." She looked over at William. "Can you put the bottles in the recycling bin on the back porch?" He nodded, gathered up a few of the bottles in his hand and went out the back door. Ann scraped the uneaten food into the garbage can wondering why Emma had thought she could eat all those mashed potatoes anyway. She turned on the hot water in the sink, tipped the dish detergent bottle to pour some soap onto the sponge, and began her version of rinsing the dishes before putting them into the dishwasher. She looked out of the kitchen window over the sink and saw the boys were done with their horse chores and were hanging on the fence talking to the animals. *I wonder if Emma had seen the same thing yesterday morning before Grant was killed.* Her stomach quaked. *What the hell am I thinking?*

"When did you get here, William?" she asked him when he finally closed the kitchen door and sat down at the table, having concluded that his part of cleaning the kitchen was completed.

"Yesterday morning."

"Yesterday morning?" Another shiver shook her shoulders. She couldn't seem to control her involuntary responses and could only imagine what Emma, who had seen Grant's mutilated body, was experiencing. She handed William a sponge she had run under the hot water and squeezed out. "Would you wipe off the table, please, and the counter?"

"Oh, sure," William said, taking the sponge from her.

"Did you arrive after Grant was killed?"

"I think I might have gotten here before that, but I'm not sure." He leaned forward and wiped off the table, pulling the crumbs of food toward his palm. He seemed far too nonchalant to her. Perhaps this complete calm was his way of dealing with horror. "I quit school," he continued, as if saying a piece he had written down and then memorized. "I drove here during the night. When I got here, I said hi to Mom, we talked for a bit and I went to bed." He dumped the crumbs into the sink and rinsed off his hand and the sponge.

Ann nodded approvingly at his cleaning method. "Do the police know you're here?" she asked, thinking what she didn't want to think, that William was at the house right at the time the murder was committed. She had to restrain herself from moving away from him.

"I think Mom said she was going to tell them, but I don't know if she did. She was really distracted yesterday. She kept flitting from thing to thing."

"I don't wonder." Ann took the various containers and small brown bags out of the large shopping bag William had put on the table then put out plates for the little soufflés, bagels and croissants she brought. She had no idea if Emma would eat, but she had tried to find something to tempt her. She took out plastic containers of cream cheese, fruit salad, plastic knives and forks, napkins. "Oh, wait, I forgot the flowers I brought! They're in the car. I'll be right back."

Ann walked through the house toward the front door as Emma was coming down the stairs. She was wearing black velvet pants, a long gray sweater and black silk Chinese slippers, no makeup or jewelry. Her eyes held the blank look of shock. *But even in grief, she looks lovely.* She waited at the bottom of the stairs for Emma and gave her a hug. Emma didn't even question the fact that her long-time admin was in her home in the early morning. *She really does seem very distracted. William's word was apt.*

"I brought breakfast. It's on the kitchen table. I forgot

the flowers in my car. I'm going to get them." Emma nodded, as if all of this was completely normal, and walked toward the kitchen. Her husband's death had made her seem tractable. Ann couldn't imagine how deep the numbness went.

She unlocked the deadbolt lock on the front door and went outside, leaving the door ajar. When she came back into the house, carrying the potted white orchids, instead of Emma at the foot of the stairs, there was a sullen adolescent, with long hair, gaunt face and glazed eyes staring at her.

It took Ann a few beats to realize who it was. "Oh, Kyle, I'm surprised to see you here. I thought you were in Mercersville."

Kyle brushed past her, walking toward the kitchen. "Yeah, well, my Dad died and all. Where else should I be?"

The only other thing Ann noticed about Kyle as he walked away from her was the hilt of a hunting knife tucked into the waistband of his jeans.

When Ann reached the kitchen, Emma was already making coffee and William was eating a bagel. Kyle put one of everything on his plate before he sat down. Ann placed the pot of orchids in the center of the table. The white flowers hung above the oak surface as a promise of hope.

Emma looked at the flowers, smiled at Ann, and said, "Thank you. They're lovely. Very thoughtful of you. All of it." She waved her hand in the air to signify her thanks for the breakfast as well.

The house phone rang and Ann, closest to it, answered, "Wodehouse residence." While she listened, she mouthed silently, "Rhonda Morewood," so that Emma would know who was calling. Emma closed her eyes and turned away from the phone. Rhonda asked to speak to

Kyle. Ann held out the phone to him and said it was his mother calling.

Kyle shook his head, no, "I can't talk to her," he said, his mouth full.

Ann asked Rhonda if she wanted to talk with Emma instead, even though Emma was vigorously shaking her head "no." Ann waited through Rhonda's loud sigh and teary agreement and handed the phone to Emma. "Sorry," she whispered.

Emma took the receiver reluctantly. Ann knew that Rhonda was the last person on earth Emma wanted to talk to today, and hated herself for not interceding. "Hello, Rhonda...Yes, he's here. He seems okay, given the circumstances." There was a long pause while everyone in the kitchen watched Emma's face as it went from annoyance to disbelief to anger to sorrow in a matter of seconds. "Yes, goodbye," she said finally and hung up the receiver.

Emma turned to Kyle, seeming to sift through several possible messages and selecting one that might be the least offensive. "Your mother says to remind you that you are supposed to take your Strattera and Prozac." She shrugged, as if the message made no sense to her. "Why are you taking those drugs, if you don't mind my asking?"

"The shrink at that crap school where Dad stashed me prescribed the drugs." He took a bite of his bagel. "They said I had ADHD and anxiety. Meds are how they subdue the inmates at that penal colony."

Emma and William both raised their eyebrows and then looked away. Emma busied herself preparing a plate of food that she would not eat. "How long have you been on the drugs?" she asked with her face turned away from Kyle.

"Couple of months. I don't think they're having the

desired effect, though. I haven't become a genius and my grades are crap."

Emma busied herself cutting a bagel and then spread cream cheese on it. No one said anything for a while. Emma stared out of the window, not touching her food. William seemed absorbed by the colors in the fruit salad. Kyle consumed what he'd put on his plate and reached for more.

It was apparent to anyone who talked to him that Grant's son was every bit as smart as his father. Somehow Kyle hadn't found a way to channel that intelligence into something productive. Emma had known for a while that the boy would never fit into the life his father had planned for him. He had no interest in law, real estate or even in making money, although he was happy to be the beneficiary of someone else's work.

Maybe he needed more freedom rather than less. She'd mentioned that a few times to Grant. It was too bad there were no more open spaces where young men could test their mettle against the environment without breaking the law, although she couldn't see Kyle forsaking his comfort to go hiking the Appalachian Trail or the Alaskan wilderness alone. That wasn't the kind of adventure he craved.

Mercersville Academy was not having the desired effect on Kyle either. He wasn't conforming to the prep school ideal, but Ann understood Grant's desire to push his kid through high school and into college by any means possible. It was preparation for the day Grant couldn't be there for his son, when Kyle would have to be self-sufficient, and a college degree meant he could earn enough money to take care of his basic needs. At least that had been the working theory. Now that day was unexpectedly here far sooner than Grant had planned.

"So are you taking the meds?" Emma asked Kyle.

"Mostly I sell them," he said defiantly. His chin tilted up as he squinted at her.

"Why would anyone buy them?" Ann asked.

"The Strattera is great for pulling all nighters before an exam. Pop a few and your brain just zooms through stuff."

"A few? Isn't that dangerous?"

Kyle laughed, looking at her as if she had just emerged from a previous century as dusty as an unread book in a library.

Emma looked at William, who nodded. "I've heard of students doing it. It seems to work pretty well, but you get addicted to the ease with which you concentrate."

"Do you take the Prozac?" Emma asked Kyle.

"Yeah, when I'm really anxious I might pop a few. But, frankly, I prefer Jim Beam." He laughed at the look on Emma's face. "Really, whiskey is better," he said seriously, happy to continue needling his stepmother. "You should try it."

Emma ignored the taunt. Kyle wanted to drag her into an argument that he would win by storming out of the house. Emma wasn't playing.

"Did your father know about the drugs the school has you on?" Ann asked.

"Who gives a damn what he knew?" Kyle yelled, suddenly irate, red in the face, the veins in his neck throbbing, his anger seeming to take him as much by surprise as it did the others. "Who the hell are you to give me the third degree?"

"Whoa, wait, hold on there," Emma said, trying to diffuse the situation. "Ann is just asking you a question. If the school didn't have Grant's permission, or your mother's, then we have an issue with them."

"Why should I answer any of your questions? Have you been looking out for me? Do you even give a damn about me?" He pushed back his chair until it fell over and he jumped to his feet. He reached around to the back of his pants and pulled the knife out from behind his back. He gripped the knife hilt firmly, making it abundantly clear that he was ready to stab anyone close to him. His knuckles were white.

"Kyle, where did you get that knife?" Emma asked the way she would ask if it was snowing outside.

"Out in the barn, where all the horse grooming stuff is."

In an instant an Arctic chill filled the kitchen. Emma, Ann and William each drew in a sharp breath. Emma knew that Grant's knife could cut through the oak table as if it was butter. All logic flew out the window and was replaced by a dark vacuum of fear. Emma tried to assess the situation, which needed diffusing. The kid was a lit fuse on a stick of dynamite.

Emma put both her arms on the table, her hands open, and said in the quietest voice she could muster, "Kyle, I have always cared about what happened to you since I met you. You are part of my family."

Kyle glared at her. "Cut the crap, bitch!" Spittle flew into her face. "You can't fool me with your crisis management voodoo." He reached over, grabbed William by the hair and held the tip of the knife under William's chin, close to his neck.

William closed his eyes, but he didn't flinch. He seemed to be mumbling something under his breath.

Kyle leaned forward. "If you don't do what I tell you to do, Willy here is going to learn how sharp this knife is. And if you don't think I will stick it into him, I can tell you I already tested it. It works really well."

Ann gripped the edge of the table. Her eyes flitted around the kitchen, fixing on the rifle. She looked at Emma. William and Emma were silent for moments that seemed to stretch to hours, waiting for Kyle's instructions.

Kyle's claim to have tested the knife set off shivers across Ann's shoulders. He was plainly menacing them. *Was he saying he has used the knife on a human being?*

"Where were you yesterday, Kyle?" Emma asked.

"What do you care?" he screamed at her. He tightened his grip on William, who kept his eyes closed, murmuring his chant.

"I'm just curious, that's all. What did you do with your day before you came here?"

Kyle laughed. The knife nudged William's neck. A drop of blood oozed from his skin and trickled down his neck. "Let's see…I hung out with Dad for a bit. Then I visited a woman. Then I was really tired and crashed in my car for a couple hours. Then I got something to eat at Mickey D's and I went up to Martinsburg and walked around that crap mall. I went to the movies and saw *Gravity*. God, what a dumb movie. Sandra Bullock as an astronaut. Yeah, that's really believable. And nothing happens. She talks to herself. Then I came back here. Day done. Got all that?"

"So then you got the knife when you were in the barn with your father?" Emma seemed perilously close to putting two horrible thoughts together. "Was that yesterday morning?" She looked him directly in the eyes.

"That's right, Emma, I got the knife when I was in the barn with Dad." Kyle laughed, two short barks. "I came to get some money I need. Dad didn't want to give it to me. Now *you* are going to give it to me. Understand?"

Emma closed her eyes, nodding—she understood completely—then glanced quickly at the rifle. It was to her right, ten feet away. She calculated how long it would take her to get to the rifle, pick it up, and point it at Kyle. She wouldn't be fast enough. Kyle would have plenty of time to stab William. She wasn't sure she could really shoot Kyle anyway and it was clear that threatening him was not going to work. She was trying to work out her options, but her brain was stuffed with steel wool. It was best to keep him talking until a plan presented itself.

"What's been going on at school, Kyle?"

"Oh, come on, you don't care about that," Kyle said, placing the tip of the knife on William's throat directly over the carotid artery, with all the curiosity of a scientist conducting an experiment. "I'm screwing up, that's what. I'm a screw up. Everybody hates me. I punched out a few people and they took it the wrong way. I just came here to get money and I'm gone. So just shut up and let me think about how I want to do this."

The doorbell rang.

Kyle's head went up, a hunting dog sniffing the air.

The bell rang again.

CHAPTER 27

8:30 a.m.:

G o see who it is, Emma," Kyle said. "Act normal, and don't forget I've got your darling boy right here at the sharp end of this knife. Don't do anything stupid."

Emma nodded, got up from the table, and walked to the front door. Her joints had forgotten how to bend. She could only shuffle her feet across the floor. When she opened the door, she saw Detective Lagarde and his associate Sergeant Black. Rigid with fear, she could barely speak.

The idea that she could behave normally in this situation was ludicrous.

Her breath came in little gasps. "Come in, detectives," she managed to get out. She hoped they were smarter than they looked.

Lagarde and Black exchanged glances and walked into the foyer. Lagarde began, "We'd appreciate a few minutes with you, Mrs. Wodehouse. We have some questions about your husband's death."

Emma nodded. She led the way into the sitting room adjacent to the foyer. She pointed to chairs and seated herself in the pearl gray Queen Anne chair nearest the arched entryway into the room. She couldn't have walked any farther.

"Do you have visitors this morning?" Black asked her as he perched on the edge of a yellow brocade wingback chair.

"Oh, yes, Ann Roberts is here."

"Is that her Honda?"

"Yes."

"Who owns the Jeep with the Massachusetts license plate?"

"That's my son's car. William. He came down from school."

"When did William arrive?" Lagarde asked.

"Oh, I forgot to tell you. Sorry. I just..." Her thought drifted out of the window with her gaze. She was waiting for them to ask her about Kyle's Audi, trying to think about what she would say. *Where was Kyle's Audi?* It wasn't visible from the window, although she could see the other vehicles.

"Forgot to tell us what, Mrs. Wodehouse?"

"I forgot to tell you about William. He arrived yesterday morning, probably before Grant was killed. He came to talk to me about school."

"You mean he was here when I first interviewed you yesterday morning? What time did he arrive?"

"Yes, he got here around 6:45. I was just making coffee. We talked, and he went to bed. I went out to find Grant. I just sort of forgot all about William, as if he had never been here." She looked blankly at them. "I can't explain it."

Lagarde and Black exchanged a look containing several messages. Black wrote in his notebook. They had another person on the property at the time of the murder, and that addition created still more possibilities for them to reconcile before they could settle on one theory of the crime.

"Could we talk with him now?" Lagarde barely kept his annoyance out of his voice. "He may have seen the assailant arrive on the property. He might be able to give us a description."

William's arrival was her alibi, Emma suddenly realized...or the police thought she and William committed the murder together.

"He's not really available right now," Emma said. *That was the truth. William* was *being held hostage at the point of a knife by her deranged stepson. Really, they were all hostages. Was there a way to convey that or were they so dense that nothing got through to them?* "Maybe you could talk with him later?"

"Would you get him, please?" Lagarde's patience was notably absent from his voice.

"Why don't you ask me the questions you had for me? Maybe he'll come in while we're talking."

"I know you're lying to us, Mrs. Wodehouse. I don't think you're doing your son a favor by trying to protect him."

Emma looked down in her lap. "You...don't...understand. I...can't."

Lagarde stood up. "Unless you bring your son to us, Mrs. Wodehouse, I will search the house for him."

Emma stood also. "Do you have a warrant to arrest him, Detective, or to search the house for that matter? The police went through my house with a fine-tooth comb yesterday."

"The police may have gone through your house, but apparently missed a man sleeping in one of the bedrooms and his vehicle in the driveway, so not so thoroughly," Lagarde retorted.

"The fact that the police failed to notice a large object,

a Jeep, parked in my driveway is not my fault, Mr. Lagarde. We weren't hiding anything. Someone could have asked me—" She looked at him pointedly. "—and I would've told him."

They glared at each other.

Black watched Lagarde and Emma lock horns. In an odd way, he admired the woman for standing her ground, even if she was making their job more difficult. It was clear that Lagarde and Mrs. Wodehouse wouldn't be able to extricate themselves from the top dog tussle Lagarde had started. They were just going to circle around each other, wasting time. As Black saw it, Mrs. Wodehouse was their best suspect, better than her son. She had motive, means and opportunity. She just didn't have the physical strength to do the job. Maybe that's what her son was for. Watching her back Lagarde off, Black thought she might in fact have the intestinal fortitude to kill someone.

"Look, we just want to rule him out. If he has an alibi, then we've checked that box and we'll move on."

Emma nodded. Without saying anything to them, she walked out of the room and down the hall to the kitchen. Lagarde and Black could hear people talking in a heated exchange but they were too far away to hear the words.

"Didn't she say Ann Roberts was here?"

Lagarde nodded.

"Then why doesn't Ann come in to say hello to us? There's something else going on here. Something's definitely not right." His detective's sixth sense didn't actually have to work very hard to notice the difference in Emma's level of cooperation between yesterday and today. She was hiding something and she was desperately afraid.

Emma came back into the room with a tall young man she introduced as her son, William Thornton. It was apparent that William had some of his mother's beauty translated onto larger planes. Black noticed he had a small, fresh cut on his neck, which seemed odd because he sure didn't shave this morning.

William sat on the loveseat by the window, pressing a napkin against the cut on his neck. His mother sat opposite him on the sofa, perhaps to signal him with her body language about what to say and what not to say.

She is a lawyer, Black reminded himself.

Black sat in the wingback chair and Lagarde stood. They took William through the hours leading up to his arrival the previous morning. William produced a credit card slip from his wallet for the coffee and croissant he purchased at three-fifteen in the morning at a New Jersey Turnpike rest stop. That proved he was on the road early on the morning of the murder. Black noticed the young man kept all his credit card receipts neatly folded in half on the right side of his wallet and didn't seem to have any cash.

He must have used it up in highway tolls, Black concluded. *And if he was paying tolls with cash, he wasn't a regular highway commuter or he'd have one of those passes that got drivers through tolls without having to stop. So this trip to see his mother was a one-off, as Emma had suggested. If William was in New Jersey at three in the morning,* Black calculated, *he might have been able to drive to his mother's house in Shenandoah Junction by 7:00 a.m., but he'd have to be in two places at once to murder Grant Wodehouse in the short time after the dead man's tryst with Elaine and before his mother said he went to sleep. Unless mother and son murdered Grant together after Elaine trotted out of the barn.*

William didn't strike Black as someone who liked to get his hands dirty, and that would include him murdering anyone.

Within ten minutes, they had essentially cleared him, at least pending a fingerprint analysis.

"Did you see anything odd around the property when you arrived," Lagarde asked, "while you were coming into the house or later from any of the windows?"

William looked down at his knees. He looked up and to the right, above his mother's shoulder and faked a yawn, covering his mouth. Black knew he was withholding something. He could hardly have been more obvious. It was almost as if he was trying to tell them something without saying a word, or he was the world's worst liar.

Emma leaned forward slightly. "William?" It could have been a question or a warning.

"No, no, I didn't see anything," William said. "I was just thinking through everything." He blinked a few times and looked directly at Lagarde. "You know, I've had my head in some very esoteric texts for the last decade. I'm probably not your best witness for anything that happens in the real world."

"All right. We might have other questions for you. We'll be back to ask them if we need to." He turned to Emma. "Meanwhile, you should know that Elaine Tabor, your neighbor, was stabbed to death yesterday a few hours after your husband was killed."

Emma groaned, tucked her head, and hugged herself.

Lagarde turned to watch William. "We think the same killer did both murders."

William sucked in his breath and looked down at his knees. He clearly had no idea what to do next.

"Do you have any other guests this morning, Mrs. Wodehouse, besides Ann Roberts?" Black asked. "We're looking for a Warren Lyles, who we think was in your barn yesterday morning, and it would be helpful to know where Grant's son, Kyle, is. We know he's not at his school."

Emma's head snapped up as if a firecracker had gone off in her sitting room. She stared at Black. "I don't know Warren Lyles. Why are you looking for my stepson?" Her tone was cold and tense as she plucked at her sweater sleeve.

Lagarde turned toward her and said in measured tones, "We want to know where everyone was at the time of the murders."

Emma shook her head slowly as if denying something to herself. "I don't know what to tell you." That statement was clearly the truth.

"What kind of car does Kyle drive?" Black asked.

"I think it's an Audi," Emma said. "I'm not sure. He's had several different cars during the last year."

Black made a note on his pad. *If the Audi spotted by Tabor parked on the side of the road was Kyle's car, then that would mean the boy was in the area at the time of Elaine's murder.* Lagarde would tell him he was leaping. Black had no idea what motive Kyle would have for killing his father's lover, but maybe he was the kind of killer who didn't need a motive. *Maybe these were thrill kills. Maybe the kid was a psychopath.* It was a discomfiting thought, particularly when they didn't know where Kyle was or if he was done with his killing spree. Black stopped his speculation. He was jumping far ahead of what the evidence they had told them.

Emma answered most of their questions factually, but was still evading the truth. Once more, they took her through the approximate time William arrived, what they had talked about, what they had done, when she had realized how long Grant had been in the barn. William, of course, corroborated her story. Black and Lagarde waited a few minutes in case she revealed any other facts, or volunteered the names of other people who happened to turn up out of the blue on the morning of the murder.

The tension in the room grew.

Both Emma and William stared out the window as if an engrossing drama was unfolding before their eyes. Met with only silence, the officers said goodbye and left the house. All their instincts told them something was wrong.

"They're lying or hiding something critical to finding the killer."

Black nodded. Walking back to their vehicle, they agreed to get the broadest possible warrant to search the house. It could take a few hours to get a judge's signature on the warrant. They felt antsy about the delay, but there was nothing they could do about it. Meanwhile, they still had to find Warren Lyles, at least to give him back his compass. At this point, they were pretty sure he was not their killer but they needed to dot those I's.

CHAPTER 28

9:15 a.m.:

The man waiting to talk to him at headquarters was homeless, the receptionist Joyce, briefly a Mrs. Lagarde, told her ex-husband. She had put the man in Interview One.

Joyce was still a lovely redhead and had no difficulty talking to Lagarde about anything. She particularly enjoyed flirting with him. After all, she had come away from the short marriage greatly enriched by the monthly alimony he would have to pay until she remarried. She had the upper hand. She could always remind Lagarde she'd seen him naked. Lagarde hadn't learned until it was too late that almost everyone at the Troop 2 Barrack had seen Joyce naked.

"He was really insistent that he had something to tell someone about the Wodehouse murder yesterday, and it's your case so I had him wait for you." She put the end of the pen in her mouth. Lagarde asked the man's name. "Oh," she said, tapping her lips with the pen, "I forgot to write it down. Sorry."

Does she even know what a pen was for? She was part of the generation born knowing how to one-hand a smart phone—another clue, if he had been thinking with his head at all, that he should never have considered having a relationship with her. He and Black walked down the corridor to the room marked Interview One, stopping for a brief run through on tactics.

"If this is the guy in the barn, we know he was in the hayloft because we have his compass, but we don't know if he was there yesterday morning or some other day. According to the forensic boys, it might have been anytime."

"It's not his prints on the weapon, so he's probably not our perp, but he may have seen something and his coming here to tell us means that he thinks he did."

"At the very least, he might fill in the story about Wodehouse for us. You get him started. I gotta hit the head."

Black guffawed. "Okay, old man, maybe you should have that prostate checked," he called after Lagarde as the older man hop-scotched down the hall. "I could buy you a pack of Men's Depends." Black chuckled at his own joke, turned, and opened the door to the interview room. The man seated at the Formica table in the purposely bland room, both hands holding a Styrofoam cup of black coffee, was dirty and ragged. He looked as if he hadn't slept indoors in a very long time, or had a bath and a decent meal. He was thin, tired, and his hair was a greasy mass of tangles. He carried a backpack of despair he never took off.

The man stood up and held out his hand. "Warren Lyles," he said, as if this was a business meeting he'd set up with a colleague.

Taken aback by Lyles's professional manner, Black found himself nonetheless taking the man's hand and giving it a short shake. As they both sat down, Black had to resist the impulse to find and use hand sanitizer. It was possible he had just shaken hands with a killer. Although if Warren Lyles was a killer, he seemed to be one of the mildest Black had ever met.

Black struggled with his sense that his automatic response to the offered hand had been the right one. Aside from the guy's appearance, Lyles had *walked* into a police station. *Either he was here to confess to the murder and surrender himself or he had something important to tell them. Or, he was crazy. Always a possibility,* Black reminded himself. *But it was also a possibility he might be an honorable man underneath the apparent hardship.*

Lagarde walked into the room and Black introduced them. "This is Warren Lyles," Black said. "Mr. Lyles, this is Detective Sam Lagarde. We understand that you have something important to tell us."

Lyles stood and offered his hand again. Lagarde shook it. Black watched Lagarde behave as if it were the most normal thing in the world for a person of interest to walk into their headquarters to talk with them.

"What's on your mind, Mr. Lyles?"

"I need to tell you what I saw yesterday morning. I was at the Wodehouse property. I slept in the barn the night before. Mr. Wodehouse said I could. There was a lot of noise, it woke me up, and, oh man, what a lot of trouble. I never saw anything like it." Warren Lyles put his hand on his forehead and looked as if he might cry. He looked up at them. "Anyway, I saw the person who stabbed Mr. Wodehouse. I'll never forget the killer's eyes. They looked right at me. I ran away because I thought I was going to be killed, too."

"You're safe here, Mr. Lyles. Take your time. Just tell us what happened, in the order it happened. We're going to video tape your statement so that we don't miss anything. Is that okay with you?"

Warren Lyles nodded yes. Lagarde reached over and turned on the video recorder.

"Would you prefer to have an attorney present?"

Warren said no.

"You understand that you have the right to be silent and that something you say may incriminate you and could be used against you in court?"

Warren nodded yes.

That was the skinny on the Miranda warning waiver, as far as Black was concerned. They might get in trouble with the prosecutor for not getting a signature on the correct form if it turned out that Lyles was more than he seemed—a brazen liar who killed and then came back to report to the police that someone else was the perpetrator, but for expediency's sake, they took that chance.

"It's October 13, 2014, 9:15 a.m. Warren Lyles, a walk-in person of interest in the Grant Wodehouse murder, interview with Lieutenant Lagarde and Sergeant Black. Go ahead Mr. Lyles."

Fifteen minutes later, after he had relayed his blow-by-blow story of the murder of Grant Wodehouse, Lyles began telling Lagarde and Black his life story from the day he was born. The man obviously felt that a police interview room was as good a confessional as any more sanctified place and he had a lot to get off his chest, none of it relating to their double murder.

Black signaled he wanted to talk to Lagarde outside the interview room. Lagarde suggested to Warren Lyles that he rest for a few minutes. He turned off the video recorder and he and Black went out of the room.

"I'm going to head over to Charles Town for my meeting with Ann," Black said, his face turned slightly away from Lagarde, his body in a half crouch to prevent any psychological blows his colleague might throw his way.

"Glad to see you're keeping your eye on what's important," Lagarde said sarcastically, grinning.

"Yeah, well," Black said, looking around the office for a place to store his embarrassment, "I'm already late leaving." He shrugged and grinned again. He couldn't seem to stop grinning even though they were in the middle of a grisly murder investigation.

Black scrutinized Lagarde's face and thought he saw impatience there. "Before I go, I'll write up the complaint showing probable cause for a more thorough search of the Wodehouse property and all outbuildings. We've got an eyewitness, an out of state car parked up there, and relationship to the victim. We just don't have motive."

"That's enough for a warrant."

"Yeah, I think so. I'll go over to the courthouse and get the warrant signed by the judge. I'll be back after my meeting with Ann and we can go back out to the Wodehouse property. Might be best if we take Emma and her son by surprise. Maybe there are more levels to this murder than we know. I've got Jen running an ownership check on all Audi 3s registered in Pennsylvania."

"Good idea. Oh, and drop in at the sheriff's office while you're in town. Maybe Harbaugh's heard something we haven't about the vehicle. Call me if anything turns up. I'm guessing Lyles is good for another fifteen minutes of talking. Then he's going to pass out. He might not mind sleeping in a cell. He's terrified that Wodehouse's killer is going to get him. We can hold him as a material witness for twenty-four hours. That'll give him time for a nap. I'll get him fed, too."

"You're getting soft in your old age."

Lagarde shook his head then said, "When Lyles is out of my hair, I'll call Kyle's mother to see if he's with her," and went back into the interview room.

Black left headquarters and drove south on Route 9 toward Charles Town. The new highway was a straight-away—a blessing in a region of hills, no sight lines, and sharp turns. Black was thinking about Ann's eyes. He sure would love to stare into them for a long time and see what happened. Somehow he drove the seven miles to the Charles Town exit in thirty seconds, although that wasn't possible. He chalked it up to a time warp and exited onto Route 340, which became Charles Town's main street, then drove another five blocks to the center of town. He parked in his favorite 'police vehicles only' parking spot next to the court house, figuring he should get that business done first, and used the employee's side door to enter the eighteenth-century courthouse.

There had been some modern modifications to the historic courthouse for electricity, heating, plumbing and more recently for computer technology, but for the most part the building kept the feel of a structure last remodeled after taking shellfire during the Civil War. This stately courthouse at the corner of George and Washington Streets was the centerpiece of Charles Town, a village originally part of Virginia and only ten minutes from that more affluent state. Black wondered if the town's inhabitants knew about their county's pre-revolutionary status as home to George Washington's less well-known siblings.

Making his way through to the judge's office, Sergeant Black was cordial to all courthouse staff, precise with the prosecutor and most respectful with the judge. Within twenty minutes, he had a signed warrant. Then he walked across George Street to see if Deputy Sheriff Harbaugh had heard anything new on the Elaine Tabor case. Harbaugh said that no one from the Le Gore household had called about a misplaced Audi on their property. They hadn't reported seeing anyone on their property at all.

He kept shaking his head, not yet recovered from seeing Elaine's mutilated body laid out on a bed of blood yesterday afternoon.

"Glad it's your case, man. How are you doing on it, anyway?"

"I think we've got it narrowed down. Fingerprint evidence strongly suggests the same killer did both victims. We've just got to identify and arrest the guy."

Harbaugh reminded Black that the sheriff's office would be happy to assist in an arrest. Black nodded. As with any hunt, the glee was in the final moments of capture. All the hunters wanted to be in at the kill. Getting the bad guys, that's what made their day.

Black thanked him and moved on.

If the Audi wasn't spotted by anyone in the Le Gore family, then the car had been moved before Albert and Marv's mother got home from work. Where did the driver go? Maybe he had committed all the murders he planned for the day and drove back to school in Pennsylvania. The real kicker would be if he moved the car onto the Wodehouse farm somewhere and they missed it. Black's intuition tingled. *If the killer was still in the area, where the hell is he? And what is he doing?*

He checked his watch, felt his heart sink a little. He was late for his appointment with Ann. From the sheriff's office, Black nearly ran to the Wodehouse-Waters office on Washington Street. He was more than ready to be conciliatory. He was glad this small, walkable town gave him a chance to stretch his legs from time to time.

He opened the front door of the office. No one was in the reception area. Ann wasn't at her desk. He called out and walked back toward the offices. He kept expecting Ann to come out of one of the rooms and surprise him with her beauty all over again. She didn't appear anywhere.

She should have been back from visiting Emma by

now. He checked the screen of his phone. No messages.

The only person in the office was Waters, overheated, perspiring and attempting to pull every hair out of his head. Ann was right to think something had gone seriously awry with this lawyer's business dealings. Black made a note to call a pal at the FBI about the lawyer's real estate venture. There might be something there the agency would find interesting.

Black leaned into Waters's office. "Is Ann in the building?"

"No, Ann's not here. Haven't seen her all day. She was supposed to be here by 9:30 the latest, according to her text message, but I haven't seen or heard from her."

"Any idea where she might be?" Black asked.

"Not a clue. Shopping maybe?" Waters shrugged as if women were a mystery put on earth to plague men.

"What did she say in her text?"

"She was bringing breakfast to Emma's and would be here in the office after that. That was at…" Waters picked his cell phone up from his desk, tapped his messages, scrolled and found the right one, "seven-forty-five a.m. She's normally a woman of her word."

"Thanks," Black said and walked out of the office. On the sidewalk, he texted Ann, "Here at your office. Sorry I'm late. Where are you?" He felt instant chagrin at his tone and sent a second text, "Don't mean to sound demanding. Sorry." And then a third text, "Are you okay?" He hated the way email and text left no room for nuance. He called her cell phone and got voice mail.

Walking briskly back to the vehicle, he phoned Lagarde to tell him Ann was missing in action and that his intuition alarm bells were going off.

Three words into their cell phone conversation, the barrack receptionist buzzed Lagarde on the office phone and said she had a weeping Mrs. Morewood on the phone

returning his call. Lagarde said to put her on hold, that
he'd get to her in a minute, and went back to his conversation with Black.

They decided Black should come back to headquarters
as planned and pick up Lagarde. They were going back
out to the Wodehouse farm. Maybe Emma knew what
was going on with Ann. Search warrant in hand, they'd
take another look around the entire property. If nothing
else, the trip might resolve the missing Audi issue. The
warrant would let them search the house and grounds.
They could walk the property and see if the car or its
owner were anywhere nearby. They disconnected.

Lagarde glanced at his email, something he didn't or-
dinarily do, but he was in a holding pattern waiting for
Black to come back and get him. There was an email
from their fingerprint analysis folks. He clicked it open
and opened the attachment.

FBI records had identified the unknown person whose
fingerprints were on the pitchfork and in Elaine Tabor's
bedroom. The prints were from the same perp, the report
said. He experienced a small twinge of annoyance. They
already knew that. He scrolled down through the attachment. Recent front and profile mug shots showed a young
man in his teens with long, curly blond hair, a handsome
face with blue eyes and the strong neck of a football
player. A good looking boy in the prime of his life mate-
rialized on Lagarde's computer screen.

"Who the hell is that?" Lagarde asked out loud, even
though no one was in the room with him.

He answered his own question by reading the text below the images. The mug shot was identified as Kyle
Wodehouse, six feet, one-hundred-eighty-four pounds,
son of Grant and Rhonda, current residence Mercersville
Academy in Pennsylvania, date of birth May 12, 1998,
booked last week for the vandalism and burglary of an

office in that small town. He was arraigned a few days ago for the burglary and was out on bail pending trial.

"Damn it!" *This particular black sheep chose yesterday to come home and didn't get the welcome he expected. Kyle Wodehouse is our killer.* Lagarde quelled the sinking feeling in his stomach, the kind he got when elevators in tall buildings took the express route to the basement, and called Black on his cell phone.

"Hope you're close. We just got the ID on the mystery prints from the pitchfork and in Elaine's bedroom. They're Kyle's." He heard Black's intake of breath. "We've got a patricide. I think I might hate this case."

He paused for a minute as he printed out the ID and queued up the right form on his computer screen. "Good thing you got the warrant. I'm putting out a four-state all-points bulletin on Kyle Wodehouse as the suspect in a double murder. Let's get some help spotting this guy from local law enforcement in surrounding states. God knows where he's gone." He clicked off the call to make sure he typed the correct letters in the correct spaces on the form.

Lagarde couldn't imagine Emma Wodehouse sheltering Kyle if she had the slightest inkling he was her husband's killer. But there was something going on at that house that he should have investigated further early this morning. He mentally kicked himself for being polite.

When he finished the BOLO, he suddenly remembered Rhonda Morewood was on hold. She would have to have a lot of patience to still be there. He picked up the office phone, pushed the right button, and identified himself to the woman, apologizing for the wait. In spite of her hysteria, she managed to tell him what he needed to know.

He called Black. "Larry, step on it. Rhonda Morewood just informed me that her son Kyle is at the Wodehouse farm. She said Emma called her last night to let her know he was there and safe. That's why Emma was so peculiar. He's there with them. She knows he's the killer."

"Shit. I'm still five minutes out," Black fumed, setting his flashers and siren going, the speedometer touching eighty-miles-an-hour on Route 9, heading for Kearneysville, and wished he could fall into that time-warp on purpose.

Lagarde looked through his pad for Emma Wode-house's phone number and dialed.

CHAPTER 29

October 12, 7:25 a.m.:

Grant was surprised that he felt no physical pain. He was in shock and the adrenalin pumping through his body was keeping the pain at bay. He couldn't seem to take a breath. He couldn't move. Something was dribbling out of his mouth, but his arms were too heavy for his hand to reach up and wipe it away. It was mildly amazing to him that he could think about his body in this detached manner. It was better this way, though. He wasn't good with pain. He felt very cold, tired, and then far away from his body.

He remembered Emma's face the first time he made love to her. With Emma, it had been an act of love and not simply lust. She wept and laughed and looked at him with such openness that he felt his heart expand. *This is how it's supposed to be.*

He remembered the faces of other women he'd had sex with over the years, too many women to remember, and it turned out they were completely inconsequential. His mind came back to Emma. How startling it was to realize at this moment, when there was nothing he could do about it, that she was the one, that romantic promise of perfect love and companionship, and that even in his careless way, he still had her in his life. He hadn't lost her.

Except now. He would lose her now. He was struck by a loss so deep that he cried out.

His mind veered away to another image: the house, his horses. *Was there enough money for her to be comfortable?* He had the delicious sensation of being astride his horse, walking out into a fine autumn day.

He saw his son's face, the fury and hatred that contorted Kyle's features. He was another person entirely. Grant was horrified by that hatred, transfixed. *Where is the little boy I used to throw into the air, the boy who giggled, laughed, and put his small arms around my neck as if I were the most wonderful person in the world? How did we get to this? What happened to my son?* He looked around the barn. Kyle was nowhere to be seen. Kyle had stabbed him and run away. Another pang of loss shot through him. *My boy left me alone.*

Rebecca. What a charming girl she had been. She was distant with him now. He had screwed up that relationship by not being with his dying wife at the end of her life. *How was it that I just couldn't wait for her to die? Noooo, I had to be out rutting some strange woman.* He *was* sick. Emma was right about that. He was sorry for the estrangement with his daughter. *All my fault. Oh, well.*

He had run out of time.

His mind went blank.

There was a single flash of white light—and then darkness.

CHAPTER 30

October 13, 9:30 a.m.:

Emma and William had walked back to the kitchen exhausted from the tension caused by deceiving police officers and reining in their own fear. For the first time in a very long time, William took his mother's hand. Emma thought he intended to reassure her and maybe himself that they could survive this crisis. She squeezed his hand the way she used to do when she walked him to the door of his grammar school, a little secret hug to remind him that she loved him and that everything would be okay. The thought of Kyle, or anyone, now cutting short her son's life made her angry enough to kill. She shook with her determination to save her son.

It surprised both William and Emma that, now that the police interview was over, they were still complying with Kyle's demands. They could have run out the front door after the officers, waving their arms, begging to be saved, but Kyle had Ann by the hair and a knife at her throat, waiting for them to get rid of the police and come back into the kitchen. Neither of them was willing to sacrifice Ann for their own safety. Their mutual and unspoken decision gave them courage, as if courage was something you might find by accident in your pocket, like a five dollar bill you had forgotten, miraculously there when you needed it.

They had no plan about how to proceed. Emma's goal was to keep them safe, to somehow defuse Kyle's fury and get him to leave the property. *How in the hell am I going to pull this off? Think. Think. I don't give a shit if Kyle gets away, if the police never find him, as long as he never comes back here again, as long as he doesn't hurt my son.* That was the bargain she was willing to make. Her goal was to try to keep Kyle talking until an opening appeared.

When they walked into the kitchen, Kyle had already nicked Ann's neck twice, as if he were practicing. Maybe he simply enjoyed tormenting her. Two lines of blood ran down to her collar. Her eyes were closed, her face gray, her mouth in a thin line. Kyle had a strange look of fascination on his face. He seemed delighted with his venture into sadistic pleasures. He was murmuring to her, "Imagine how you would look if I cut that pretty face." He looked up at them. "Did you know that Miss Perfect here fucked my dad?"

Emma and William shook their heads.

"Yeah, she did. She told me. Interesting how a knife at your throat will get you to tell the truth. She had him when he was young and strong. Way before you, Emma. Didn't you, Ann? He was porking her when he was married to my mother. Right?" He jabbed her with the tip of the knife.

Ann's entire body shook. "Yes," she whispered.

"I think she got the better deal, don't you, Emma? Dad was a hunk in his forties, six pack abs and all. What do you think?"

"I didn't marry him for his muscles," Emma said and then instantly regretted it. She didn't want to spar with

Kyle. Anything could trigger him into more violence.

"I'm really helping you out if I do her, aren't I, eliminating all your competition. I did that little ho he was boffing in the barn, easy as slicing into a pie." He grinned. "Although, really, you can't compete if there's nothing to win. Isn't that right, Emma?"

Emma nodded, searching her mind for a way into his manic conversation that could turn the situation around.

William eyed the shotgun. Kyle was so focused on what he could do with a knife that he didn't seem to notice the gun. It had been leaning against the counter since before Kyle arrived. It blended into the appliances, cups and saucers, as part of the kitchen's equipment. William walked over to the cupboard, opened it and reached for a cup. "Want some coffee, bro?"

Kyle threw his head back and laughed but he never let go of his grip on Ann's hair. His fingers were tangled in it down to the roots. "Helluva time to begin paling around with me, Willy."

"Yeah," William said, as if resigned to his failure. He closed the cupboard door, picked up the rifle and aimed it at Kyle's chest. "Now, get the fuck away from her. Just back your ass up to the wall right there and don't move."

Kyle's hands came down to his sides. Ann slid out of the chair and rushed to Emma's side near the back door. The women clung to each other. Surprise momentarily took the place of fear in Emma's face. *Where did my son get the courage to do this?*

"Go on, Mom, go out the back door, get to your car with Ann. Get out of here," William commanded. "Drop the damn knife," he shouted at Kyle.

Emma had never felt so proud of her son or so terrified for him. He was not a fighter. She had no idea whether he knew how to use the bolt action Remington but she remembered she had loaded it with five rounds

234 Ginny Fite

yesterday. At this range, if he pulled the trigger, he would hit something, although maybe not Kyle. The rifle had a terrible kick. He probably didn't know he had to pull the bolt to reload for a second shot. Maybe he was hoping to scare Kyle into backing down. She looked over at Kyle. His chin was raised and he was squinting. This look she now recognized as calculating. The boy was thinking through the possibilities of evading being shot and re-gaining the upper hand. She couldn't leave her son alone with a killer. She wouldn't.

"Ann, go on, get to the car. Get help," Emma insisted.

"I'm not going without you," Ann said, her teeth clenched. But she unlocked the back door and opened it. "We're all going together. William, you, too. Walk over here."

Emma's cell phone, laying on the kitchen table, buzzed. They all jumped then froze. Ten seconds later, the house phone rang. Emma looked at the clock on the wall. *Slightly after ten. Who would be calling?*

In those seconds, as William looked at the phone on the table, Kyle lunged toward William and stabbed him in the shoulder just above his heart. He pulled out the blade. Blood gushed from the wound. William looked down at his chest. His face paled. He groaned and sank to his knees, hitting the back of his head against the cupboard counter. The rifle clattered to the floor. Kyle grabbed the rifle, fitted the stock to his shoulder and pointed it at Emma. Emma, her hands outstretched toward her son, her mouth open but unable to emit a sound, stood stock still.

They heard the house phone message machine click on. Lagarde's voice said, "Mrs. Wodehouse, call me back immediately. You may be in danger."

Kyle sniggered. "Wow, the light bulb went on for that old dude. Took him long enough." He trained the rifle on William. "Don't think I don't know how to use this rifle,

Emma. Remember all those buddy trips Dad took with me when I was young. We knew you'd freak out if we told you he taught me how to shoot. But he did. Now just fucking stand there and don't breathe while I figure out what's next."

Emma watched the second hand on the clock move across its face with infinitesimal slowness. William groaned. Ann, without thinking of the possible consequences to herself, grabbed the dishtowel hanging from the handle under the sink, folded it over and knelt down to press it against William's wound.

"We need to call for an ambulance," she said, her voice shaking but stern.

"I'll decide what happens here," Kyle said, sounding more insane by the second. "I don't give a damn if he dies. The fewer heirs, the more money for me." He grinned at Emma. "Isn't that how it works, Emma?"

Emma nodded. Her mind wasn't working. She could see no options.

"Now where does Dad keep his cash? I know he's got money stashed here somewhere."

"In his office, in the safe. Maybe. I'm not sure. I'll have to find the combination first. I don't know where he wrote it down. I'll have to look for it. It's written down with his passwords in his office somewhere."

"How much money is in there?" His breath came out in snorts.

"I think he keeps about ten thousand in cash in the house."

"Good enough. You open the safe. I'll stay here and watch your William bleed to death if you don't hurry."

CHAPTER 31

10:15 a.m.:

Lagarde had called Emma's cell phone and got her voicemail. He left a message. He called her house phone and got the message machine. He left the same message. *Does she have her cell phone on mute?* He texted the same message he left on voicemail. *The text message might show up on the screen of her cell phone without making any noise.* Every smart phone was different. He had no way of knowing if she would get any of the messages, but had to try all possible avenues.

He figured she already knew that she was in danger. That would account for her stiff reception of them two hours ago at her home. *Why hadn't he read the signs?* The woman simply annoyed him. Now he was annoyed at himself for letting his personal reaction to a suspect get in the way of his judgment. He walked outside the building to wait for Black who pulled up within minutes. Lagarde got into the car and they sped away. They had ten miles to drive, most of it on winding roads with one-hundred-year-old trees on the perimeter. Black wouldn't be able to drive faster than fifty-miles-an-hour without risking T-boning the car into a tree. Ten miles could take twenty minutes and twenty minutes could be enough time for Emma to be dead and the killer gone by the time they arrived. Local law enforcement and the state troopers they'd called in for backup wouldn't get there any sooner than they did. Lagarde had told them 'No sirens' hoping they could take control of the scene without more bloodshed.

"What're you thinking?" Lagarde asked Black while they were still on straight, flat road, and Black could talk and drive simultaneously.

"Kyle Wodehouse is the killer. We've got the prints to prove it. He drove here in a frenzy yesterday morning, maybe hopped up on illicit drugs readily available to him at school, maybe to demand money from his father. Spur of the moment, nothing planned. But he thought he wouldn't be welcomed and maybe he wanted to take his father by surprise. That's why he parked so far from the house."

Black slowed the car slightly and took a sharp left onto Jones Valley Road.

"I think when he got to the barn, where he expected his father to be, doing his morning horse chores, he saw Wodehouse having sex with Elaine and it infuriated him, tripped him past all reason. He forgot all about the money he wanted, hid in one of the empty stalls while his father did his thing, and jumped out at him when it was over to demand the money. For whatever reason, Wodehouse wouldn't give him the money, inflaming Kyle even more, and the kid stabbed him with the closest weapon to hand. He may not have wanted to kill his father, may not have known he wounded him mortally, but he left him for dead."

Black negotiated the first hairpin turn.

"Then he hid in the woods and instead of calming down or feeling guilty, something went wrong and he got more infuriated. He kept thinking about Elaine and his father. Maybe he thought about all the times Wodehouse was unfaithful to his mother. Maybe he equated Wodehouse's infidelity to abandoning him. He thought about all the times his father wasn't there for him, that he never felt safe or loved. But that might be too deep. Whatever the cause, he wanted to get revenge on his father and killing him wasn't enough. Frankly, I'm still not clear on motive. Killing his father could've been spontaneous, even accidental, but killing Elaine Tabor was another thing entirely. That was deliberate murder."

He paused to take the next hairpin turn. Lagarde braced himself with his hands and feet just in case Black flipped the car taking the turn at sixty-miles-an-hour. They were close to the property now. Black slowed the vehicle. "Drive right up to the house or be more covert?"

"Park sideways at the end of the driveway where they can't spot us. That'll also slow his exit if he gets to his car and tries to exit the property that way. It'll also stop our guys from steaming up the drive just as things go sideways inside. We'll go through the woods for cover. Go in the back door."

Black looked through his rear view mirror at the road behind them and at his watch. All his instincts were telling him that things had already gone sideways. "Backup should be here soon." He was praying they would.

Lagarde got out of the car and looked through the dense trees toward the house. Between the rhododendron and holly, they'd have enough cover to not be spotted immediately from any of the house windows, if anyone was looking. But there was a thirty-foot cleared area around the house and if Kyle was anticipating they might come back, he'd see them. Just in case, Lagarde drew his weapon, clicked off the safety and held the gun down at his side. Black saw Lagarde pull his weapon and did the same. They ran through the bushes and stopped just short of the lawn around the house.

"Big house, lots of windows," Black whispered.

Lagarde nodded. "They don't have any lights on. We can't see inside."

Lagarde ran out from the cover of the woods toward the back of the house, moving quickly until he was up against the stone wall of the house. Black followed.

It was very quiet.

Then a horse snorted and whinnied in the paddock, as if warning those who dared to enter.

They sidled around the building, ducking when they passed below the large windows of the parlor. They were within ten feet of the back porch when they heard glass break.

Light glinted off the muzzle of a rifle jutting out of a dining room window. "Gun!" Lagarde yelled before he heard the blast.

They dropped to the ground then crab-walked backward around the corner of the house. There was a second shot. Kyle had seen them before they even got close. They had lost the element of surprise. It wouldn't take Kyle long to run through the house and locate them from another window. They were at a clear disadvantage trying to shoot upward and through a window when they couldn't see the target. They had no idea how many bullets he had loaded. They couldn't time when he might have to stop to reload. Their only chance was that he thought they had retreated.

It was clear Kyle didn't plan to flee. He had hostages. Lagarde had no intention of negotiating. The guy had already killed two people. Adding a few more to his total wouldn't faze him, and wouldn't change the law's response to his killing spree. He was still doing life in prison. To get the upper hand, Lagarde and Black had to storm the house from the back door, and somehow regain the element of surprise. Lagarde figured the kid would run through the house, going from window to window to get a better shot at them. He wouldn't expect them to rush the house. He signaled Black with his head, 'this way.' They crept back to the porch keeping low to the ground.

Lagarde took one side of the back door and Black the other. The door was open a crack. Lagarde could see the body of a man on the floor. He recognized Emma's son, William, blood covering his shirt. Black pushed in the door. Lagarde rushed in, swung his gun in the direction he looked, and made a fast assessment of the situation. Emma was not in the kitchen. William was lying on the floor with blood pulsing out of a wound in his chest. Ann knelt next to him, her hands pressing down on a folded towel on top of William's chest. Her face was drawn, her eyes wide. She motioned with her head toward the door leading to the dining room. Lagarde looked through the kitchen doorway and saw a young man striding toward them with a rifle. He instantly assumed this was Kyle from his resemblance to Grant Wodehouse and the mug shots he'd recently viewed.

Lagarde and Black raised their arms and aimed their guns at Kyle.

The entire room fell away. There was only Kyle Wodehouse at the end of a short tunnel with a rifle aimed in their direction. Lagarde could see every blond hair on the kid's head, how some of the long curls twisted right and some left. The boy had very long eyelashes. They made a shadow on the ridge of his cheek bones. Kyle was barely out of the peach fuzz phase. The boy was too young to have killed two people and be working on his third murder.

Time slowed. Every breath they took was in slow motion. Lagarde saw the boy fingering the rifle trigger. He remembered how quickly Kyle had re-chambered another bullet when he shot at them from the window. *How many shots? Three? What does that rifle hold?* As slowly as time moved, it didn't seem to Lagarde there was time enough to talk the kid out of shooting anyone but Lagarde had never shot anyone in his long career as a detective. He didn't want to start now.

"Put it down, Kyle." Lagarde's voice was calm. "We're the police. It's over. Put down the gun, son."

Kyle continued his advance. "Sorry, old man, I don't know if you've noticed but I don't take orders from anyone anymore." He aimed the rifle at Ann. "Put down your guns or the nice lady who brought us breakfast gets it in the head."

Black's finger tightened on his trigger. "Put. The. Rifle. Down."

Lagarde could hear only his own breathing.

Kyle ignored Black, locking in the next round in the rifle chamber. The sound of metal moving against metal was an excruciating gong going off in Lagarde's head. He heard Ann gasp behind him. Lagarde was a hair's breadth from squeezing the trigger on his gun. He still hoped he wouldn't have to do it.

Emma rushed up behind Kyle, an iron poker raised over her head. She brought the pointed end of the poker down, with all her strength, toward the boy's head. Kyle twitched and the poker missed his head, slamming against his shoulder.

The boy lurched forward, took two steps to regain his balance, shook off the pain, whipped around, and pulled off a shot as he turned. The bullet grazed Emma's shoulder. She staggered back several feet. She dropped the poker, gripping her shoulder, and fell to her knees. Kyle instantly reloaded without thinking, spinning back toward the police officers. Black and Lagarde never hesitated, firing straight into the teenager's chest before he could take another shot.

Kyle collapsed on the floor.

Lagarde put his hand up. "No more shots." He shook his head, leaned down, and removed the rifle from within the boy's reach. "Enough. We've had enough."

Emma lay beside Kyle, blood blooming on her sweater, the poker on the floor at her side. She reached over with her good arm and stroked Kyle's hair. "I didn't see another way," she said, shaking her head. "I'm so sorry, Kyle. I couldn't think of anything else to do."

Lagarde leaned over Kyle's inert body and felt for a pulse on the boy's neck. Dead. He told Black to tell the forensic techs to come in to work the scene. They were probably all waiting at the bottom of the drive.

He put his hand on Black's shoulder. "It's okay, Larry. It was appropriate use of deadly force."

Lagarde's haggard face displayed the same look of sudden sorrow that showed in Black's. It would take them both a while to process the shooting. Maybe they wouldn't feel guilty about defending themselves and the other people in the house, but they would always wonder if there had been a way they could have arrested the boy instead of killing him. For Lagarde particularly, who had prided himself on never discharging his weapon during a murder investigation, shooting Kyle would cost him emotionally.

These ten minutes would come back to them at night when they were trying to sleep, sitting in the car driving to another crime scene, and even at their desks filling out paperwork. Ten minutes would stretch out to infinite time in their minds as they went over every second of their response to the situation. The memory of the shooting might not haunt them, but it would stay with them for a long time. Killing the boy would affect their work. They would either be overly cautious in the future or more reckless. They would have to monitor their behavior from now on, so would their supervisors. Nothing would be the same for them.

CHAPTER 32

10:30 a.m.:

Seemingly within minutes, for the second day in a row, police swarmed all over the Wodehouse property. Emma pulled herself up off the floor, grabbed the edge of the dining table for support and stood. She walked into the kitchen and sank to her knees by her son. She put her palm on William's cheek. "It's over, sweetheart. It's over. He won't hurt anyone ever again."

She looked over at Ann, who only now relinquished her pressure on the wound, handing that job over to Emma. She couldn't think of what to say to this stalwart friend. "Thank you," she whispered. Until the emergency medical technicians bundled William into the ambulance, she stayed on the floor next to her son.

Watching all the activity around her, Emma said out loud to no one in particular that the police reminded her of grackles that periodically swarmed the roof of the house and the grounds, perpetually moving, cawing and pecking the ground. Perhaps she was telling William. His eyes were closed, his face paler than she had ever seen it. She was talking simply so he could hear that she was there.

She had a flesh wound, the emergency medical tech told her. She was 'lucky,' no major organs or arteries were affected, but the wound would need cleaning and dressing. Emma grimaced at his choice of words. She didn't think of this as luck.

The EMT cut off her sleeve and applied a temporary dressing to hold her until she got to the emergency room doctor. She was in shock now, he said, and the adrenalin coursing through her body was concealing her pain, but she would feel it soon. "Stay put," he told her as they put William on a gurney to transport him. "We'll come back for you in a minute."

She sat on the floor in her kitchen impatient for someone to tell her what was going to happen next, whether or not they were going to charge her with assault. She was numb, her body, her brain, even the slow thump of her heart in her chest seemed suppressed. She couldn't weep. She couldn't think. In the space of two days, her entire life had changed. The two people she loved most in the world had been attacked by her stepson. She could not begin to understand Kyle's behavior. *Was this all about money? That couldn't be.* Something else was at work but no matter how she tried to find the logic, she failed. She was reduced to breathing in and out, waiting.

Lagarde came over, squatted down next to her and told her that the medical examiner's first take on Kyle's death was that the bullets from their guns had killed him, not her blow to the boy's head. It was not really a relief. She had struck her stepson with the intent of stopping him in his tracks, whether that killed him or not. In her own mind, she was guilty. She didn't think Kyle originally intended to kill her. *Hell, he could have done that while I was sleeping last night, could have killed William, for that matter.* Kyle *doesn't even know what he* wants. *He's desperate, terribly alone, medicated, and armed—a lethal combination for anyone.* Something had triggered his breakdown, and not only would she never know what it was, there was nothing she could do about it anyway.

She had thought she had experienced all the sadness she could bear when Grant was murdered. She had been wrong. There were new levels of grief waiting for her. She saw her stepson stabbing her son over and over in an endless loop every time she closed her eyes.

She would remember forever that look of defiance and hatred, or was that complete panic, in Kyle's eyes as he shot her.

CHAPTER 33

10:45 a.m.:

S heriff's deputies found Kyle's Audi parked in the hayloft of the Wodehouse barn. In the back of the Audi, they found his school clothes, the cuffs of his blue button-down shirt stained with someone's blood. Black slapped himself on the head. *I am an idiot! I should have checked the barn this morning.* If he had done a simple search, he might have prevented the stabbing of an innocent victim, might have prevented the perp's death. He seemed to have forgotten how to do the simplest kind of investigative work and blamed himself for the shooting. There should have been another way. He questioned his choice of career, his competence, even his basic intelligence. He had failed badly. His failure would make him second-guess himself from now on. A detective who didn't trust his instincts was useless.

Forensic techs pulled the ought-six bullet from the Remington that had sped past Emma's body out of the wall in the dining room. They found two shell casings on the floor in the kitchen from where Kyle had shot through the window at Lagarde and Black. They found the bullets in the ground very close to where Lagarde and Black had scurried for cover. They took the sheets and cover from the bed Kyle slept in, the clothes he wore to Emma's house, the toothbrush he used in the bathroom and bagged the knife Kyle used to stab William. They would test it to see if it also had Elaine Tabor's blood on it. Regardless of the fact that the killer was dead and his killing spree over, the forensics team would still examine all the evidence from these crimes so that a complete report on the murders and the suspect could be filed. Later, the DNA evidence they pulled from the toothbrush and the blood on his school shirt would be used to prove that it was Kyle Wodehouse who bludgeoned a Mercersville teenager into a coma with his fists the day before he killed his father.

Black half-carried Ann into her car and clicked her seat belt into place. She protested that she wanted to go with Emma and William wherever the ambulance was taking them, but Black wasn't waiting for that. Blood had accumulated along her collarbone and soaked into her dress. He couldn't bear to see her enduring without a whimper the knife wounds Kyle had inflicted on her. He slid behind the wheel of her car and drove her to the emergency room at Jefferson Memorial Hospital to make sure she didn't need stitches on her neck, and in general to see if she was suffering from more than shock. It wasn't normal procedure for him to take her, but he didn't care. He had simply waved at Lagarde from the car and his lieutenant had nodded. He knew Lagarde would understand. Black could file his paperwork later. There was a certain freedom in giving up on his career as a detective.

On the drive to the hospital, Ann kept saying to him, "My kids, are my kids okay? Someone needs to check on my kids."

Although he expected that Ann's children were unharmed and unaware of the trauma their mother had endured this morning, Black called for a trooper to head over to the children's school to make sure they were fine. He tried to get Ann to focus on giving him details of their encounter with Kyle.

For a while, Ann couldn't concentrate on anything but her children's safety. She replayed for Black the images of her morning: the sharp flick of the knife against her skin, the sight of a lunatic stabbing her boss's son. Held at knife point and toyed with by a boy who seemed to have lost all his humanity, she was unable to stop him. "I'll never be able to take my safety or the safety of my kids for granted. The ground rules have changed."

Kyle had been a normal teenager and then he snapped, she said. He transformed from a normal person with inhibitions to a callous monster with no regard for human life. If it could happen to Kyle, it could happen to anyone. "I saw it happen right in front of my eyes. It could happen to one of my children's teachers, their school bus driver, the principal at the school, the librarian, or the janitor." She turned her face up and looked at Black, seeming uncertain for a second that she could trust him.

Black listened but took no notes. He would never forget her narrative of the events.

"Kyle was possessed." She sniffled and shuddered. "He couldn't be reasoned with. We were sure he was going to kill all of us. And all he really wanted was money. He did all that killing just to get money. It doesn't make any sense."

Ann shook her head and pressed her face into Black's shoulder. She let Black put his arm around her while they waited for her to be seen by the doctor. She leaned against him. As far as Black was concerned, she could go on leaning against him for the rest of his life. It didn't matter to him that what brought them together was her fear. Only for a second did it occur to him that later, when she regained her courage, she might rethink the choices she made in terror.

CHAPTER 34

11:00 a.m.:

Kyle was taken by the medical examiner for autopsy, as required in an officer-involved shooting. The ME would also check for toxins, alcohol and drugs in his body. Her exam would reveal his entire physical history and determine the cause of death, even if at the moment he dropped to the floor, the shooters and the witnesses were absolutely certain it was the two bullets from the police-issued weapons that killed him. Before they moved him, the medical examiner did a quick search of Kyle's body for identification, even though there were living witnesses who would swear this was Kyle. She found a gold chain with a diamond-studded heart in Kyle's jeans pocket. She held it up in one gloved hand for Lagarde to see.

He nodded. As he had suspected, Kyle wanted trophies. That necklace must have been Elaine's. "Bag it, but when you're done with it, let me know. I know a little girl who would love to have that."

Lagarde and Black had surrendered their weapons and submitted to an on-scene gunpowder residue test to confirm that they had fired their guns. There would be one bullet from each of their guns in the dead body. Later, there would be reams of reports and seemingly countless interviews to confirm their story of how the shooting occurred. Their memory of the events leading up to the shooting would be probed separately and there would be counseling. They had two-days cooling off time before the very long interviews would take place. As in other officer-involved shootings, they expected that they would be cleared of any wrong-doing and that the prosecutor's office would decline to indict them. They had two good witnesses and Kyle Wodehouse had been on a rampage. They had shot him in furtherance of preventing another murder. But it was never possible to predict the panel's finding in advance and it was best not to try. They just needed to calmly tell what happened as they experienced it, minute-by-minute, and answer the questions.

Lagarde wasn't worried about the interviews or the panel's decision. Frankly, their opinion didn't matter to him. He was deeply saddened by the fact that he had killed someone. It might be called a justified shooting, but the boy was still dead, and he had made him that way. He would have to live with that for the rest of his life. He didn't need to have nightmares to know that this feeling of horror would never go away.

CHAPTER 35

1:30 p.m.:

William was taken first to the local hospital where he was stabilized and then transported by helicopter to the Winchester, Virginia hospital, barely in time for the operation that saved his life. He was weak from loss of blood and in a lot of pain. He would have to endure physical therapy to get the strength back in his chest, shoulder and arm, but he would recover.

Lagarde made sure Emma knew her son was okay before she left the hospital where her own wound was patched. Another detective took her to an interview room in the nearby sheriff's office for questioning about her assault on her stepson and to provide an account of what had happened at the Wodehouse farm prior to and including the officer-involved shooting.

Lagarde had no intention of letting anyone book her on assault, much less send a case against her to the prosecutor on any charge. It was clear she had acted out of a sense of immediate life-threatening danger to her son, herself, and her friend. Even if she hadn't realized by then that Kyle killed his father, she had acted in self-defense. It was Lagarde's fault that the situation had gotten so far out of hand that she thought she had to act. She had been through enough. It was time to let her move on with her life, if it was possible to gather enough shreds of it together to make a shelter in which she could survive.

Emma was driven home from the hospital by a state trooper at Lagarde's request. She didn't even look around the house. She found she didn't care about the house at all. She changed her clothes, got into her Lexus, and drove one-handed for the thirty miles to Winchester, Virginia, to be with her son at the hospital.

The hospital was vast compared to the small county facility in Ranson where she'd been treated. Stopping at reception to learn William's room number, she headed to the surgical recovery suite.

The nurse looked up at Emma's pale face, arm sling and obvious discomfort. "He made it through the surgery just fine," he reported, consulting William's chart on the computer screen. "He's under sedation and he's sleeping, but you can sit with him in recovery if you wish. In a few hours, we'll move him to his room."

Emma nodded. "Yes," she said, tears rolling down her cheeks. "That's what I wish."

The nurse pointed to the curtained bay where a very pale man with dark curly hair lay against white sheets. His lips were white. Tubes snaked from him to various bags of liquid and monitors. His shoulder and chest were bandaged. Behind him, various screens showed graphs with constantly moving dots and blips. Numbers flashed on the other screens.

Emma sucked in her breath. Her dear, brilliant boy looked fragile and tenuous, as if life were deciding whether to reside in that body or float away. He couldn't die. She couldn't lose the two people she loved like this. She walked over to the bed and stood at the foot of it. If she could will life back into him, she would do it. She walked to the side of the bed and sat in the chair the nurse brought into the curtained area. She took his hand and kissed it. "I'm here, sweetheart. I'm here. Don't worry about anything."

William's eyelids fluttered, but he didn't wake. Emma leaned her head on the bed and closed her eyes. The idea of making her living by suing people for divorce and squeezing from some guy all the wealth he had accumulated now seemed criminally foolish and vapid. There had to be something else she could do that would keep her and her son living in comfort. For now, they could just breathe together and recover. She would figure everything out later.

CHAPTER 36

1:45 p.m.:

Warren Lyles was awakened in the holding cell, having had the first deep sleep he could recall in a long time.

He was informed that he was free to go. He would not be needed to testify at a trial. They already had his statement for the record.

He asked the officer what had happened to the killer.

"Cop-assisted suicide," the officer said.

Warren shook his head, struck by the officer's black humor. "What? I don't get it. You're saying the guy who killed Mr. Wodehouse is dead?"

"Yep, dead as a doornail."

"Killed by the police?" Warren asked, suddenly feeling the fragility of his own life.

The officer was more circumspect with this answer. "Line of duty shooting," he said tersely, putting a hand on Warren's shoulder, handing him his backpack, and moving him along.

"Who was he, the killer?" Warren ventured to ask.

"The dead guy's son."

They walked from holding down the corridor to the

front door. Warren thought the bright light coming in through the glass doors was the best thing he had ever seen.

"Oh, wait, I forgot something," the officer said. "Stand right here."

Warren did as he was told.

The officer stopped at the receptionist's desk and talked to the redhead for a minute. She picked a small baggie up from the counter and handed it to him. He walked back to Warren and handed him the baggie. "Lieutenant Lagarde said this was yours, to make sure you got it back."

Warren looked at the object in the baggie. It was his compass. *A miracle.* He thanked the officer, thinking the man was far too callous about someone else's life, shoved the compass in his pocket without removing it from the bag, shouldered his backpack, and walked out of the Troop 2 Command Post, feeling as if he had better do something more useful with his own fragile life than run away.

CHAPTER 37

2:00 p.m.:

Lagarde had yet another uncomfortable call to make and he knew he should do it in person. He had to let Rhonda Morewood know that her son Kyle was dead and that he had shot him. He dreaded this encounter. For a few minutes, he considered sending two other troopers to do the job. He could probably get his Maryland counterparts to do the notification, save the State the cost of gas for the round-trip drive to Burkittsville. In a way, that made sense. The Maryland officers would be dispassionate, simply informing the mother that her son had been shot and killed while attempting a murder. They would tell her who to contact when she was ready to claim the body. They would be calm and polite and get out of there quickly.

But he couldn't pass off the task. This, gut-wrenching as it was, was also part of his job. He called Black on his cell phone, but he didn't pick up. Lagarde left a message saying he was heading out to Kyle's mother's house. He didn't have to say anything else, Black would understand.

Lagarde found he couldn't get himself to drive faster than fifty-five miles an hour for the fifteen-mile trip over the bridges that crossed the Shenandoah and Potomac Rivers and then east on the highway into Maryland. His chalked it up to the fact that his body was reluctant to leave the Panhandle. He didn't want to examine his own psyche farther than that.

The road opened up wide and well kept on the Maryland side, framed by large farms and low rising hills sweeping back toward the mountains that hugged the rivers he'd left behind him in the rear-view mirror. He turned off the highway onto Burkittsville Road and drove north toward the centuries-old historic town with its cobbled streets and brick and stone cottages situated on half a square mile, surrounded by rolling pastures dotted with cows. This was about as picturesque as the Maryland landscape got.

He found the Morewood's timber and stone house a block from the single intersection that was the center of the town. He parked on the street, took a few deep breaths to steady himself, walked up to the door and knocked. The house was in good condition. It appeared that the stone had been recently re-pointed. There was a garden walk leading from the side toward a large backyard. A stone wall separated the Morewood residence from their neighbors. He remembered that Beverly had once lived in Burkittsville. Maybe the Morewoods knew her. This house, older than his own, was built some twenty miles outside of Frederick in the mid-eighteenth century. Except for the occasional car bumping over the cobbled intersection, Lagarde might have been in an old English village.

Rhonda opened the door wearing a fire-red caftan. She was looped. Lagarde's entire English village fantasy fell away. Kyle's mother had begun her drinking early. By 2:00 p.m., when Lagarde arrived, it seemed to him she would barely feel the wood floor under her feet.

She leaned against the door and said, "Well, hello there, handsome. What can I do for you today? If you've got brushes, I'm buying." Her red lipstick was smeared across her cheek. Her blue eyeliner had either been applied too generously or had migrated away from her eyes when the alcohol began to make her sweat.

"Mrs. Morewood, I'm Detective Sam Lagarde. I was assigned to investigate the murder of Grant Wodehouse." He displayed his badge.

She nodded, stepped away from the door, and waved him into the house. It was dark in the small front room. The antique furniture was clearly not meant for sitting on. She pointed toward a small hallway that opened to the kitchen, dining room and an expansive great room beyond it, clearly an addition to the historic home. *She doesn't have bad taste, just unseemly behavior.*

"I need to tell you about your son."

She nodded and waved in the direction of comfortable looking chairs in the great room. The large casement windows revealed a carefully tended garden outside. "My husband's hobby," she said, slurring her words. "Being mayor doesn't take a lot of time." She dropped onto her plush chaise. Her bottle and glass waited on the nearby side table. She topped off her glass. "Now—" she asked, smiling at Lagarde and jiggling the glass. "—what do you want to tell me?"

He shook his head "no" to the offer of a drink, perched on the edge of a seat, and said, "I'm sorry to tell you that your son, Kyle, is dead."

"No, no, you're confused. It's my husband—oh, my *ex*-husband—" she exclaimed, with huge emphasis on the ex, "—who's dead."

"I'm sorry, Mrs. Morewood. Your son Kyle was shot and killed at the Wodehouse farm earlier today."

"What?" She spilled her drink, threw her legs off the

chaise, and rose, shaking, to her feet. "This can't be true. You must have it wrong."

Lagarde stood. He wanted to walk out of the house. "I was there, Mrs. Morewood. I shot him. He was going to kill me, or I was going to kill him. I got my shot off before he did."

Rhonda's mouth opened, but not a sound emerged. She bent at the waist, lower and lower until she could have grasped her legs in her two arms. She drew in breath, finally, and from her mouth came what Lagarde would think of later as cawing, an inarticulate choking sound, devoid of language, an inchoate wail, the sound a mother makes when breath departs her child's body.

There was no speaking into that sound. There would be no hearing. He tried anyway. "Is there someone I can call to be with you?" wishing now that he had taken the easy way out and had the Maryland state police deliver this message.

The sounds issuing from her throat continued. He put both hands on her shoulders and maneuvered her to her chair. He removed the vodka bottle and brought her a glass of water. He looked at the small bulletin board on the kitchen wall and called the number for the town hall. He told the young woman who answered the phone that the mayor needed to come home immediately, that his wife was in great distress. He waited the five minutes, until Rhonda's husband arrived, and then explained what had happened. He saw the blood drain out of the man's face, which locked into a grimace, the look—he understood—of a man clamping down on every emotion. Lagarde left his business card on the counter in the kitchen and let himself out of the Morewood's home as Rhonda's husband knelt down next to her and put his arms around her. The sound of her wailing followed Lagarde out the door.

CHAPTER 38

October 16, 10:00 a.m.:

Three days later, the official autopsy on Kyle Wodehouse came in. Lagarde and Black drove out to the Wodehouse farm to let Emma know what the medical examiner had found. He did not have a similar urge to inform Rhonda face-to-face. A copy of the medical examiner's report was *sent* to her.

The boy had high enough levels of Atomoxetine in his body to drive him crazy, the ME had told them in language even they could understand. A normal dose of the drug prescribed to manage attention deficit disorder could make some susceptible children nearly ten times more violent than other medications of the same type would. Kyle was apparently taking enough of the drug intermittently to increase its residual accumulation in his bloodstream. Add to that the Prozac that was in his system, another drug that increased a propensity to aggression in some patients, and the boy had almost no ability to control his moods. The ME said he would have been having suicidal thoughts as well as homicidal ones.

"The kid couldn't win," she told them. "He had been chemically altered. Whatever was going on psychologically, add roaring adolescent hormones, a broken home, and no real friends, and he had no control over his aggressive tendencies."

Lagarde waited while the information sunk in. Emma had gotten a life's worth of horror in a two-day period. He didn't know how she would react to the new information. Even though she wasn't really his problem now, he was determined to tie up all the loose ends in a case, and what had pushed Kyle over the edge was one of those ends. He didn't know if she felt guilty or relieved but he could see from her pallor and the dark circles under her eyes that she was suffering.

Emma shook her head. "What a waste. What a waste."

She thanked Lagarde, shook his hand and opened the front door of her house to usher him out. "I should thank you for saving our lives, but I can't right now. I'm sorry." She held her hand up in a kind of salute and closed the front door.

Lagarde thought it might take a long time before she could thank him for saving her life. And he wasn't so sure she should ever do it.

Lagarde's other loose end on this case was Ron Tabor. He called Tabor after they got the medical examiner's report and told him they had captured his wife's killer. Lagarde didn't go into details Tabor didn't need to know.

"We won't need you for further interviews. You're not under suspicion for either of the murders."

Lagarde explained to Tabor that they had recovered a necklace from the killer's pocket they thought was his wife's. There was no point in telling Tabor that it looked expensive enough to have been a gift from his wife's lover, no need for him to be reminded of his dead wife's infidelity.

The man had plenty to deal with already. Lagarde said maybe Molly would like to have the necklace and Ron should just let him know when he was ready for a quick visit.

Tabor sobbed at the news. Lagarde got the feeling the man was sobbing frequently these days. He could hear Molly say in the background, "It's okay, Daddy, it'll be okay."

Tabor insisted on thanking Lagarde five times before he could get off the phone.

CHAPTER 39

12:00 Noon:

Lagarde took circular sweeps with the curry comb from his horse's crest through to his buttocks. Over and over, he stroked the horse's coat with the comb, lifting it when he got to the hip and bringing it back to the Paint's neck. He would work Jake's entire body this way. It was a hypnotic process, one that almost always put him in a semi-trance state. The horse shifting his feet or raising and lowering his head, nickering from time-to-time, were the only other things Lagarde noticed besides his arm moving in its long arc. It had been a week since he had ridden and both he and Jake were ready for some time together. Lagarde was counting on this ride to get him right. He had had enough blood and sorrow. He needed to leave everything behind him for a couple hours. The only way he knew how to get right with the world was to sit astride his horse and move out.

The currycomb would loosen all the dirt, hay, leaves and other debris the horse's coat had accumulated while Jake ran around in the field or rolled on his back in the meadow during the last week. The process was also a good way for him to examine the horse and make sure he had no sores or injuries. By the time he finished brushing Jake off, the horse's coat would gleam and that tangled mane would lie neatly against Jake's neck. Before he saddled him, Lagarde would pick out the horse's feet with a hoof pick.

Lagarde talked to Jake while he combed him, told him about his case, not in detail, but sketching out the high points. It helped him to think about the case from Jake's point of view, to keep in mind what was really important. A young man had killed his father and his father's lover, shot his stepmother and stabbed his stepbrother in some kind of sustained dissociative state. It reminded him of an outline of an old Greek tragedy.

"Yeah, I know you don't know what dissociative means, Jake. Neither do I, really, but I have a feeling it means that if we hadn't shot him, he might have gotten out of going to jail for killing his father and Elaine Tabor. Not guilty by means of mental disease or defect." Lagarde nodded as if Jake had said something. "I know. Just because you're crazy doesn't mean you didn't kill someone. It shouldn't be a reason for getting out from under your punishment. I totally agree. Still, I feel sorry for the kid. Helluva way to end a young life."

Jake shook his head and whinnied. Lagarde patted his rump. It was good to have a friend who understood you.

When he had finished grooming Jake, he placed a fleece blanket on the horse's back then the saddle, which he cinched up, put on the bridle, and removed the halter. Holding onto the bridle, he unhooked the leads that kept Jake in the grooming area of his barn. No matter how good your horse was, Lagarde reminded himself whenever he was tempted to trust Jake with a little freedom, he was always a horse and he could spook and run at the slightest change in the atmosphere. Lagarde had no intention of spending all day trying to corral a runaway horse.

He led Jake out of the barn to the mounting block, Lagarde's concession to old age and stiffening joints. He stepped up on the mounting block, swung himself up into the saddle, got comfortable in the stirrups and clucked to the horse to move out. Steering with one hand, the other hand resting on his thigh, Lagarde looked out over the long distance toward the mountains. That's where he was heading, toward the southern horizon. 'Look at where you want to go.' Those were the instructions for steering a horse. They were pretty good directions for how to lead your life. He and Jake would walk for a while until they got used to each other again. Jake's ears were pointed forward, a good sign that he was happy with the world and glad to be walking with Lagarde. He wished they could walk until they found a place where no one killed anyone.

Half a mile from the house, at a comfortable trot, Lagarde's cell phone buzzed in its holder on his belt. He had half an impulse to ignore it, but too much of a conscience to do that. He hoped it wasn't another dead body. That was the last thing he needed today.

"Whoa," he said to Jake, pulling the horse to a stop, and yanking his phone out of its holder at the same time. On the screen, the caller was identified as Beverly Wilson. Lagarde's heart stopped for a second. He pressed accept. "Yes?" he said to the phone, afraid to assume anything.

"Sam?" Beverly ventured hesitantly. "I've been thinking about you. I don't know why, but I thought it might be a good day for riding out."

Lagarde's face broke into a smile that would stay there for another week, at least. It was, of course, the best day for riding, he told her.

THE END

About the Author

Ginny Fite is an award-winning journalist who has covered crime, politics, government, healthcare, art and all things human. She has been a spokesperson for a governor and for a member of Congress, a few colleges and universities and a robotics R&D company. She has degrees from Rutgers University and Johns Hopkins University and studied at the School for Women Healers and the Maryland Poetry Therapy Institute. She resides in Harpers Ferry, West Virginia. *Cromwell's Folly* (Black Opal Books 2015) was her first Sam Lagarde mystery/thriller set in Charles Town, West Virginia.

CPSIA information can be obtained
at www.ICGtesting.com
Printed in the USA
BVOW06s1954011116
466640BV00002B/5/P